# POSTAL

### CREATED BY MATT HAWKINS

## VOLUME 7

PUBLISHED BY TOP COW PRODUCTIONS, INC.
LOS ANGELES

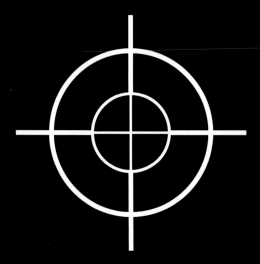

**For Top Cow Productions, Inc.**
For Top Cow Productions, Inc.
**Marc Silvestri** - CEO
**Matt Hawkins** - President & COO
**Elena Salcedo** - Vice President of Operations
**Henry Barajas** - Director of Operations
**Vincent Valentine** - Production Manager
**Dylan Gray** - Marketing Director

To find the comic
shop nearest you, call:
**1-888-COMICBOOK**

Want more info? Check out:
**www.topcow.com**
for news & exclusive Top Cow merchandise!

# IMAGE COMICS, INC.

**IMAGECOMICS.COM**

POSTAL, VOL. 7. First printing. August 2018. Published by Image Comics, Inc. Office of publication: 2701 NW Vaughn St., Suite 780, Portland, OR 97210. Copyright © 2018 Top Cow Productions Inc. All rights reserved. Contains material originally published in single magazine form as POSTAL #25, Postal: Mark & Postal: Laura. "POSTAL," its logos, and the likenesses of all characters herein are trademarks of Top Cow Productions Inc., unless otherwise noted. "Image" and the Image Comics logos are registered trademarks of Image Comics, Inc. No part of this publication may be reproduced or transmitted, in any form or by any means (except for short excerpts for journalistic or review purposes), without the express written permission of Top Cow Productions Inc., or Image Comics, Inc. All names, characters, events, and locales in this publication are entirely fictional. Any resemblance to actual persons (living or dead), events, or places, without satirical intent, is coincidental. Printed in South Korea. ISBN: 978-1-5343-0803-9.

# POSTAL™

CREATED BY MATT HAWKINS

## POSTAL #25

Writer: BRYAN HILL

Artist: ISAAC GOODHART

Colorist: K. MICHAEL RUSSELL

Letterer: TROY PETERI

## POSTAL: MARK

Writer: MATT HAWKINS

Artist: RAFFAELE IENCO

Letterer: TROY PETERI

## POSTAL: LAURA

Writer: BRYAN HILL

Artist: ISAAC GOODHART

Colorist: K. MICHAEL RUSSELL

Letterer: TROY PETERI

Cover art for this edition by:

ISAAC GOODHART & K. MICHAEL RUSSELL

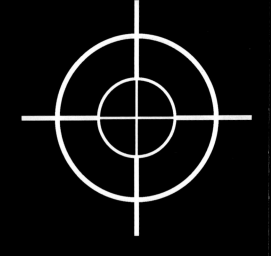

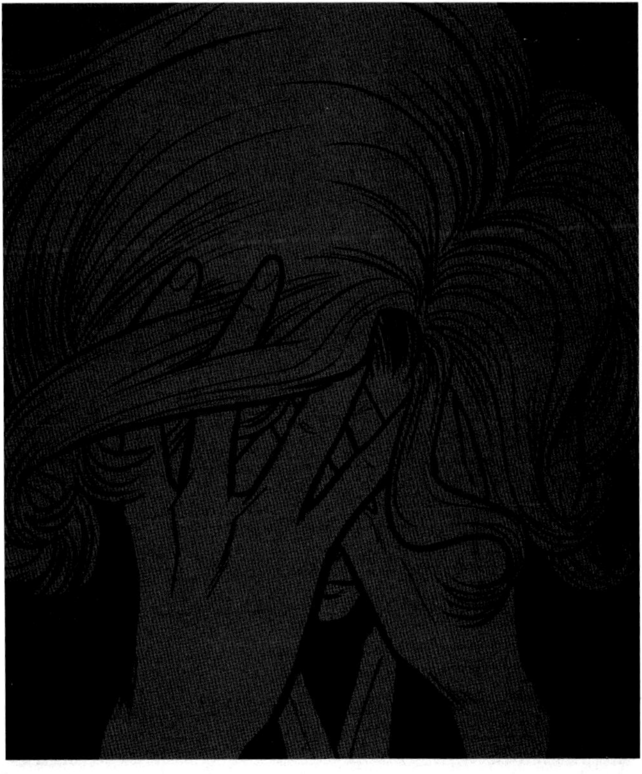

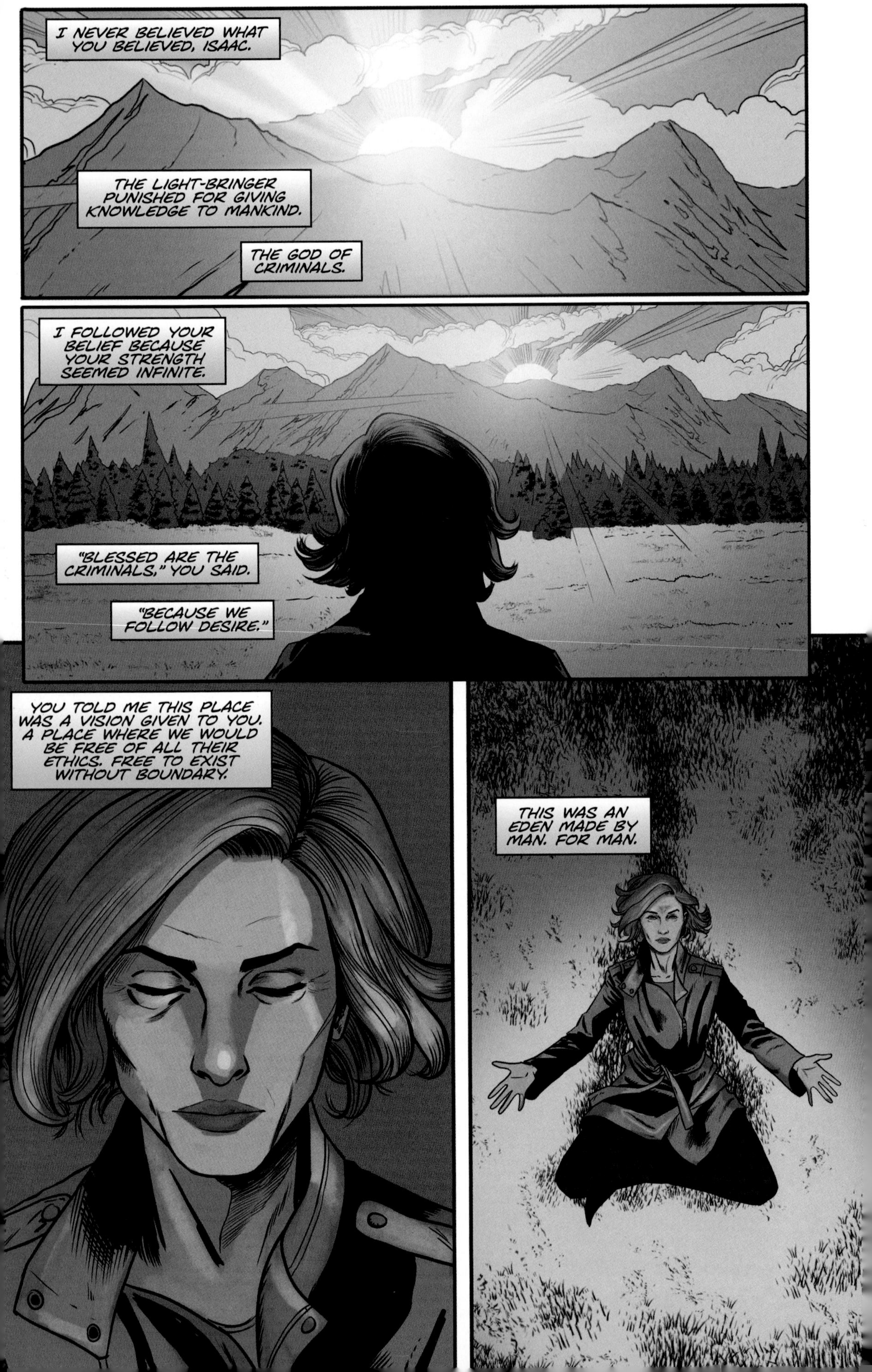

I NEVER BELIEVED WHAT YOU BELIEVED, ISAAC.
THE LIGHT-BRINGER PUNISHED FOR GIVING KNOWLEDGE TO MANKIND.
THE GOD OF CRIMINALS.
I FOLLOWED YOUR BELIEF BECAUSE YOUR STRENGTH SEEMED INFINITE.
"BLESSED ARE THE CRIMINALS," YOU SAID.
"BECAUSE WE FOLLOW DESIRE."
YOU TOLD ME THIS PLACE WAS A VISION GIVEN TO YOU. A PLACE WHERE WE WOULD BE FREE OF ALL THEIR ETHICS. FREE TO EXIST WITHOUT BOUNDARY.
THIS WAS AN EDEN MADE BY MAN. FOR MAN.

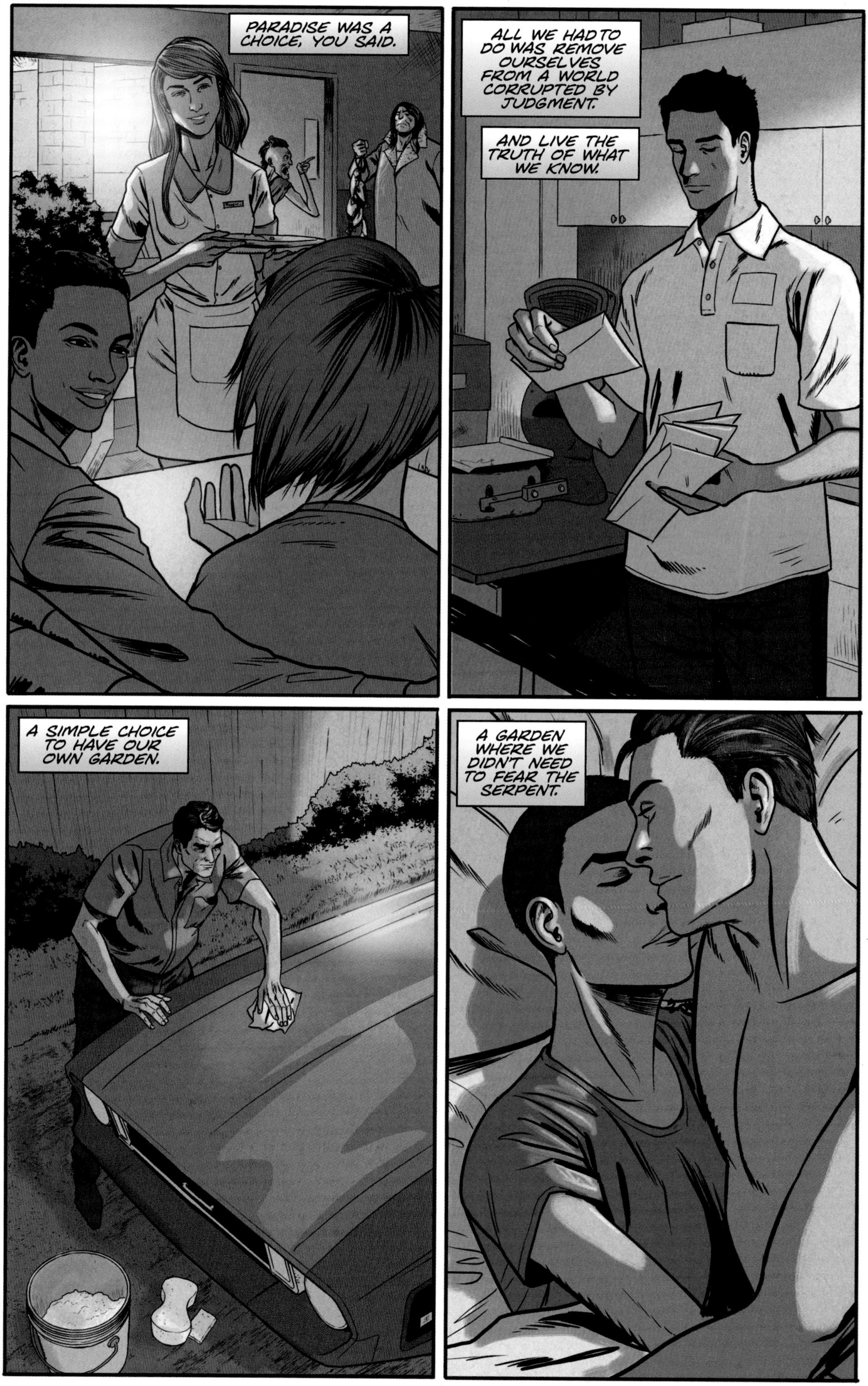
PARADISE WAS A CHOICE, YOU SAID.
ALL WE HAD TO DO WAS REMOVE OURSELVES FROM A WORLD CORRUPTED BY JUDGMENT.
AND LIVE THE TRUTH OF WHAT WE KNOW.
A SIMPLE CHOICE TO HAVE OUR OWN GARDEN.
A GARDEN WHERE WE DIDN'T NEED TO FEAR THE SERPENT.

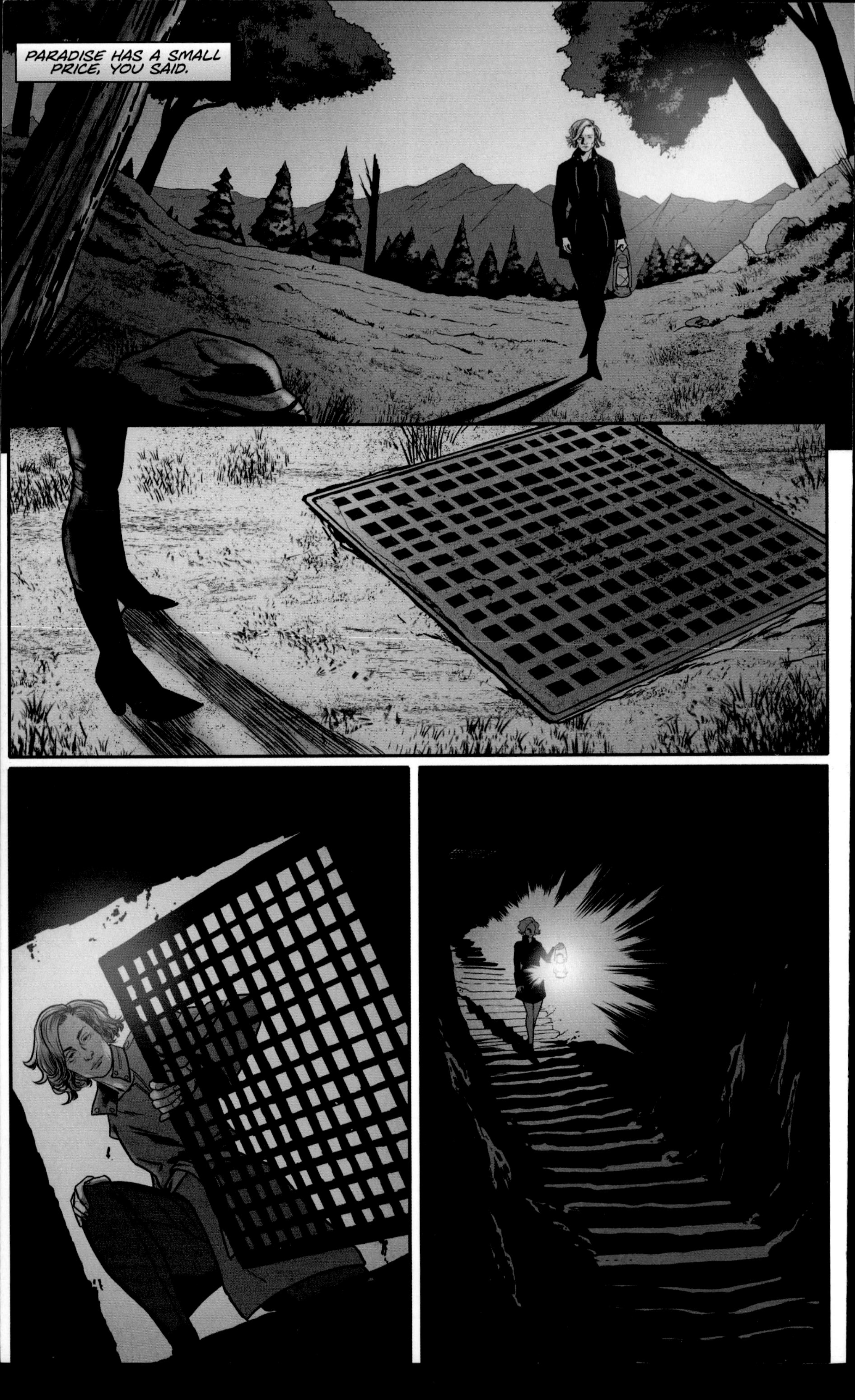
PARADISE HAS A SMALL PRICE, YOU SAID.

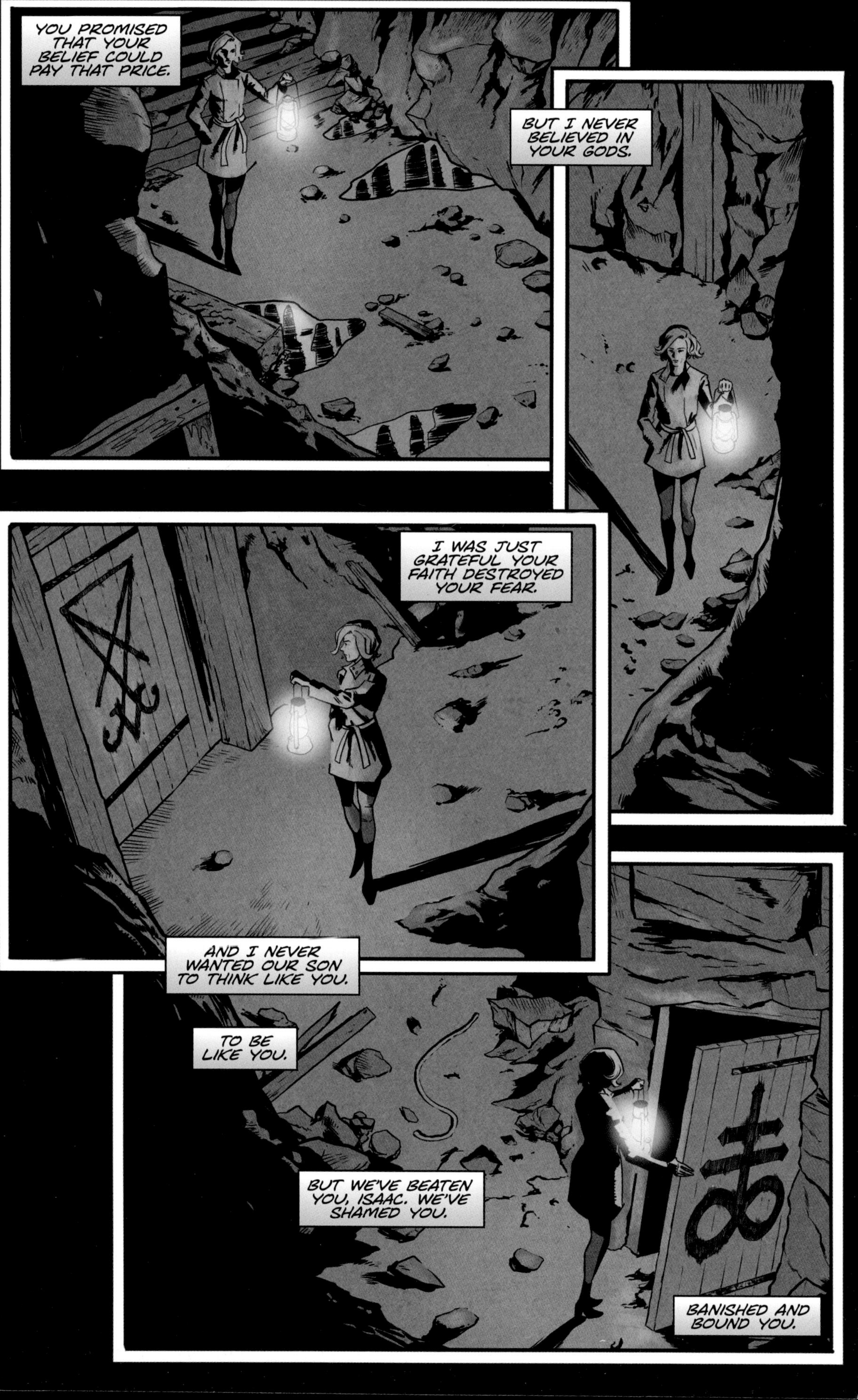
YOU PROMISED THAT YOUR BELIEF COULD PAY THAT PRICE.
BUT I NEVER BELIEVED IN YOUR GODS.
I WAS JUST GRATEFUL YOUR FAITH DESTROYED YOUR FEAR.
AND I NEVER WANTED OUR SON TO THINK LIKE YOU.
TO BE LIKE YOU.
BUT WE'VE BEATEN YOU, ISAAC. WE'VE SHAMED YOU.
BANISHED AND BOUND YOU.

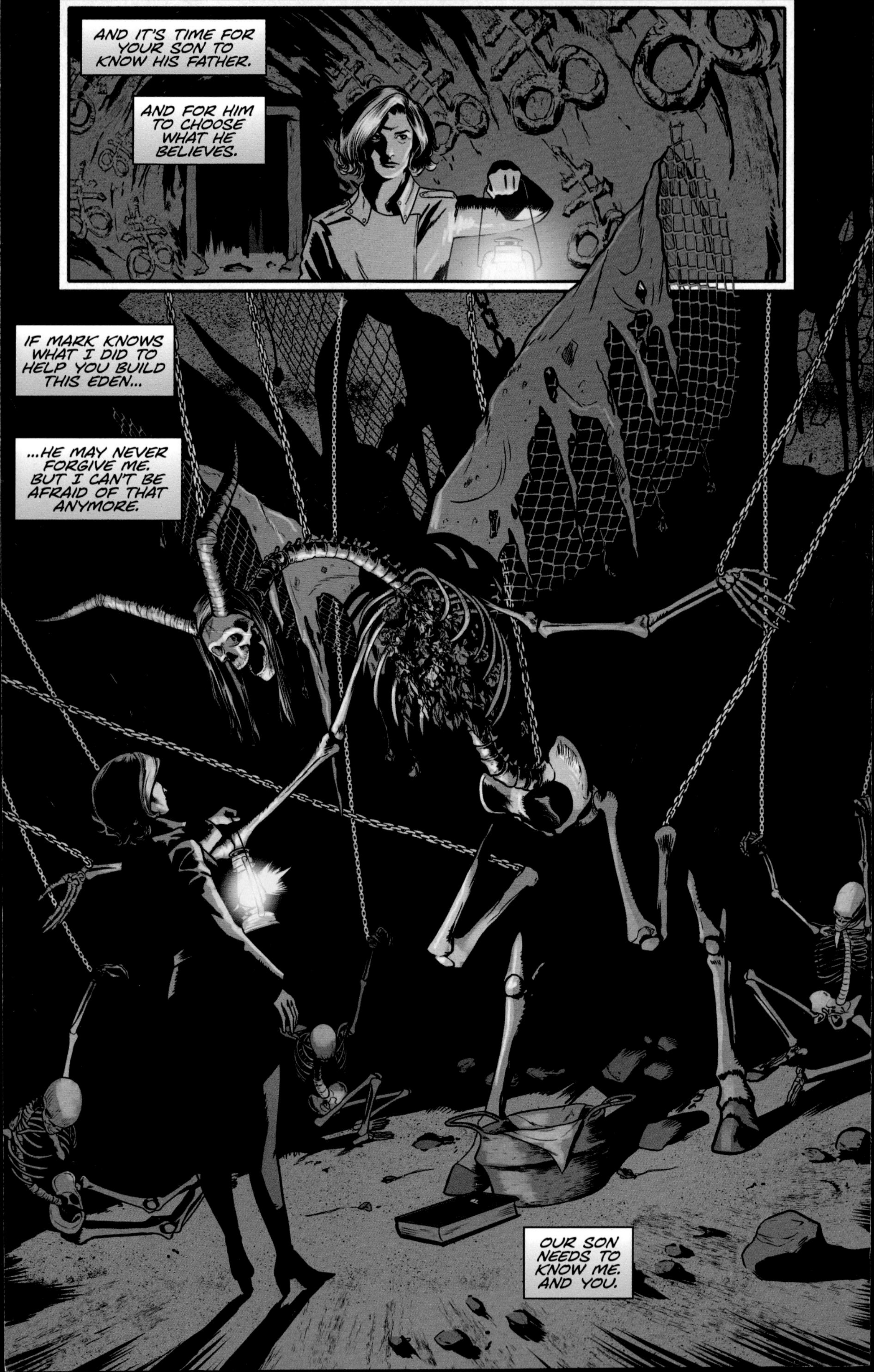
AND IT'S TIME FOR YOUR SON TO KNOW HIS FATHER.
AND FOR HIM TO CHOOSE WHAT HE BELIEVES.
IF MARK KNOWS WHAT I DID TO HELP YOU BUILD THIS EDEN...
...HE MAY NEVER FORGIVE ME. BUT I CAN'T BE AFRAID OF THAT ANYMORE.
OUR SON NEEDS TO KNOW ME. AND YOU.

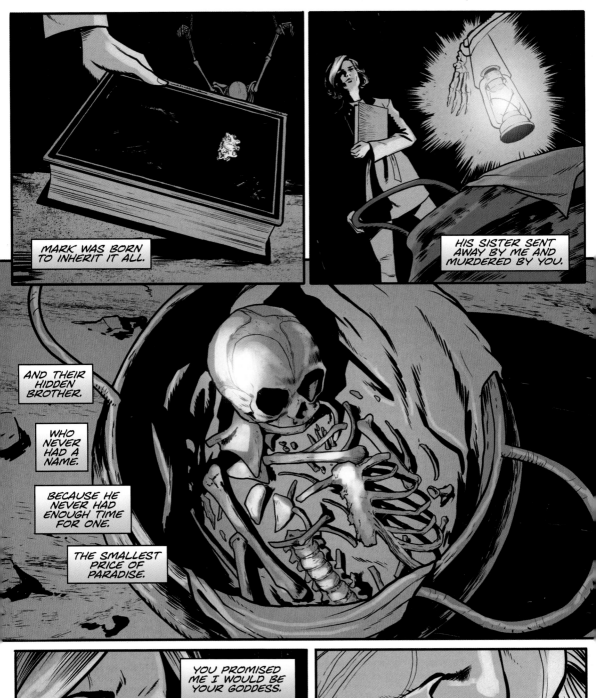

MARK WAS BORN TO INHERIT IT ALL.

HIS SISTER SENT AWAY BY ME AND MURDERED BY YOU.

AND THEIR HIDDEN BROTHER.

WHO NEVER HAD A NAME.

BECAUSE HE NEVER HAD ENOUGH TIME FOR ONE.

THE SMALLEST PRICE OF PARADISE.

YOU PROMISED ME I WOULD BE YOUR GODDESS.

AND I WAS.

BUT IT'S TIME FOR THE GODS TO DIE.

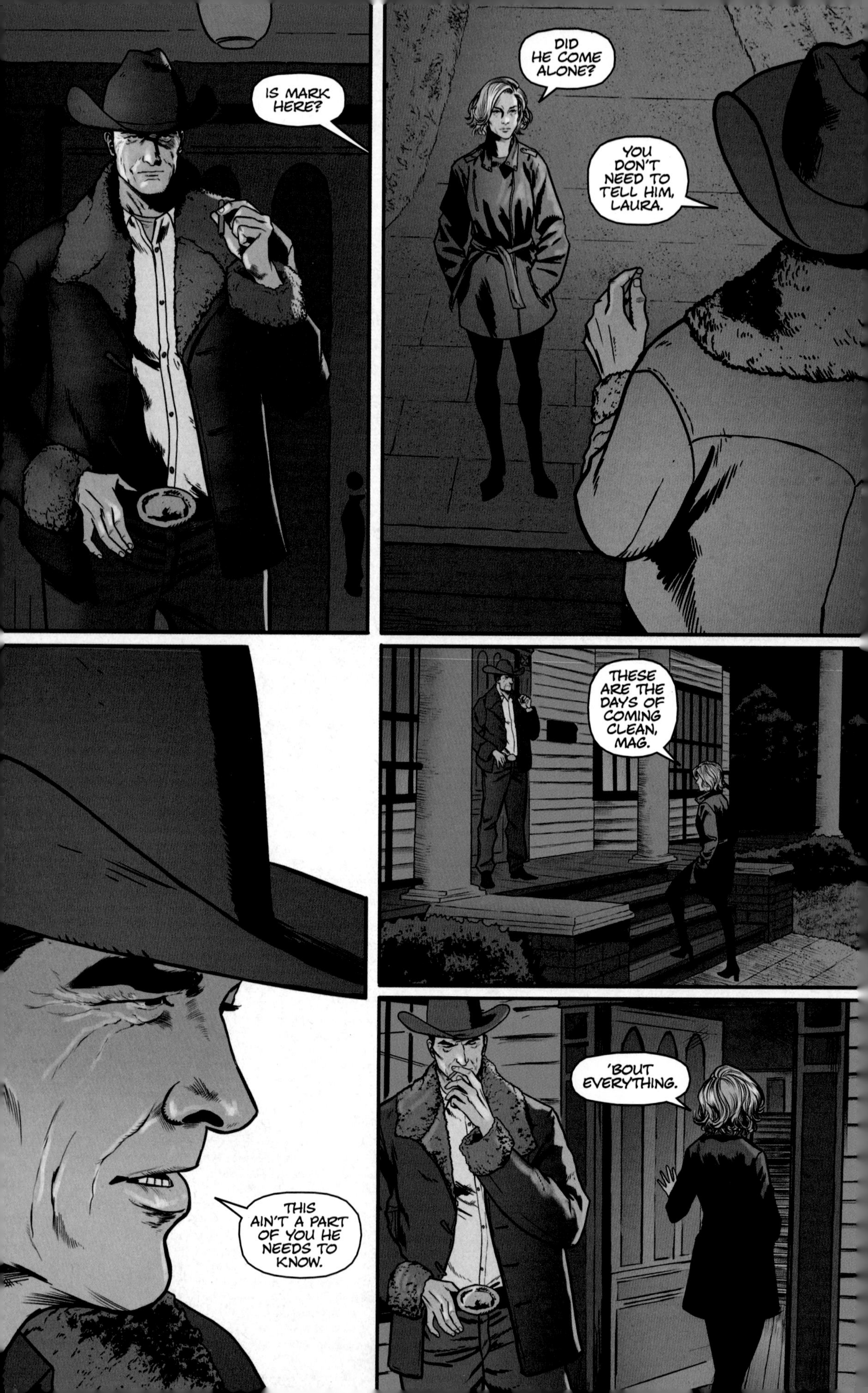
IS MARK HERE?
DID HE COME ALONE?
YOU DON'T NEED TO TELL HIM, LAURA.
THIS AIN'T A PART OF YOU HE NEEDS TO KNOW.
THESE ARE THE DAYS OF COMING CLEAN, MAG.
'BOUT EVERYTHING.

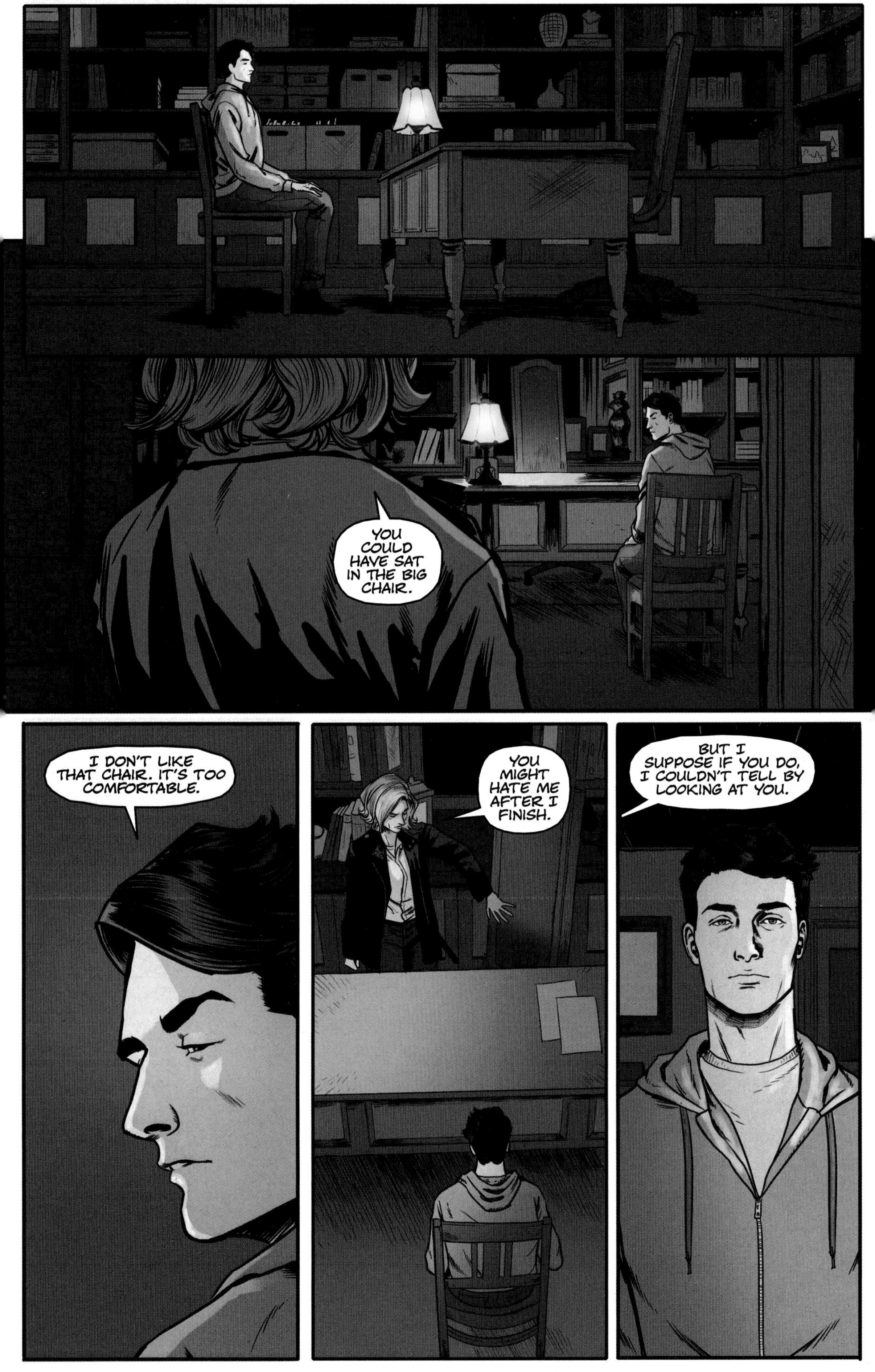
YOU COULD HAVE SAT IN THE BIG CHAIR.
I DON'T LIKE THAT CHAIR. IT'S TOO COMFORTABLE.
YOU MIGHT HATE ME AFTER I FINISH.
BUT I SUPPOSE IF YOU DO, I COULDN'T TELL BY LOOKING AT YOU.

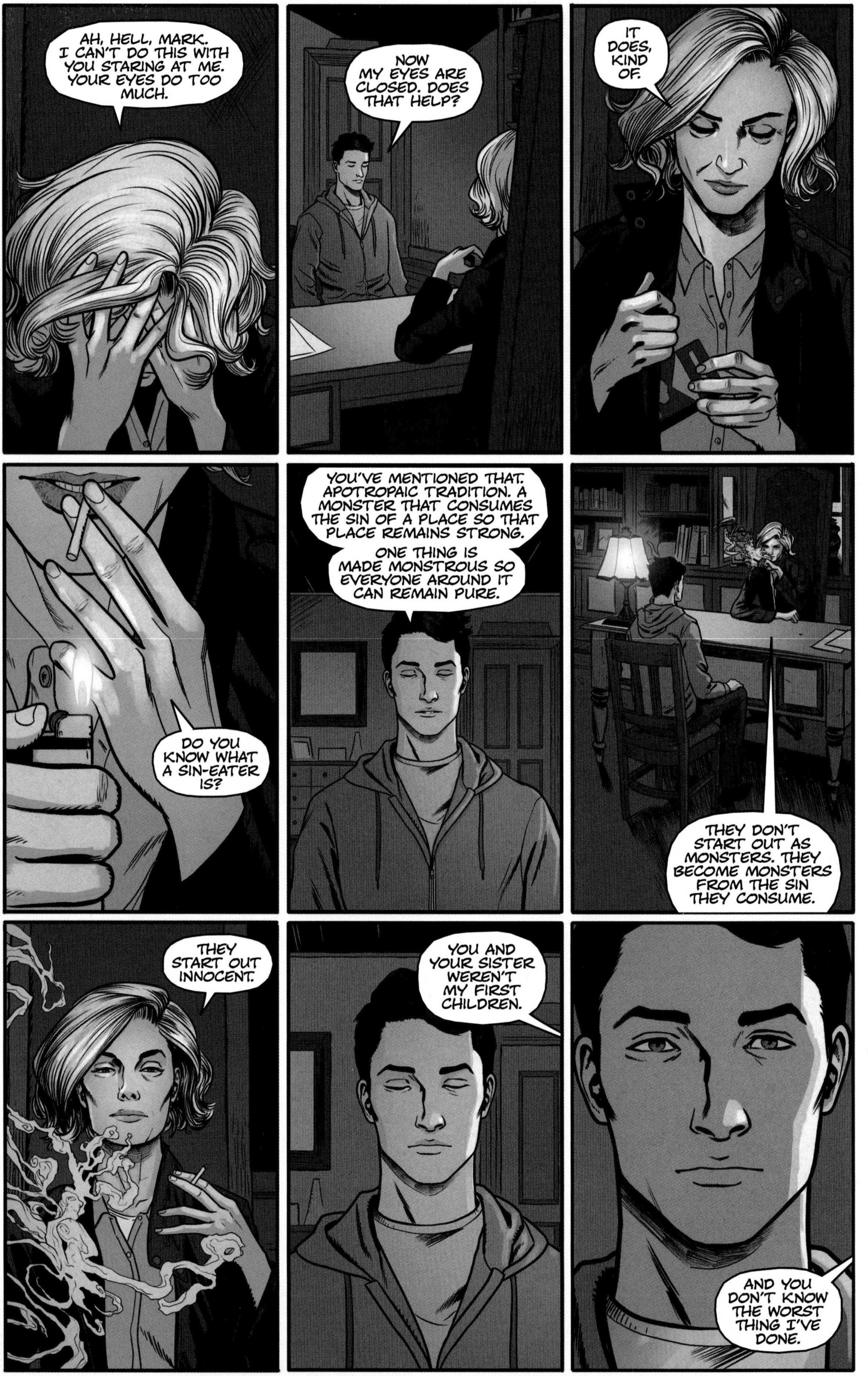
AH, HELL, MARK. I CAN'T DO THIS WITH YOU STARING AT ME. YOUR EYES DO TOO MUCH.
NOW MY EYES ARE CLOSED. DOES THAT HELP?
IT DOES, KIND OF.
DO YOU KNOW WHAT A SIN-EATER IS?
YOU'VE MENTIONED THAT. APOTROPAIC TRADITION. A MONSTER THAT CONSUMES THE SIN OF A PLACE SO THAT PLACE REMAINS STRONG.
ONE THING IS MADE MONSTROUS SO EVERYONE AROUND IT CAN REMAIN PURE.
THEY DON'T START OUT AS MONSTERS. THEY BECOME MONSTERS FROM THE SIN THEY CONSUME.
THEY START OUT INNOCENT.
YOU AND YOUR SISTER WEREN'T MY FIRST CHILDREN.
AND YOU DON'T KNOW THE WORST THING I'VE DONE.

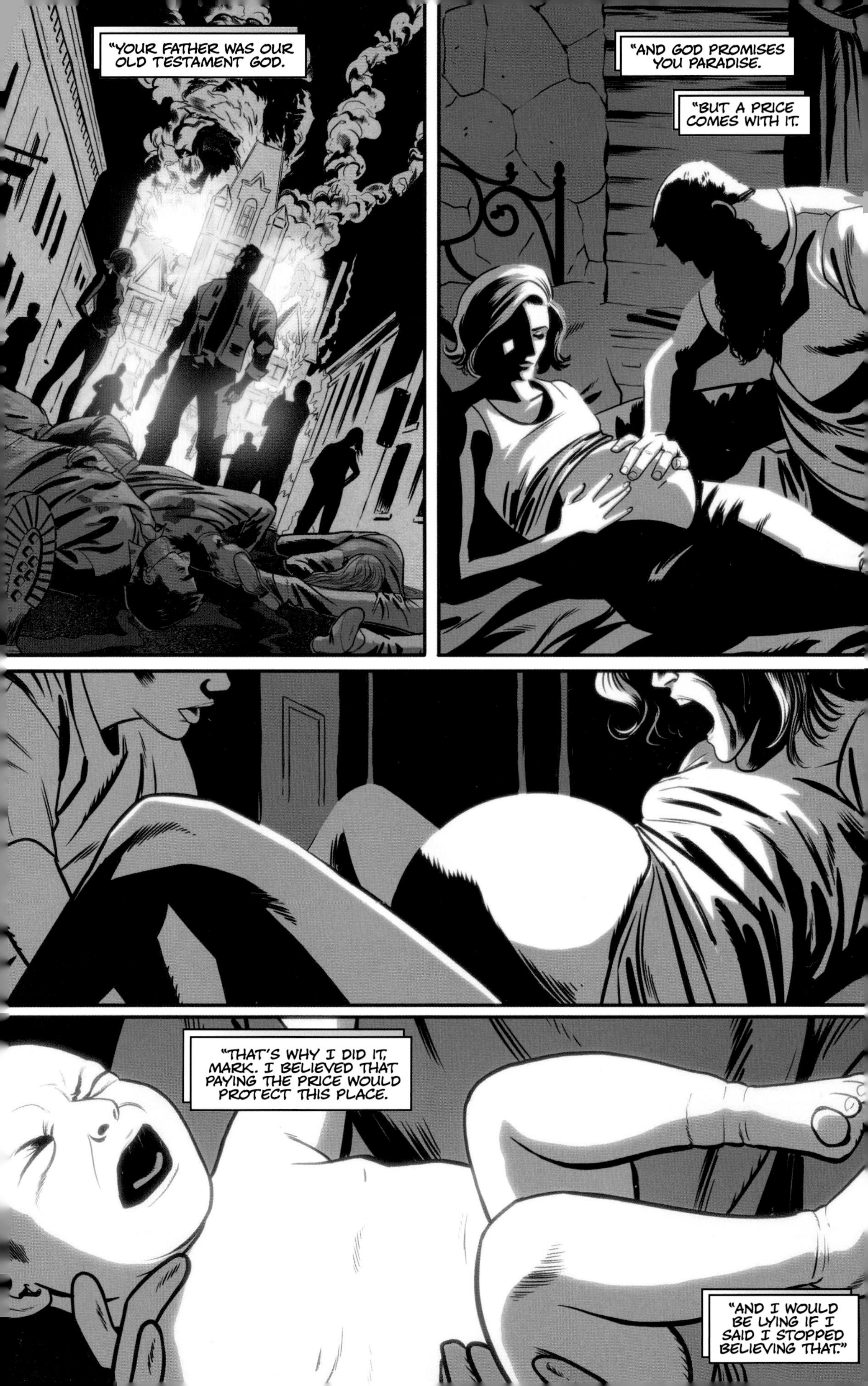
"YOUR FATHER WAS OUR OLD TESTAMENT GOD.
"AND GOD PROMISES YOU PARADISE.
"BUT A PRICE COMES WITH IT.
"THAT'S WHY I DID IT, MARK. I BELIEVED THAT PAYING THE PRICE WOULD PROTECT THIS PLACE.
"AND I WOULD BE LYING IF I SAID I STOPPED BELIEVING THAT."

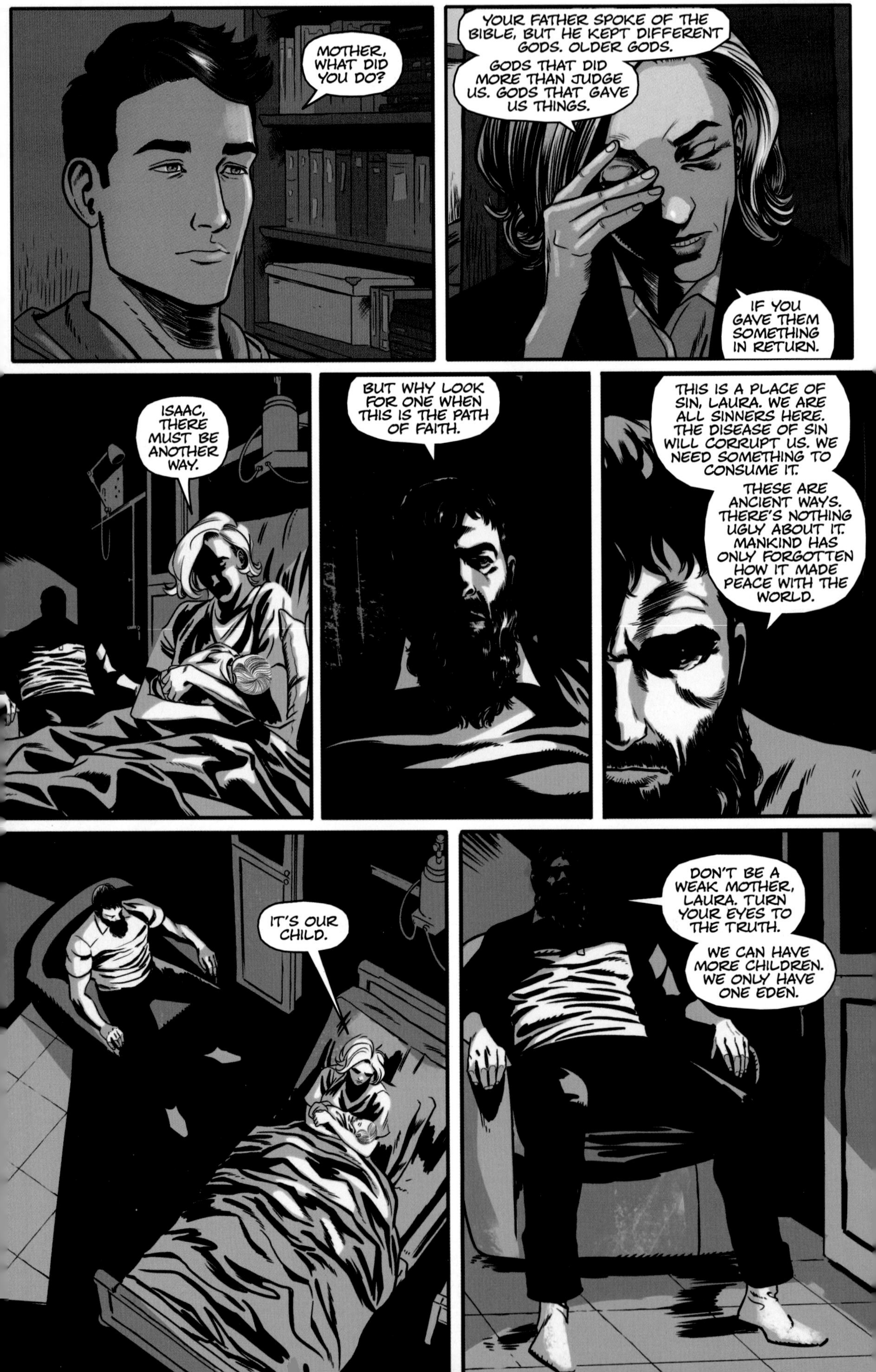

MOTHER, WHAT DID YOU DO?
YOUR FATHER SPOKE OF THE BIBLE, BUT HE KEPT DIFFERENT GODS. OLDER GODS.
GODS THAT DID MORE THAN JUDGE US. GODS THAT GAVE US THINGS.
IF YOU GAVE THEM SOMETHING IN RETURN.
ISAAC, THERE MUST BE ANOTHER WAY.
BUT WHY LOOK FOR ONE WHEN THIS IS THE PATH OF FAITH.
THIS IS A PLACE OF SIN, LAURA. WE ARE ALL SINNERS HERE. THE DISEASE OF SIN WILL CORRUPT US. WE NEED SOMETHING TO CONSUME IT.
THESE ARE ANCIENT WAYS. THERE'S NOTHING UGLY ABOUT IT. MANKIND HAS ONLY FORGOTTEN HOW IT MADE PEACE WITH THE WORLD.
IT'S OUR CHILD.
DON'T BE A WEAK MOTHER, LAURA. TURN YOUR EYES TO THE TRUTH.
WE CAN HAVE MORE CHILDREN. WE ONLY HAVE ONE EDEN.

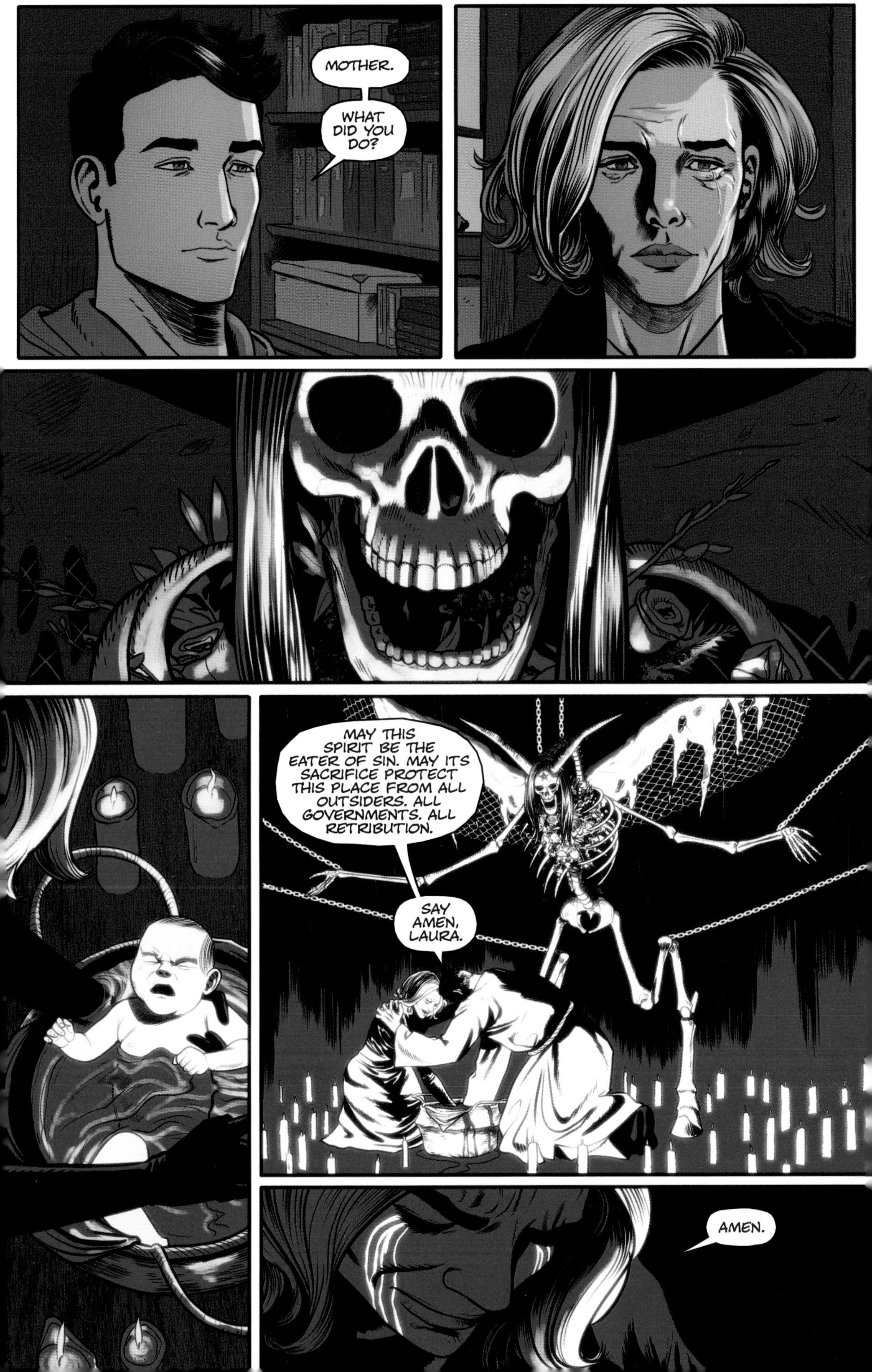
MOTHER.
WHAT DID YOU DO?
MAY THIS SPIRIT BE THE EATER OF SIN. MAY ITS SACRIFICE PROTECT THIS PLACE FROM ALL OUTSIDERS. ALL GOVERNMENTS. ALL RETRIBUTION.
SAY AMEN, LAURA.
AMEN.

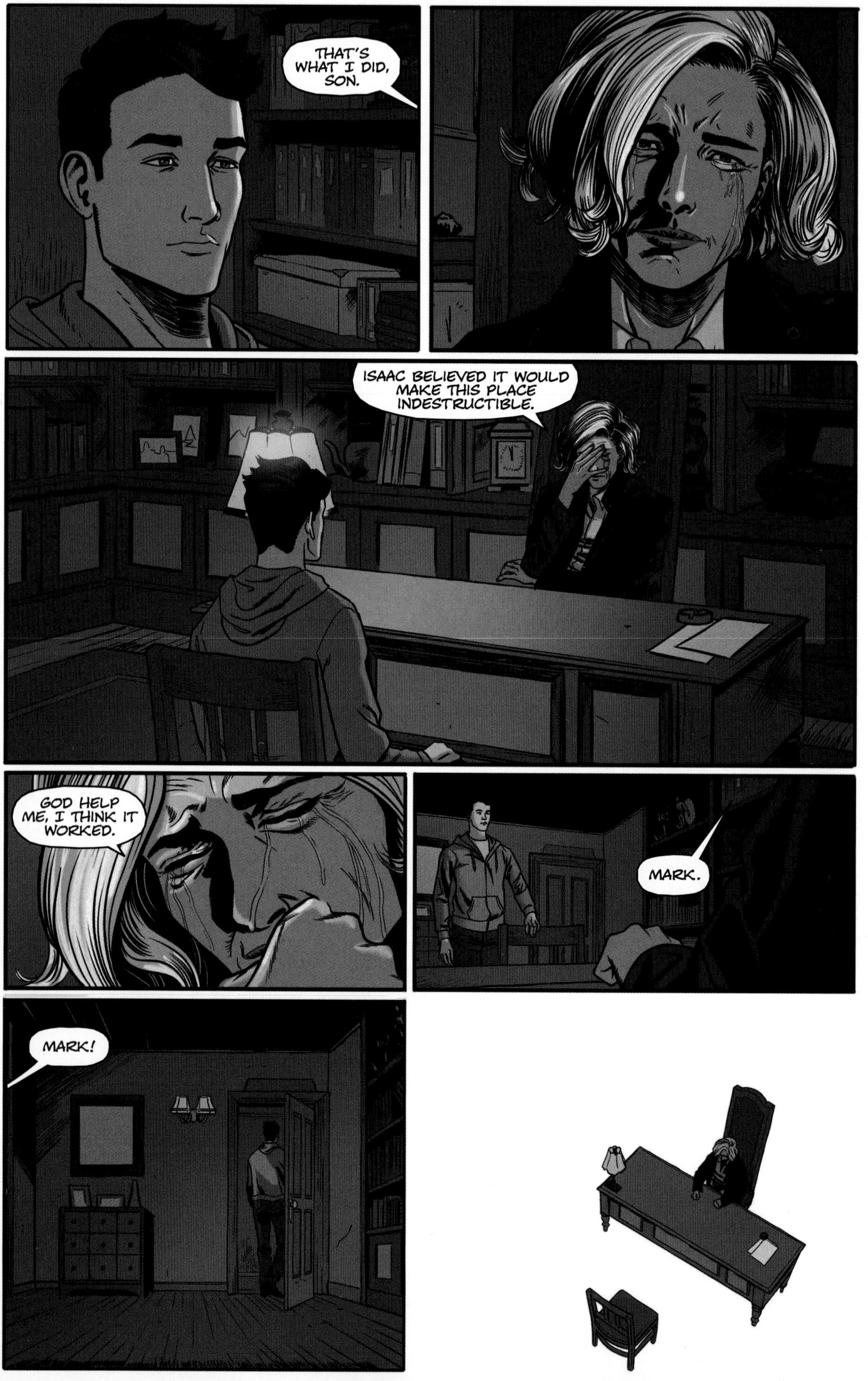
THAT'S WHAT I DID, SON.
ISAAC BELIEVED IT WOULD MAKE THIS PLACE INDESTRUCTIBLE.
GOD HELP ME, I THINK IT WORKED.
MARK.
MARK!

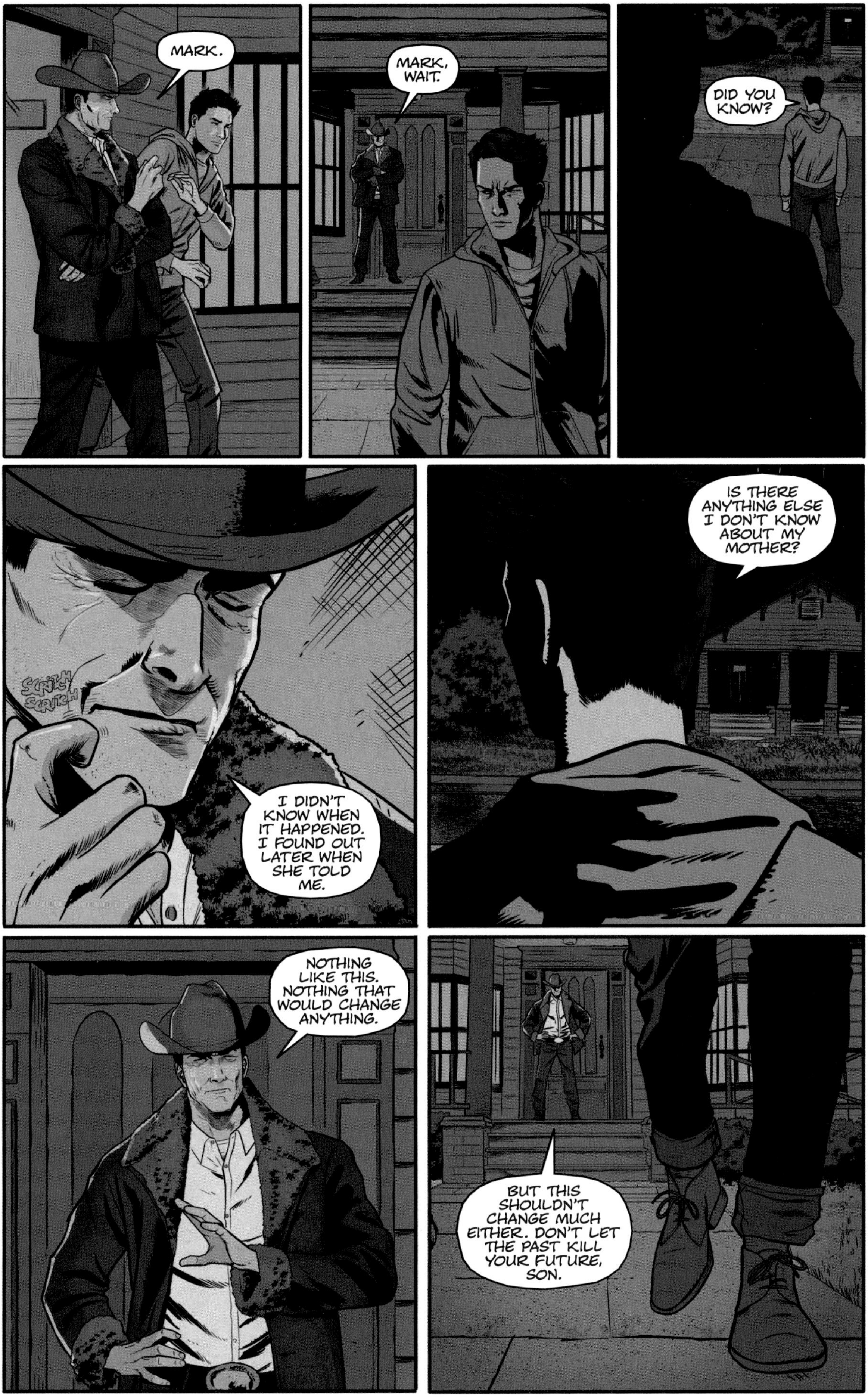
MARK.
MARK, WAIT.
DID YOU KNOW?
SCRITCH SCRITCH
I DIDN'T KNOW WHEN IT HAPPENED. I FOUND OUT LATER WHEN SHE TOLD ME.
IS THERE ANYTHING ELSE I DON'T KNOW ABOUT MY MOTHER?
NOTHING LIKE THIS. NOTHING THAT WOULD CHANGE ANYTHING.
BUT THIS SHOULDN'T CHANGE MUCH EITHER. DON'T LET THE PAST KILL YOUR FUTURE, SON.

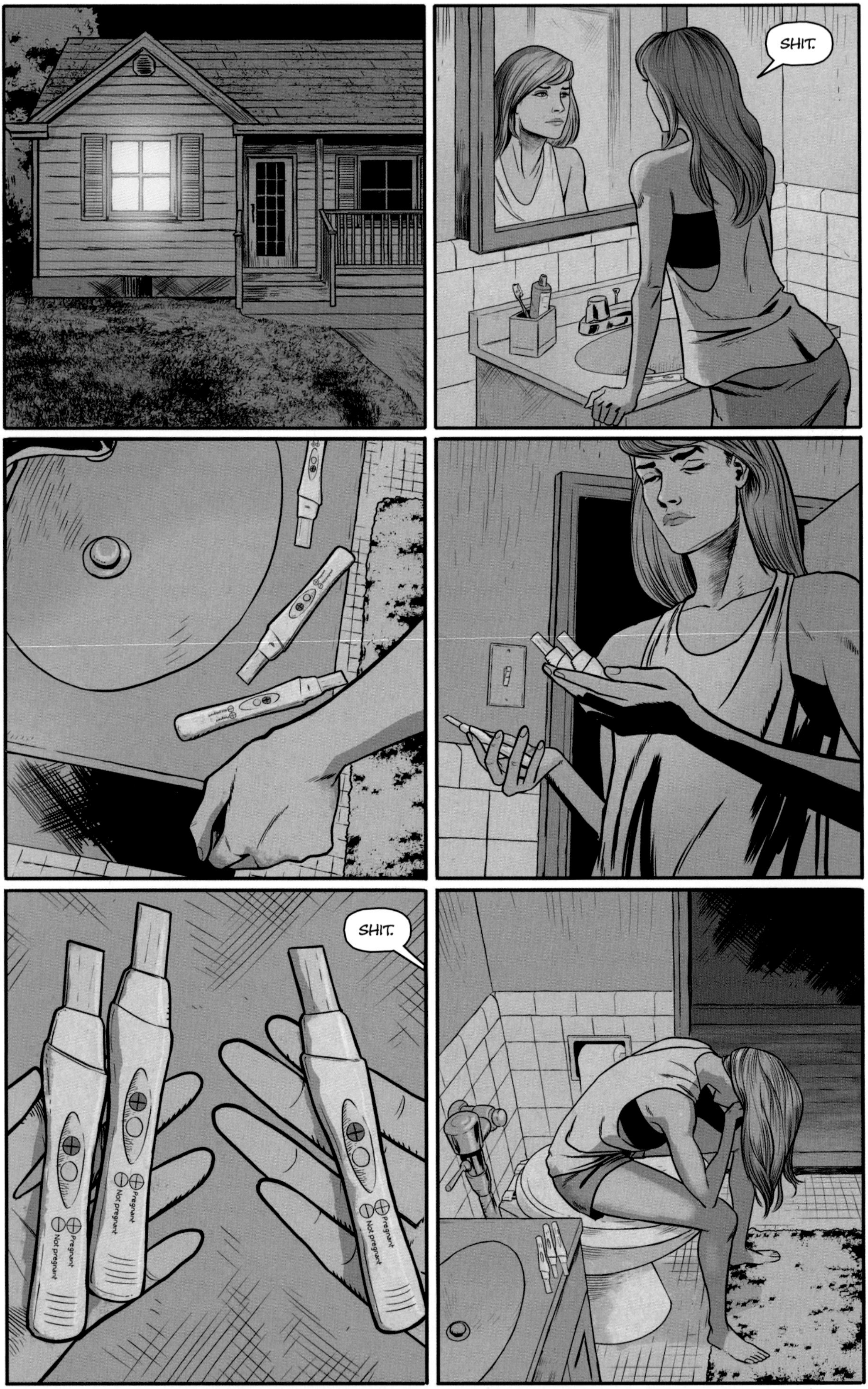
SHIT.
SHIT.
Pregnant
Not pregnant
Pregnant
Not pregnant
Pregnant
Not pregnant

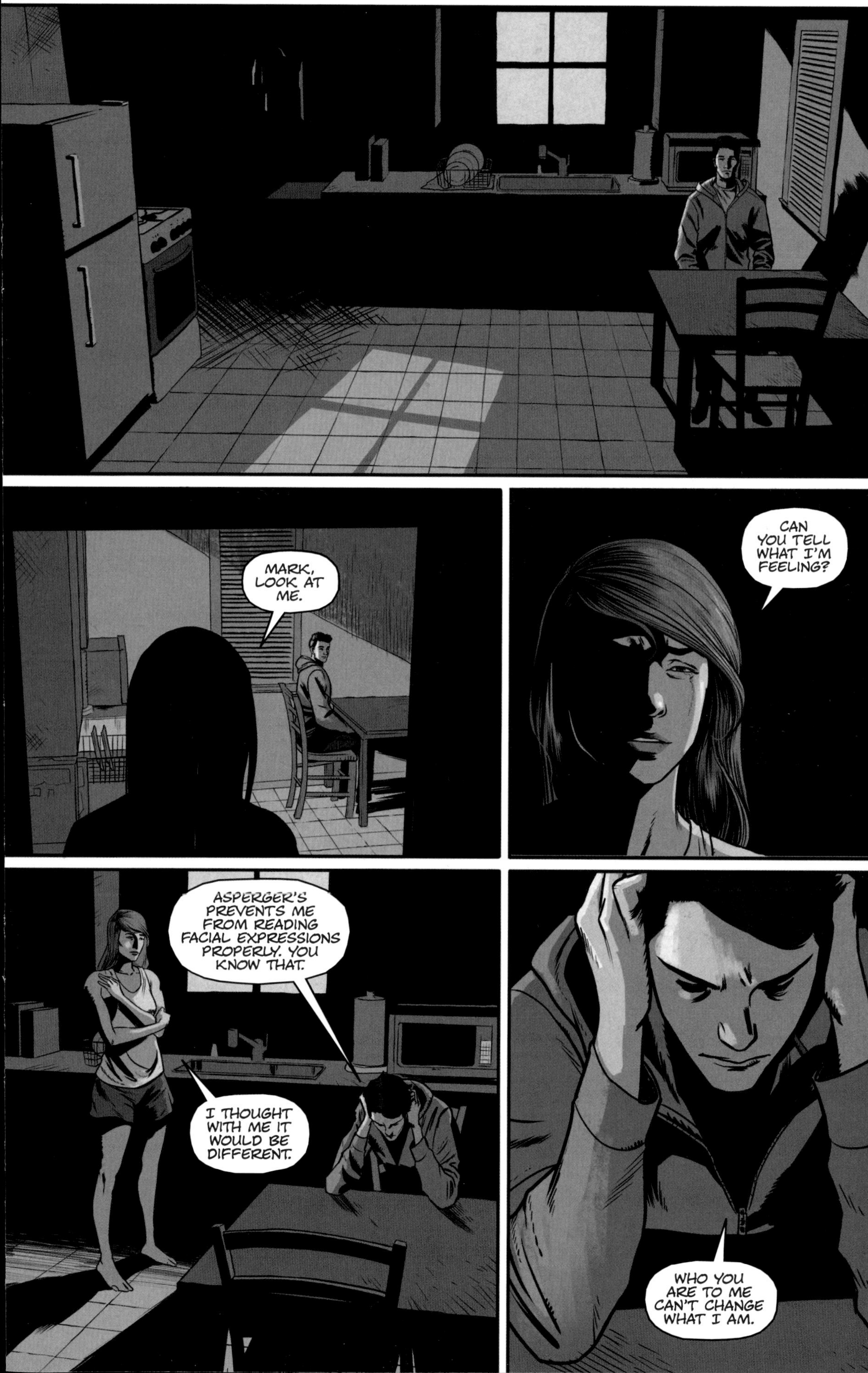
MARK, LOOK AT ME.
CAN YOU TELL WHAT I'M FEELING?
ASPERGER'S PREVENTS ME FROM READING FACIAL EXPRESSIONS PROPERLY. YOU KNOW THAT.
I THOUGHT WITH ME IT WOULD BE DIFFERENT.
WHO YOU ARE TO ME CAN'T CHANGE WHAT I AM.

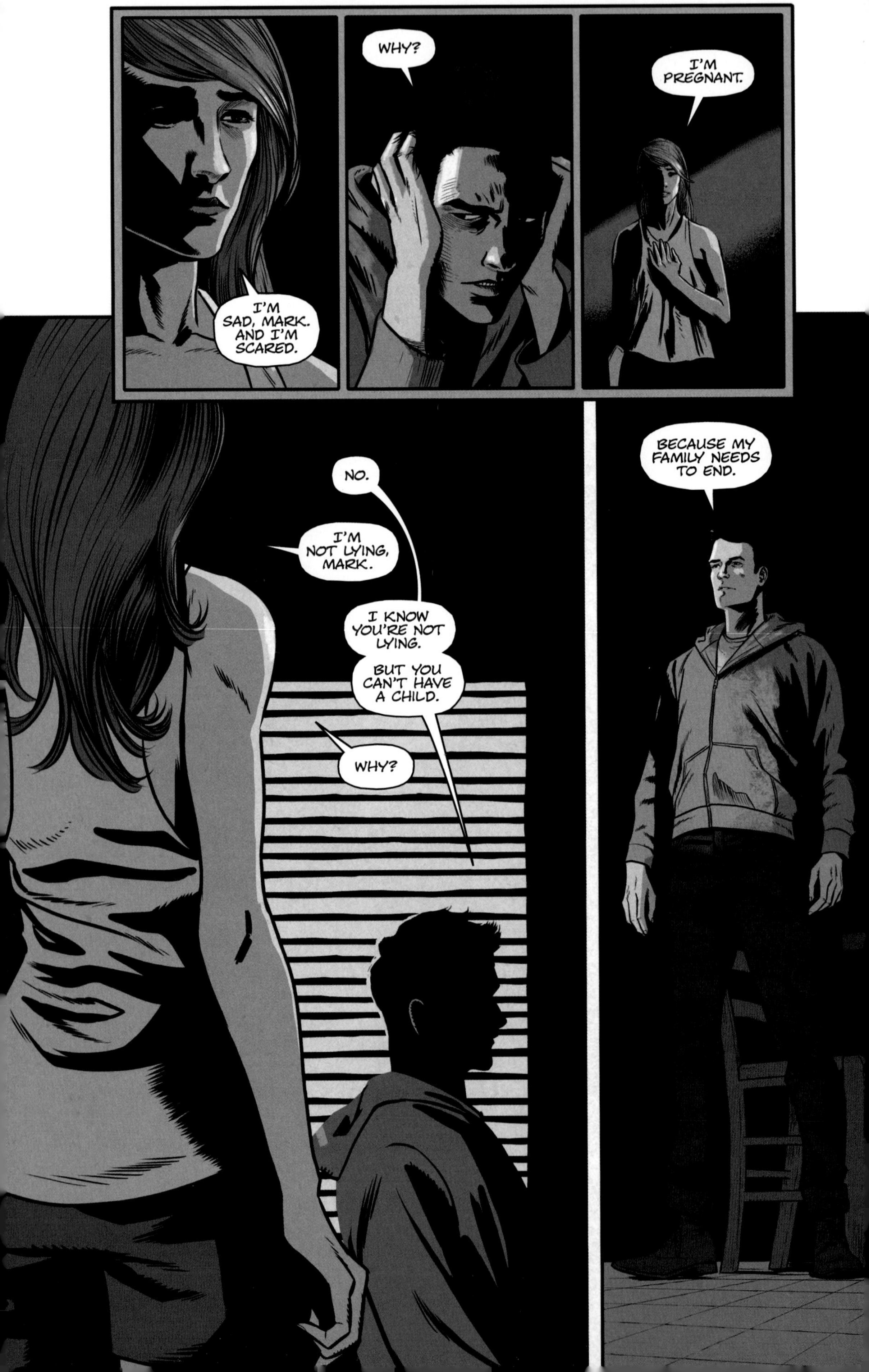
I'M SAD, MARK. AND I'M SCARED.
WHY?
I'M PREGNANT.
NO.
I'M NOT LYING, MARK.
I KNOW YOU'RE NOT LYING.
BUT YOU CAN'T HAVE A CHILD.
WHY?
BECAUSE MY FAMILY NEEDS TO END.

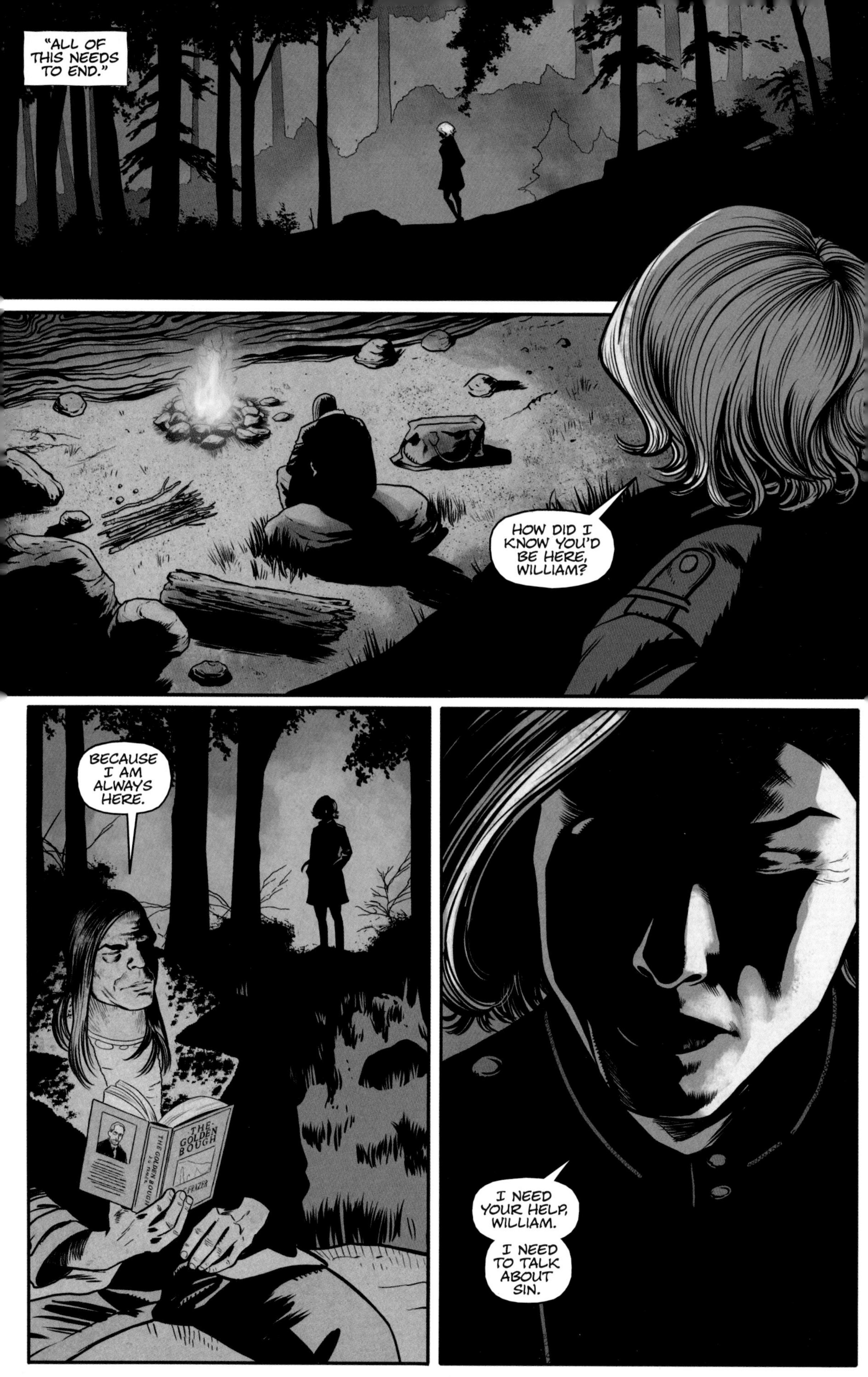
"ALL OF THIS NEEDS TO END."
HOW DID I KNOW YOU'D BE HERE, WILLIAM?
BECAUSE I AM ALWAYS HERE.
THE GOLDEN BOUGH
FRAZER
I NEED YOUR HELP, WILLIAM.
I NEED TO TALK ABOUT SIN.

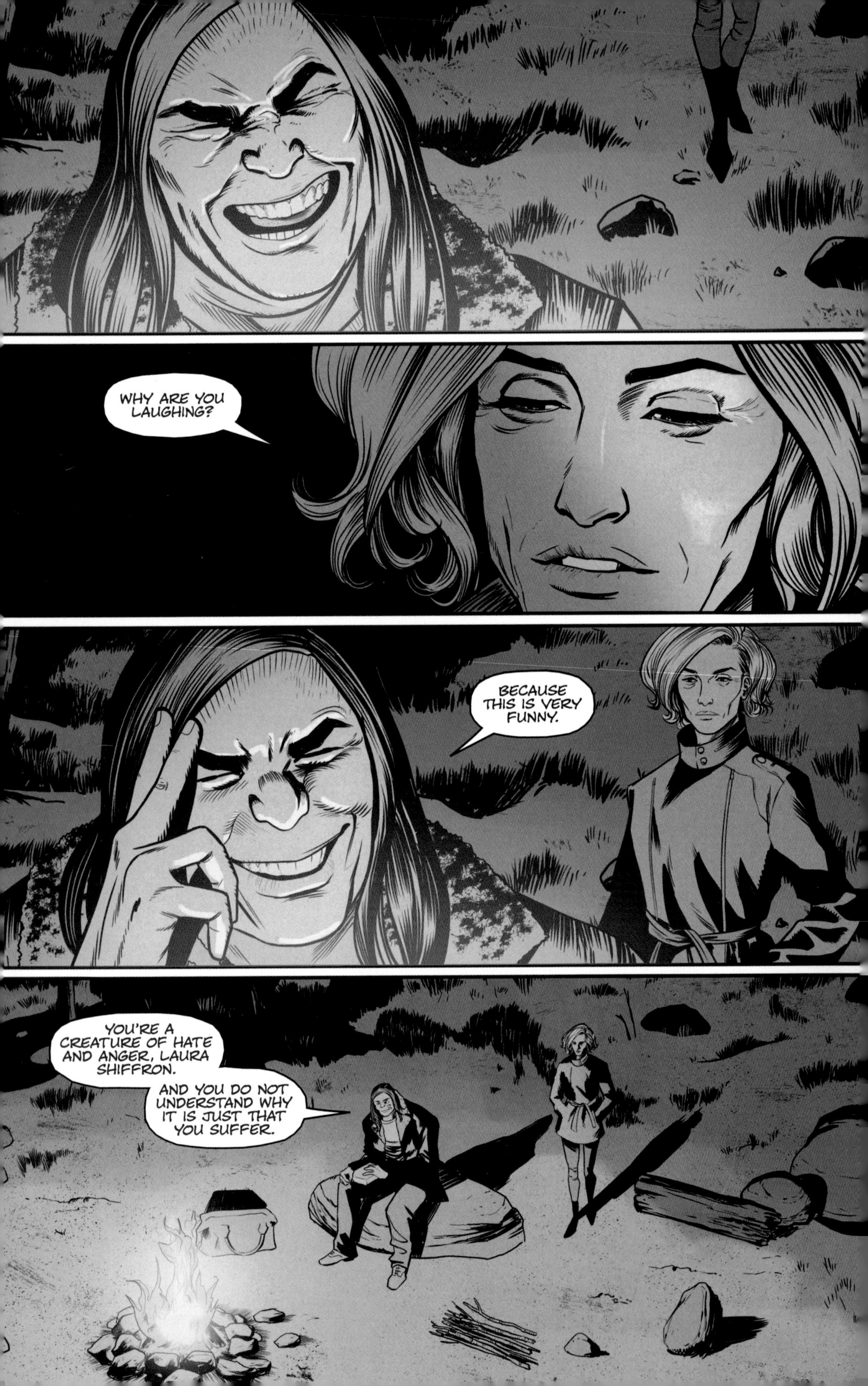
WHY ARE YOU LAUGHING?
BECAUSE THIS IS VERY FUNNY.
YOU'RE A CREATURE OF HATE AND ANGER, LAURA SHIFFRON.
AND YOU DO NOT UNDERSTAND WHY IT IS JUST THAT YOU SUFFER.

I UNDERSTAND IT, WILLIAM.
BUT I NEED IT TO STOP.
MY SON HATES ME. AND I KNOW HE SHOULD.
I KILLED MY OWN CHILD.
I KILLED MY OWN CHILD.
YOU SPEAK OF THE BONES IN THE BASKET.
HOW...DO YOU KNOW ABOUT THAT?

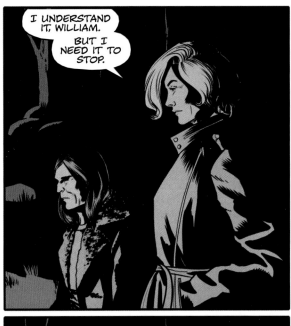

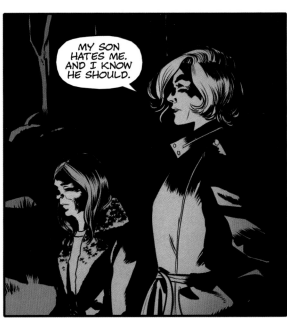

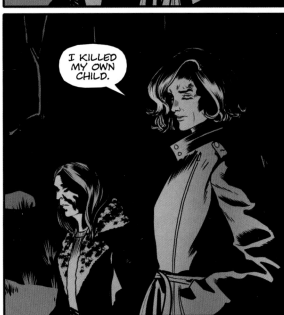

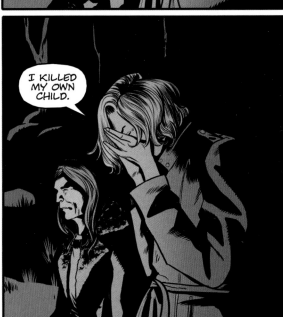

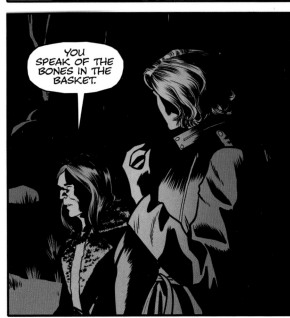

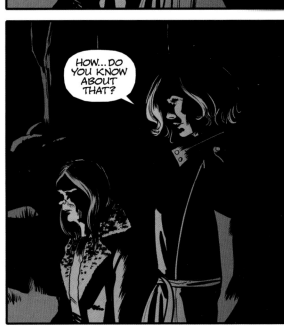

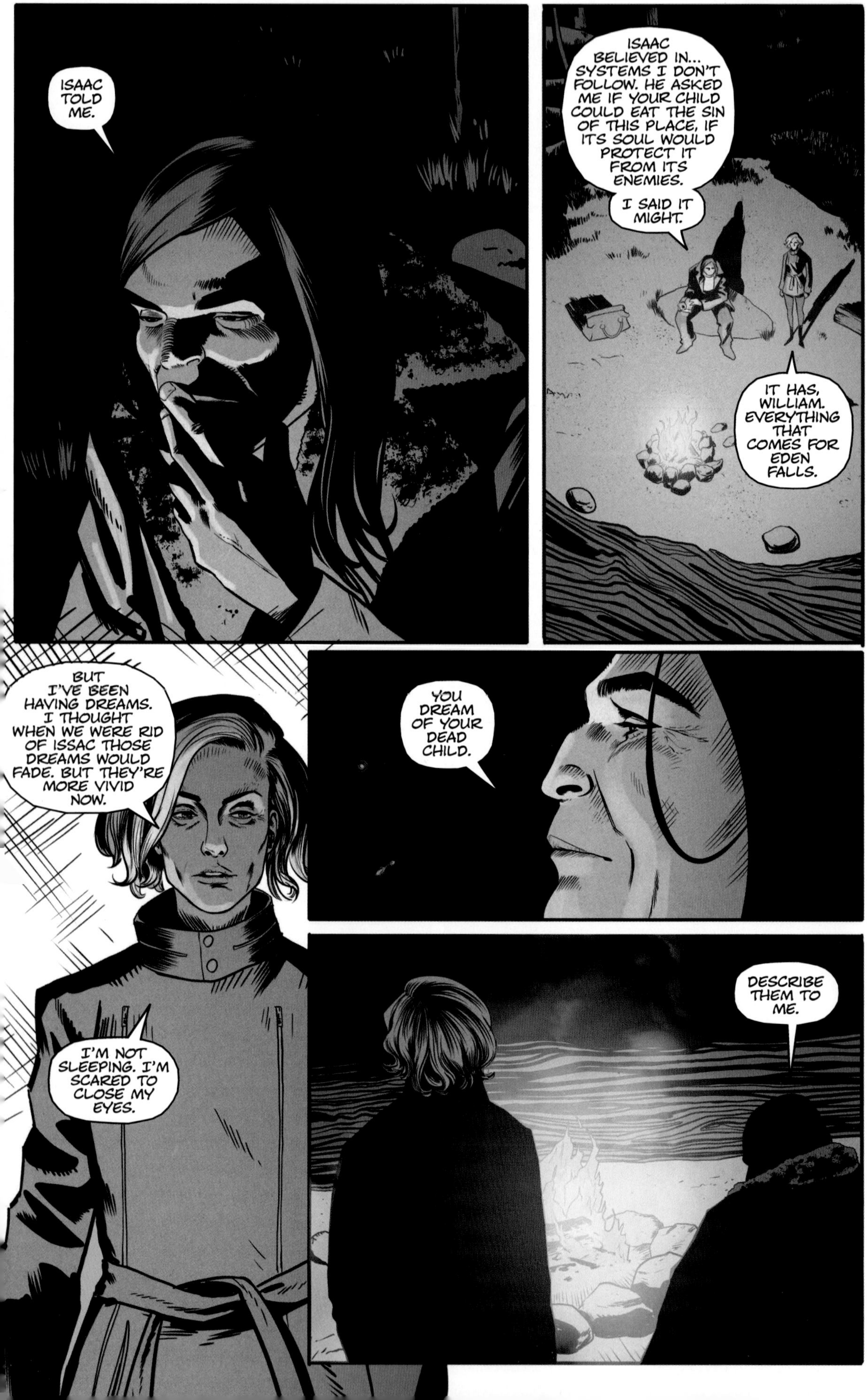
ISAAC TOLD ME.
ISAAC BELIEVED IN... SYSTEMS I DON'T FOLLOW. HE ASKED ME IF YOUR CHILD COULD EAT THE SIN OF THIS PLACE, IF ITS SOUL WOULD PROTECT IT FROM ITS ENEMIES.
I SAID IT MIGHT.
IT HAS, WILLIAM. EVERYTHING THAT COMES FOR EDEN FALLS.
BUT I'VE BEEN HAVING DREAMS. I THOUGHT WHEN WE WERE RID OF ISSAC THOSE DREAMS WOULD FADE. BUT THEY'RE MORE VIVID NOW.
YOU DREAM OF YOUR DEAD CHILD.
I'M NOT SLEEPING. I'M SCARED TO CLOSE MY EYES.
DESCRIBE THEM TO ME.

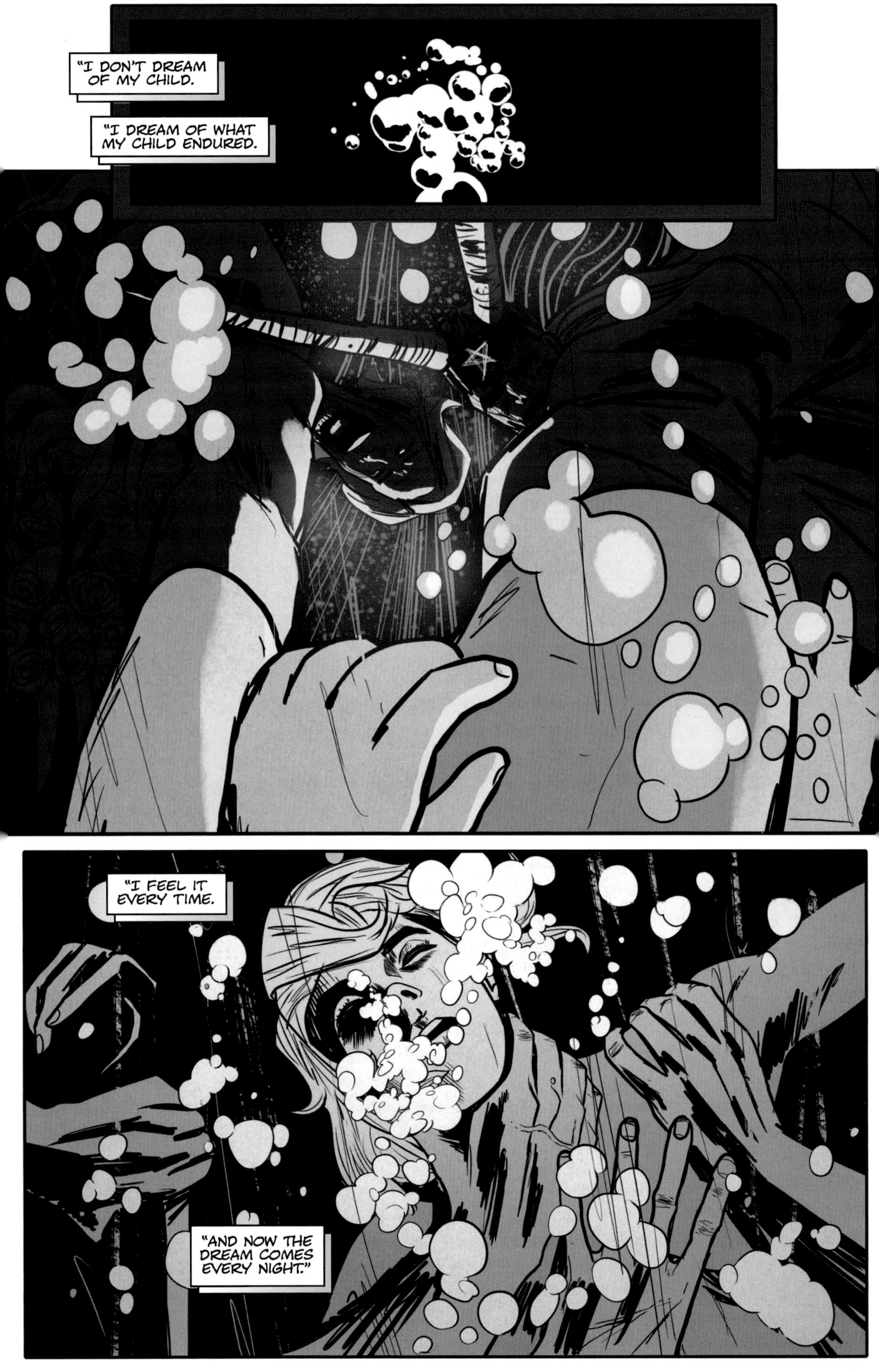
"I DON'T DREAM OF MY CHILD.
"I DREAM OF WHAT MY CHILD ENDURED.
"I FEEL IT EVERY TIME.
"AND NOW THE DREAM COMES EVERY NIGHT."

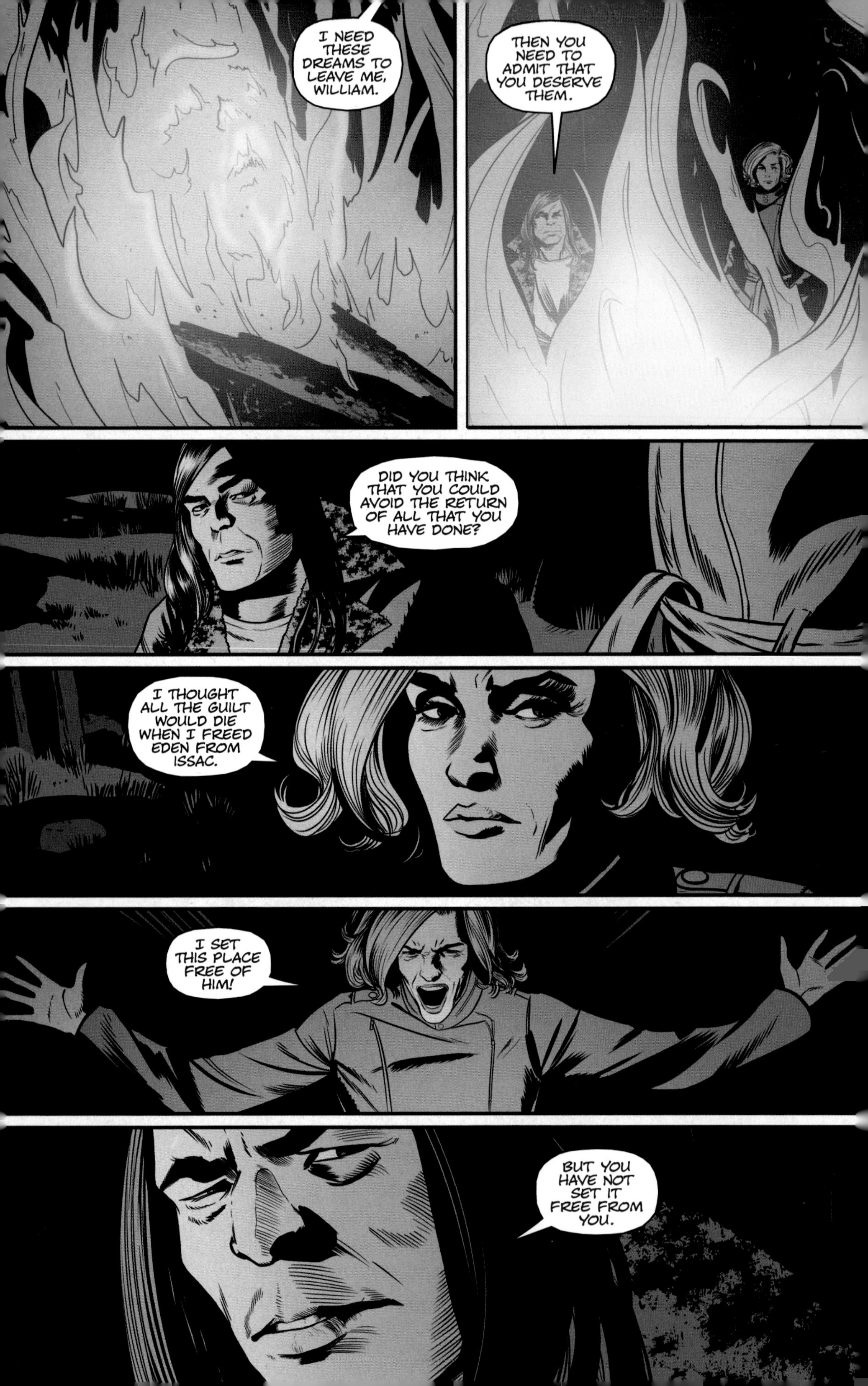

I NEED THESE DREAMS TO LEAVE ME, WILLIAM.
THEN YOU NEED TO ADMIT THAT YOU DESERVE THEM.
DID YOU THINK THAT YOU COULD AVOID THE RETURN OF ALL THAT YOU HAVE DONE?
I THOUGHT ALL THE GUILT WOULD DIE WHEN I FREED EDEN FROM ISSAC.
I SET THIS PLACE FREE OF HIM!
BUT YOU HAVE NOT SET IT FREE FROM YOU.

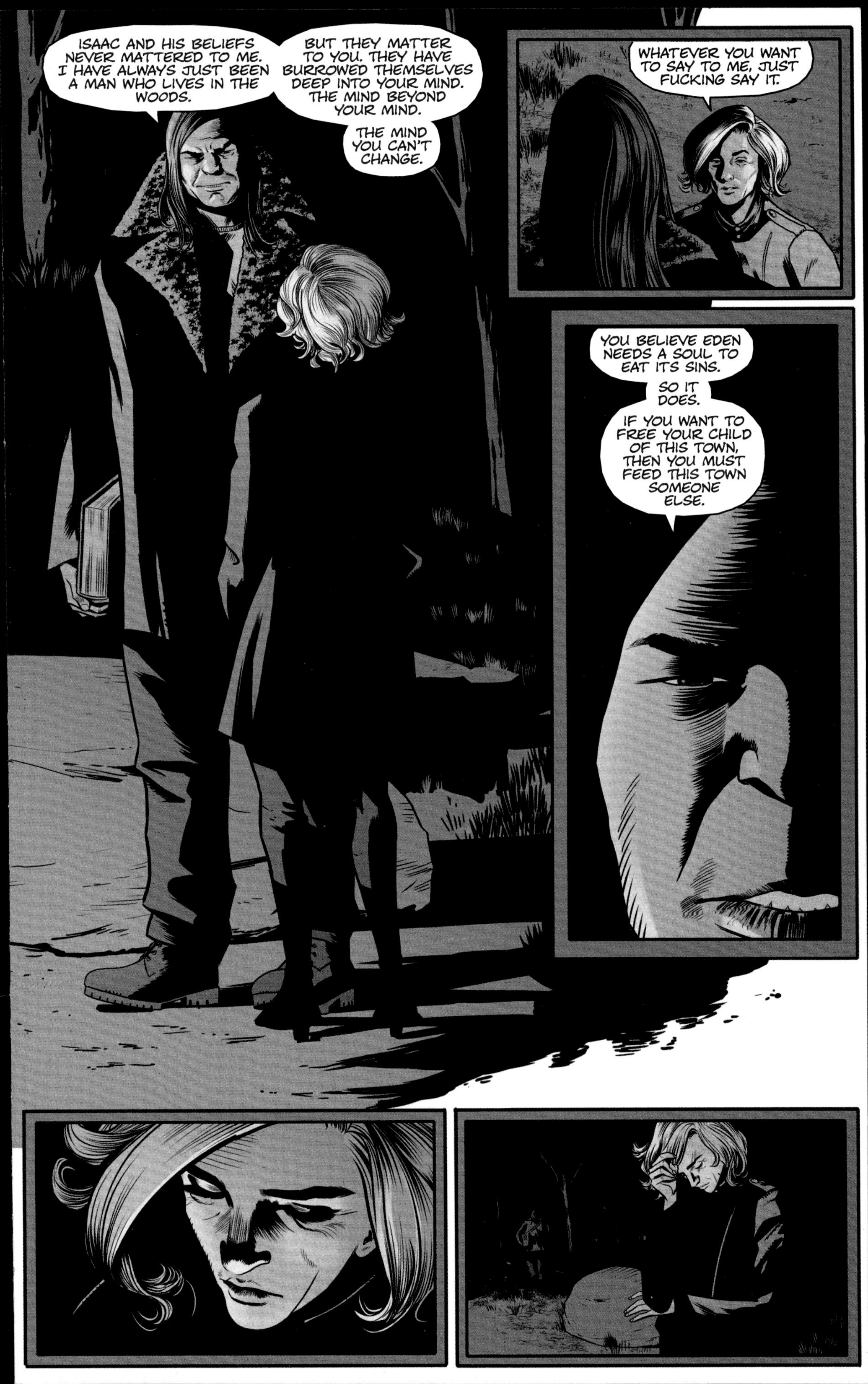
ISAAC AND HIS BELIEFS NEVER MATTERED TO ME. I HAVE ALWAYS JUST BEEN A MAN WHO LIVES IN THE WOODS.
BUT THEY MATTER TO YOU. THEY HAVE BURROWED THEMSELVES DEEP INTO YOUR MIND. THE MIND BEYOND YOUR MIND.
THE MIND YOU CAN'T CHANGE.
WHATEVER YOU WANT TO SAY TO ME, JUST FUCKING SAY IT.
YOU BELIEVE EDEN NEEDS A SOUL TO EAT ITS SINS.
SO IT DOES.
IF YOU WANT TO FREE YOUR CHILD OF THIS TOWN, THEN YOU MUST FEED THIS TOWN SOMEONE ELSE.

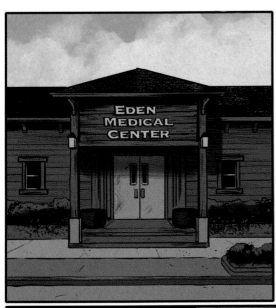

EDEN MEDICAL CENTER

AND YOU'VE BOTH CONSIDERED THIS?

WE'VE SPOKEN ABOUT IT. YES.

THIS IS THE BEST WAY.

YOU KNOW THAT THERE'S NO GUARANTEE YOUR CHILD WOULD BE ON THE ASPERGER'S SPECTRUM.

IT COULD BE NORMAL.

IT COULD BE A GENIUS AND GIFTED IN THE ARTS. BUT THAT'S UNLIKELY.

WHAT IS LIKELY IS THAT IT WOULD HAVE SOME OF MY DIFFICULTIES.

WHAT IS CERTAIN IS THAT IT WOULD HAVE MY MOTHER AND FATHER'S LEGACY.

THAT LEGACY DESERVES TO END.

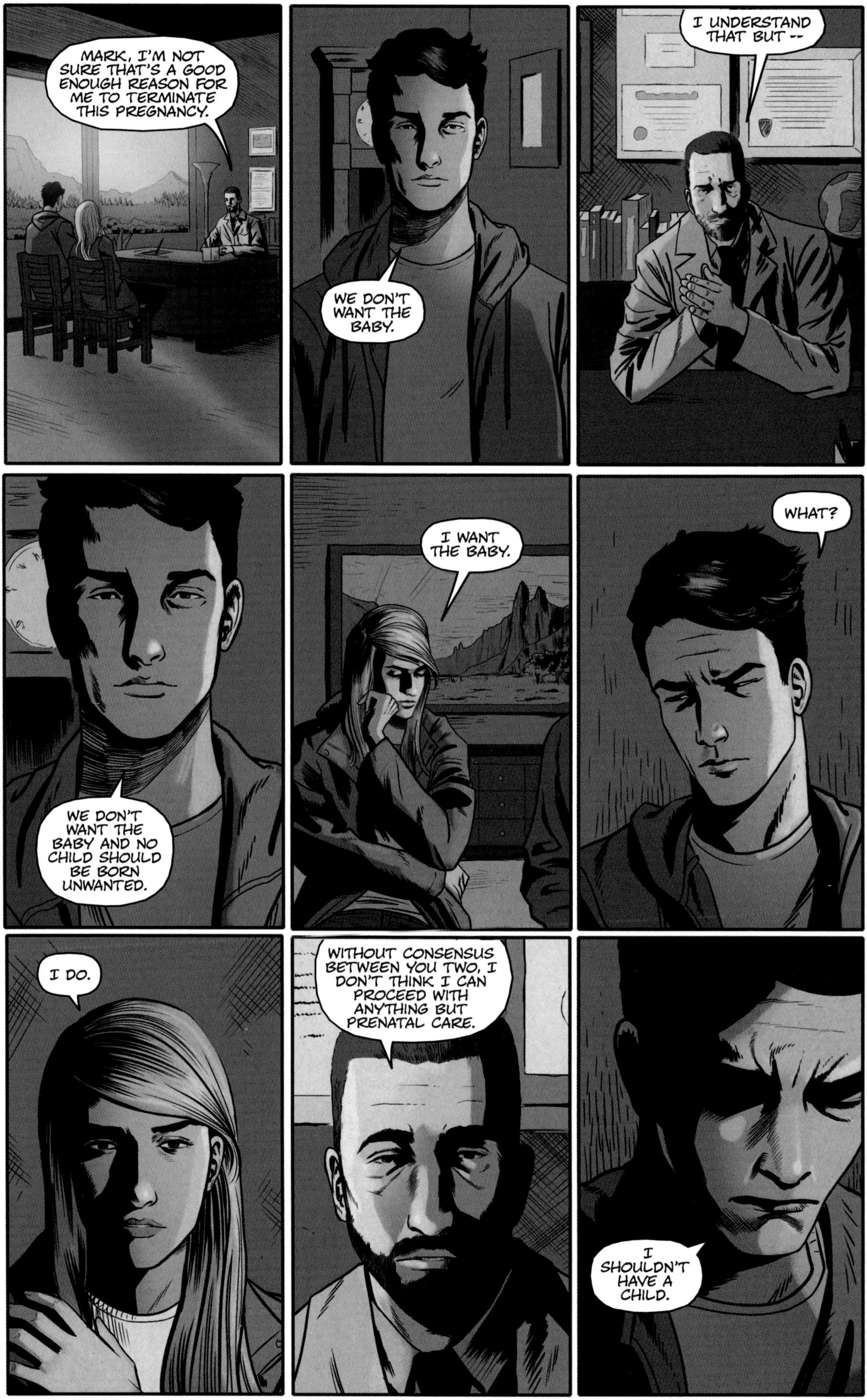
MARK, I'M NOT SURE THAT'S A GOOD ENOUGH REASON FOR ME TO TERMINATE THIS PREGNANCY.
WE DON'T WANT THE BABY.
I UNDERSTAND THAT BUT --
WE DON'T WANT THE BABY AND NO CHILD SHOULD BE BORN UNWANTED.
I WANT THE BABY.
WHAT?
I DO.
WITHOUT CONSENSUS BETWEEN YOU TWO, I DON'T THINK I CAN PROCEED WITH ANYTHING BUT PRENATAL CARE.
I SHOULDN'T HAVE A CHILD.

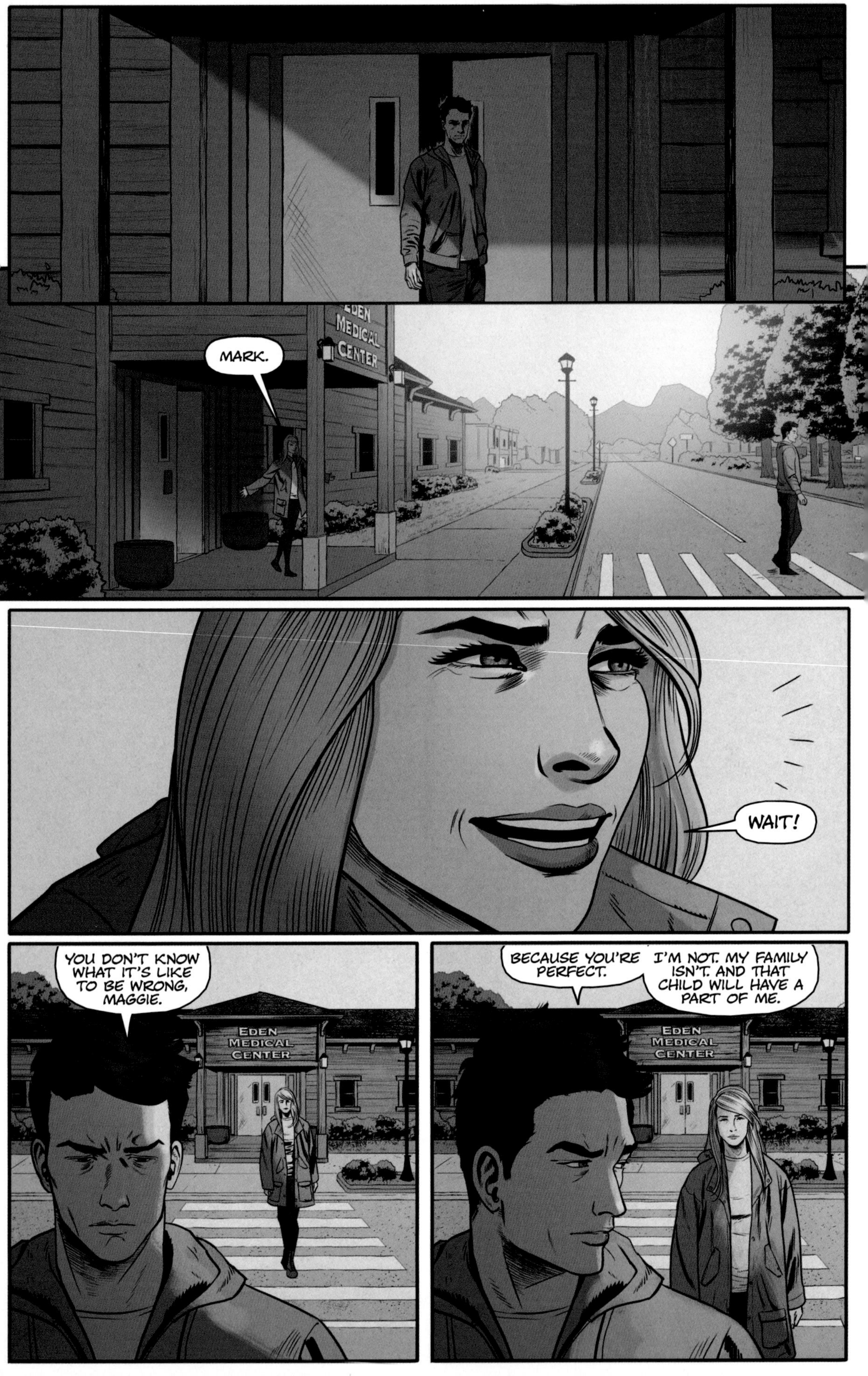
EDEN MEDICAL CENTER
MARK.
WAIT!
YOU DON'T KNOW WHAT IT'S LIKE TO BE WRONG, MAGGIE.
EDEN MEDICAL CENTER
BECAUSE YOU'RE PERFECT.
I'M NOT. MY FAMILY ISN'T. AND THAT CHILD WILL HAVE A PART OF ME.
EDEN MEDICAL CENTER

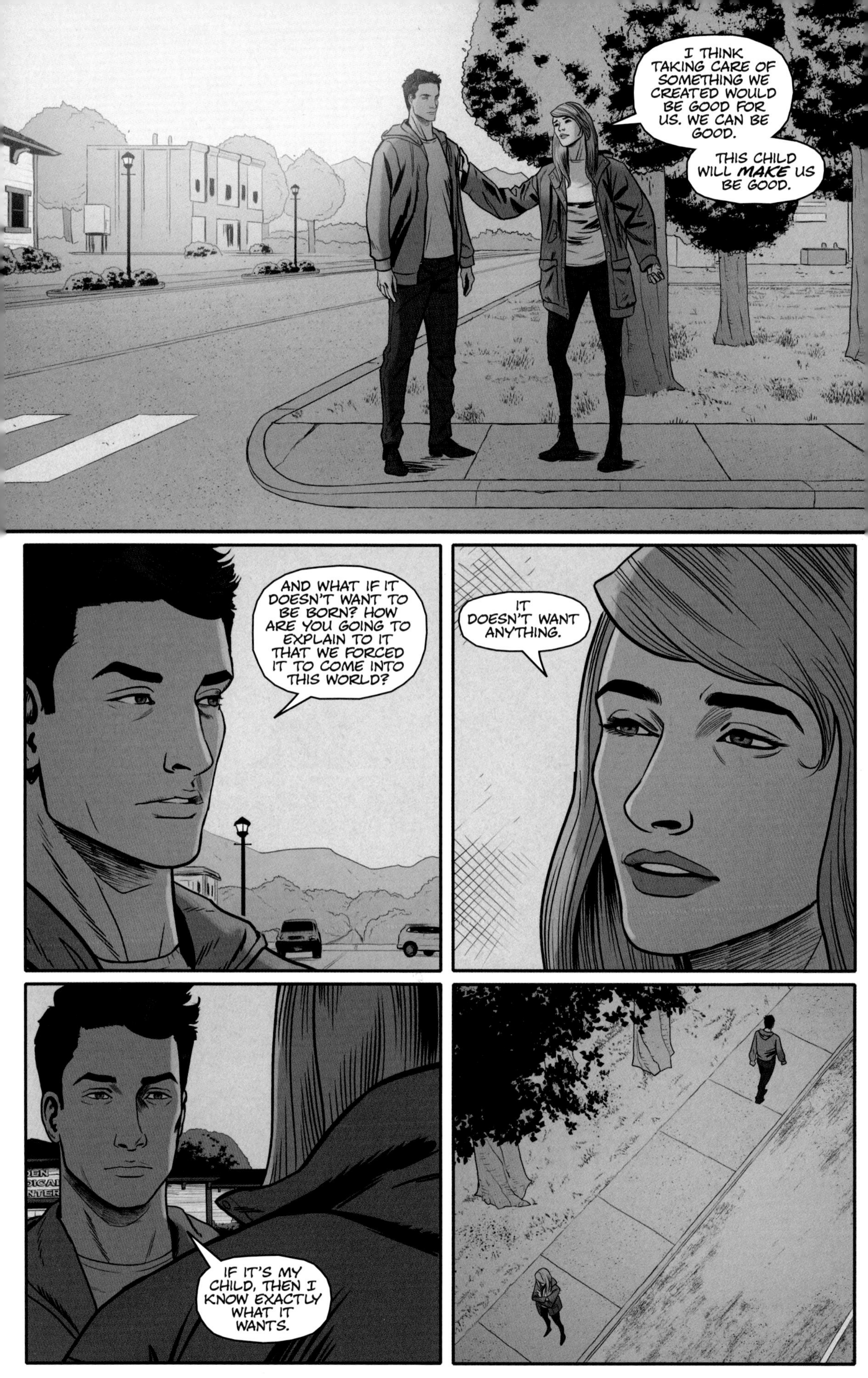
I THINK TAKING CARE OF SOMETHING WE CREATED WOULD BE GOOD FOR US. WE CAN BE GOOD.
THIS CHILD WILL MAKE US BE GOOD.
AND WHAT IF IT DOESN'T WANT TO BE BORN? HOW ARE YOU GOING TO EXPLAIN TO IT THAT WE FORCED IT TO COME INTO THIS WORLD?
IT DOESN'T WANT ANYTHING.
IF IT'S MY CHILD, THEN I KNOW EXACTLY WHAT IT WANTS.

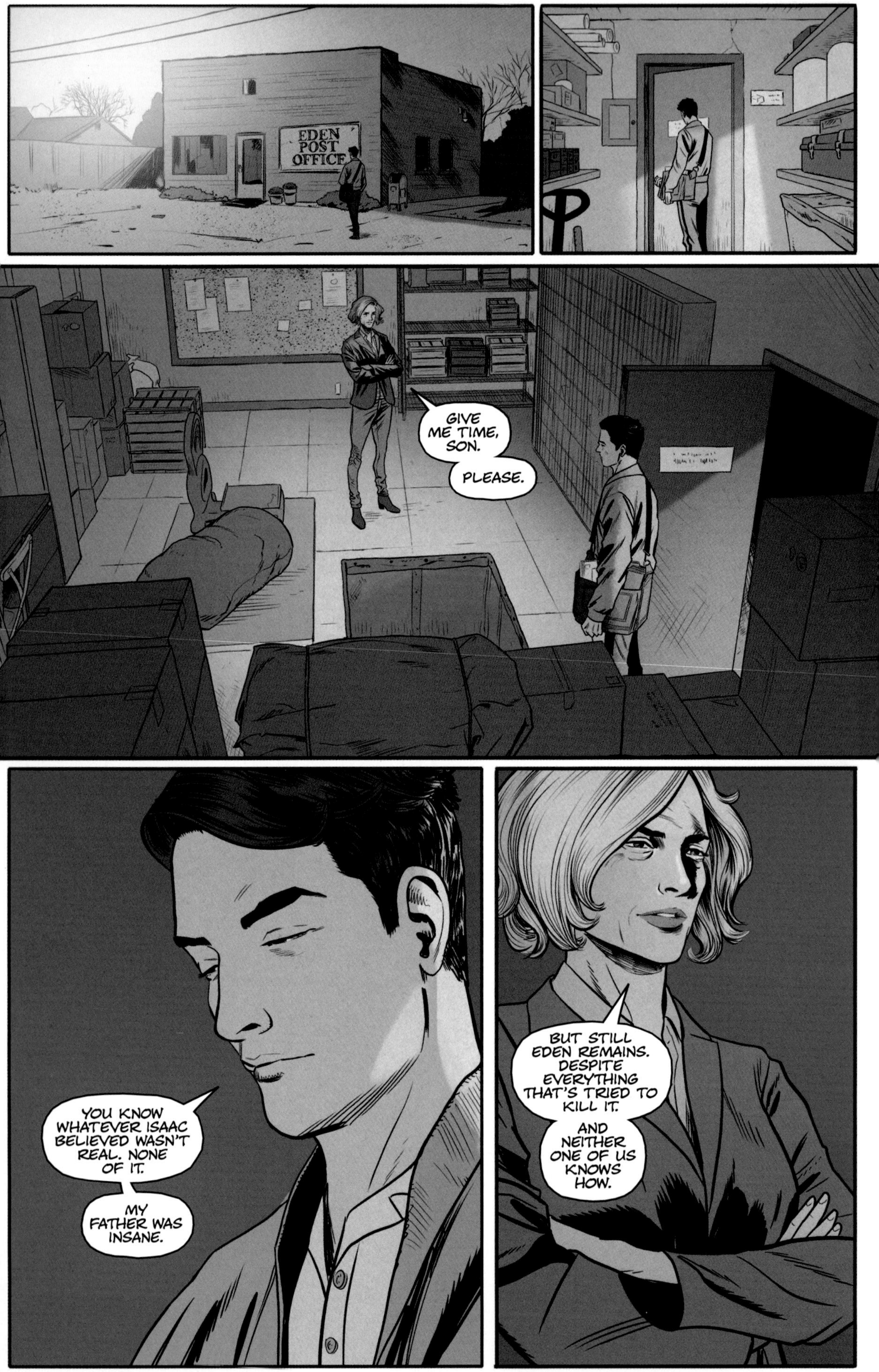
EDEN POST OFFICE
GIVE ME TIME, SON.
PLEASE.
YOU KNOW WHATEVER ISAAC BELIEVED WASN'T REAL. NONE OF IT.
MY FATHER WAS INSANE.
BUT STILL EDEN REMAINS. DESPITE EVERYTHING THAT'S TRIED TO KILL IT.
AND NEITHER ONE OF US KNOWS HOW.

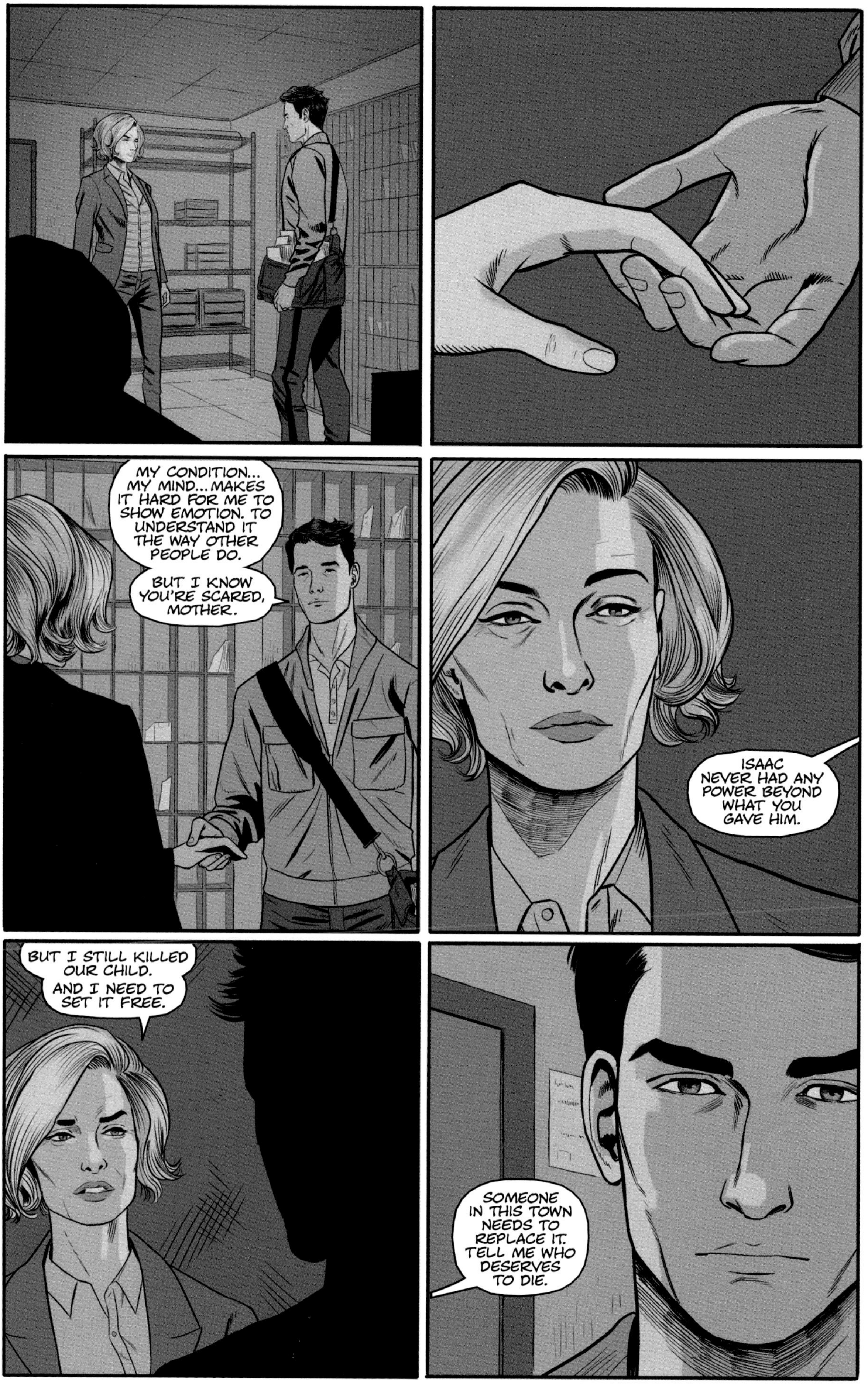
MY CONDITION... MY MIND...MAKES IT HARD FOR ME TO SHOW EMOTION. TO UNDERSTAND IT THE WAY OTHER PEOPLE DO.
BUT I KNOW YOU'RE SCARED, MOTHER.
ISAAC NEVER HAD ANY POWER BEYOND WHAT YOU GAVE HIM.
BUT I STILL KILLED OUR CHILD. AND I NEED TO SET IT FREE.
SOMEONE IN THIS TOWN NEEDS TO REPLACE IT. TELL ME WHO DESERVES TO DIE.

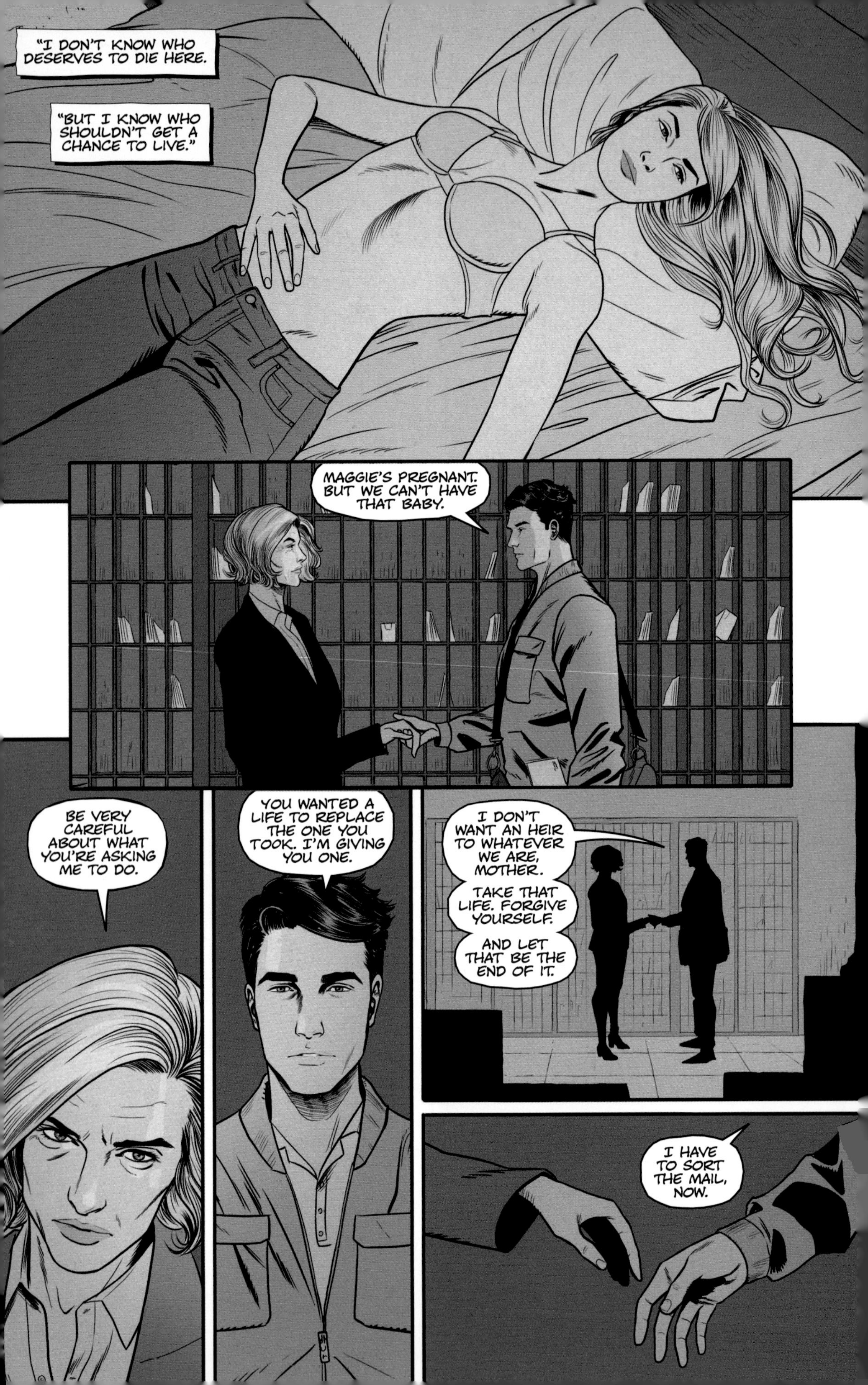
"I DON'T KNOW WHO DESERVES TO DIE HERE.
"BUT I KNOW WHO SHOULDN'T GET A CHANCE TO LIVE."
MAGGIE'S PREGNANT. BUT WE CAN'T HAVE THAT BABY.
BE VERY CAREFUL ABOUT WHAT YOU'RE ASKING ME TO DO.
YOU WANTED A LIFE TO REPLACE THE ONE YOU TOOK. I'M GIVING YOU ONE.
I DON'T WANT AN HEIR TO WHATEVER WE ARE, MOTHER.
TAKE THAT LIFE. FORGIVE YOURSELF.
AND LET THAT BE THE END OF IT.
I HAVE TO SORT THE MAIL, NOW.

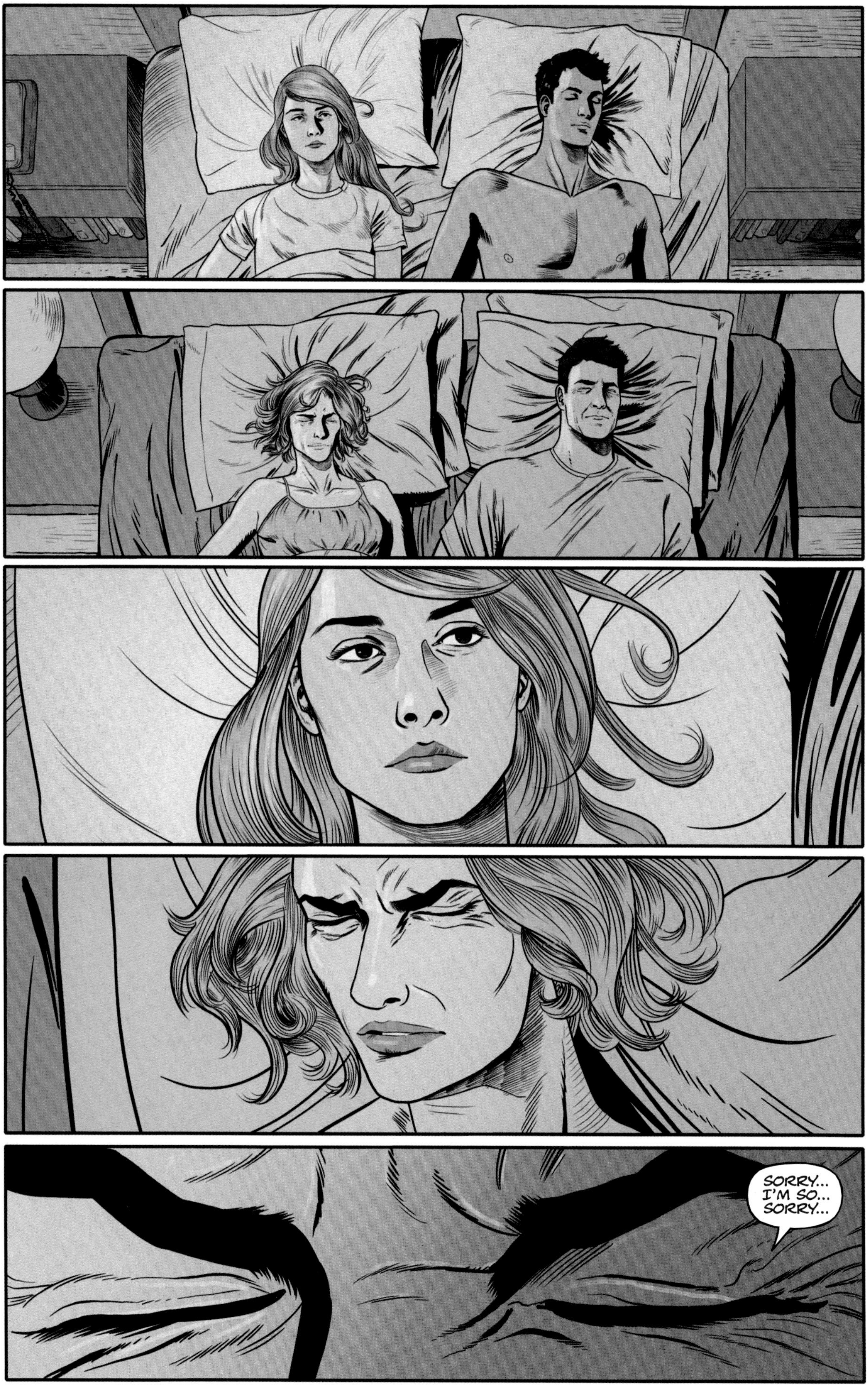
SORRY... I'M SO... SORRY...

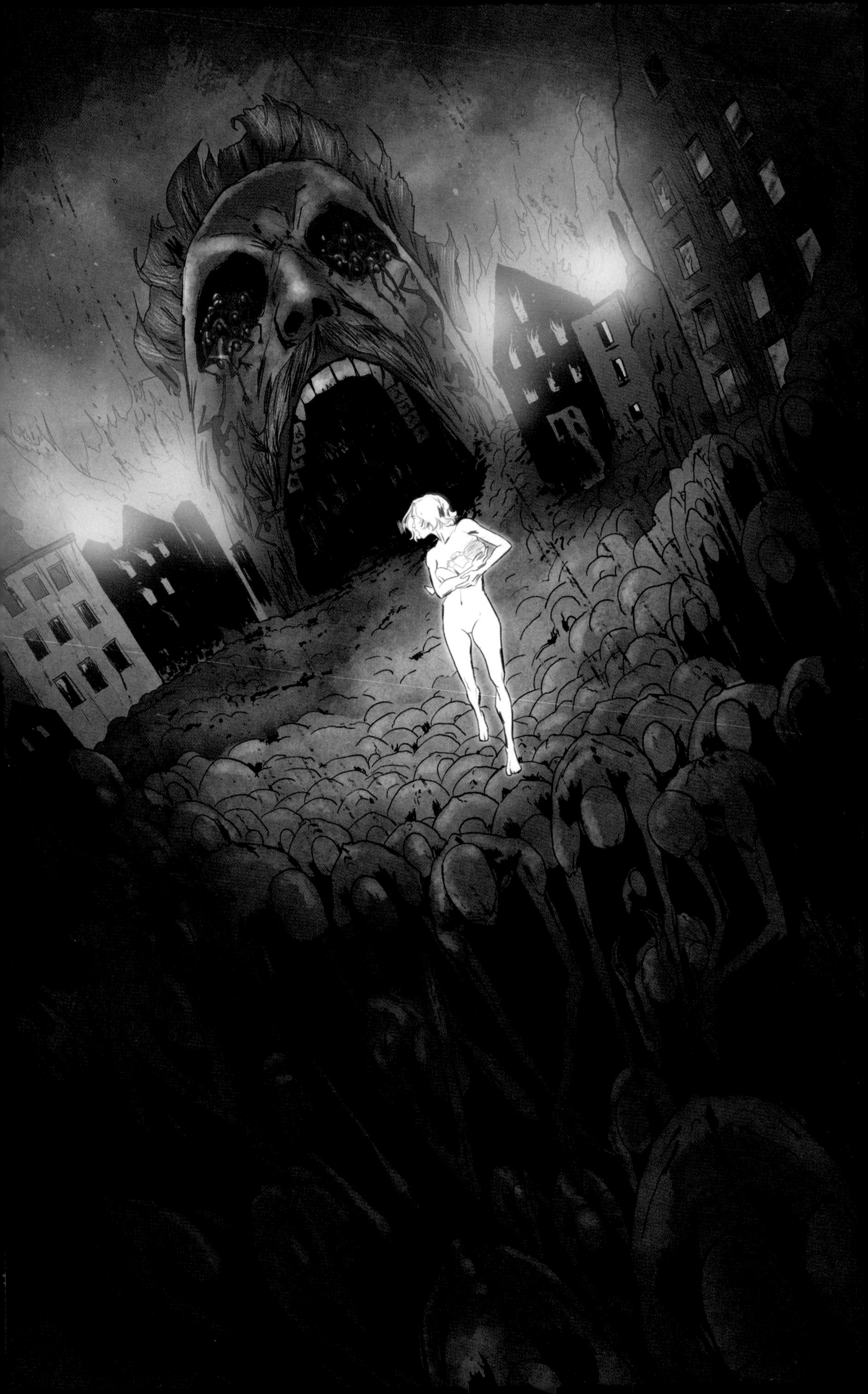

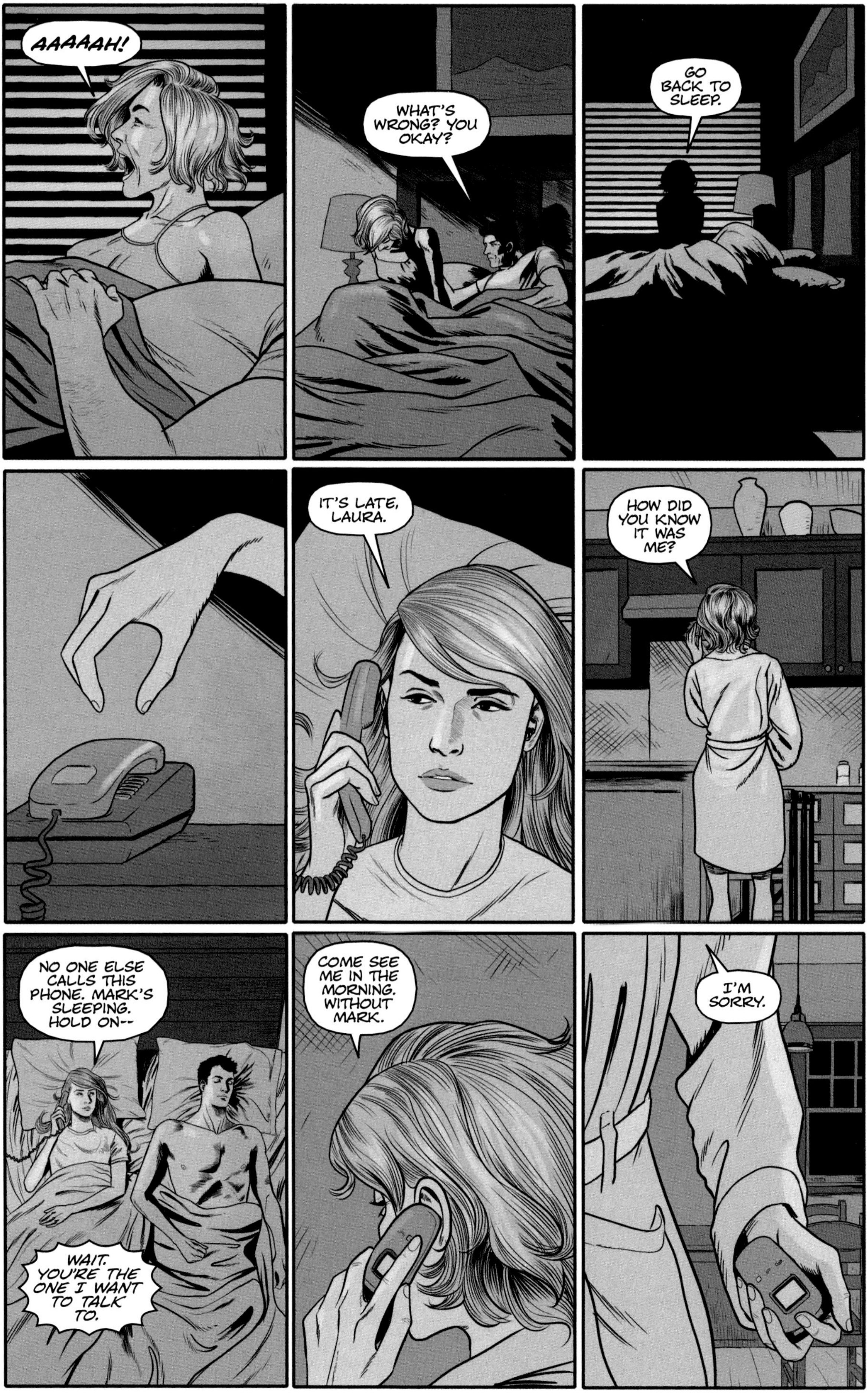
AAAAAH!
WHAT'S WRONG? YOU OKAY?
GO BACK TO SLEEP.
IT'S LATE, LAURA.
HOW DID YOU KNOW IT WAS ME?
NO ONE ELSE CALLS THIS PHONE. MARK'S SLEEPING. HOLD ON--
WAIT. YOU'RE THE ONE I WANT TO TALK TO.
COME SEE ME IN THE MORNING. WITHOUT MARK.
I'M SORRY.

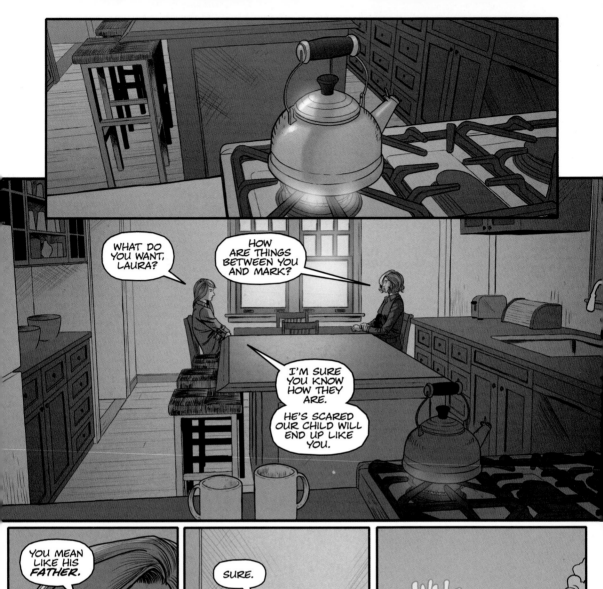

WHAT DO YOU WANT, LAURA?

HOW ARE THINGS BETWEEN YOU AND MARK?

I'M SURE YOU KNOW HOW THEY ARE.

HE'S SCARED OUR CHILD WILL END UP LIKE YOU.

YOU MEAN LIKE HIS *FATHER*.

SURE.

WHEEEEEEEE

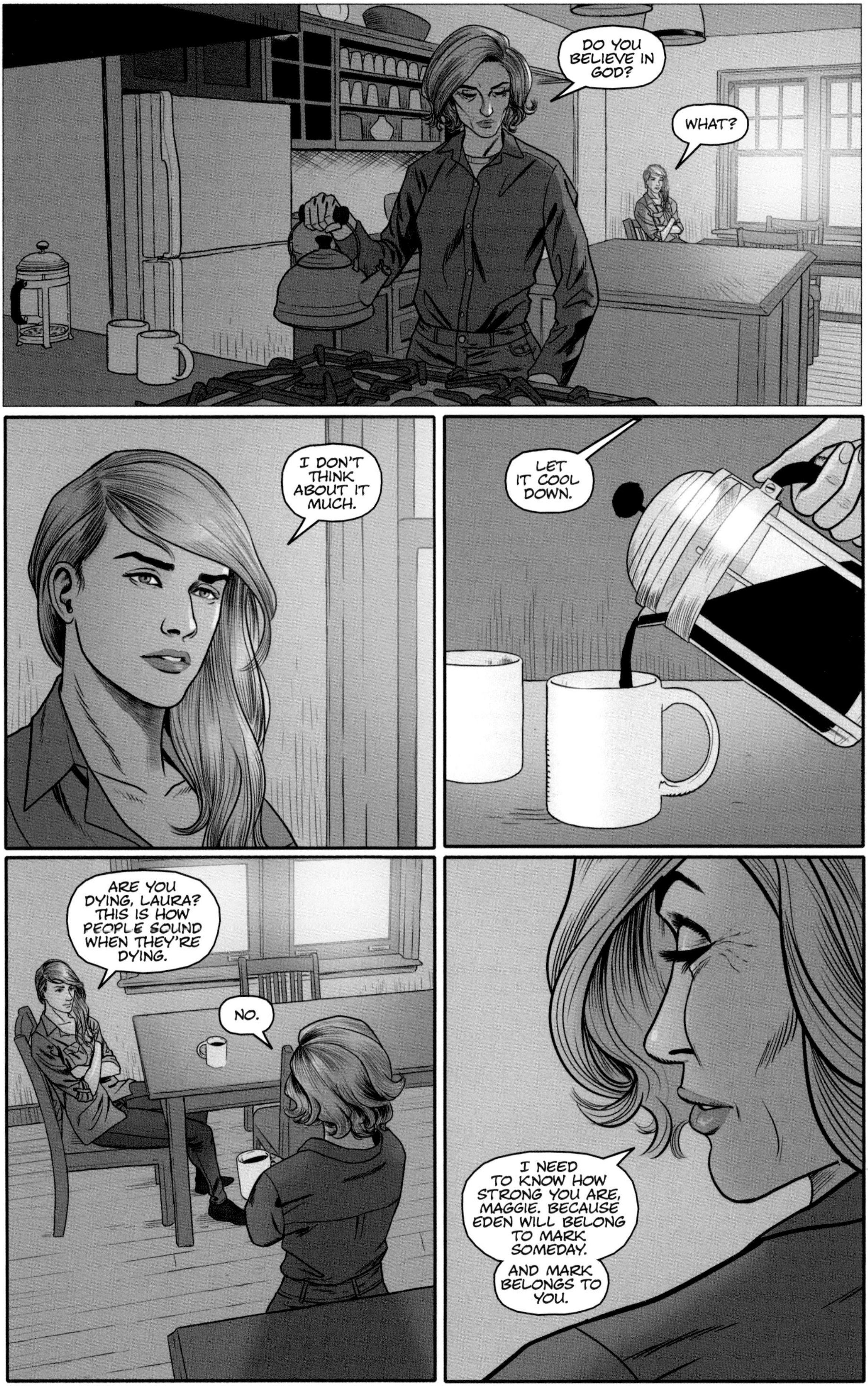
DO YOU BELIEVE IN GOD?
WHAT?
I DON'T THINK ABOUT IT MUCH.
LET IT COOL DOWN.
ARE YOU DYING, LAURA? THIS IS HOW PEOPLE SOUND WHEN THEY'RE DYING.
NO.
I NEED TO KNOW HOW STRONG YOU ARE, MAGGIE. BECAUSE EDEN WILL BELONG TO MARK SOMEDAY.
AND MARK BELONGS TO YOU.

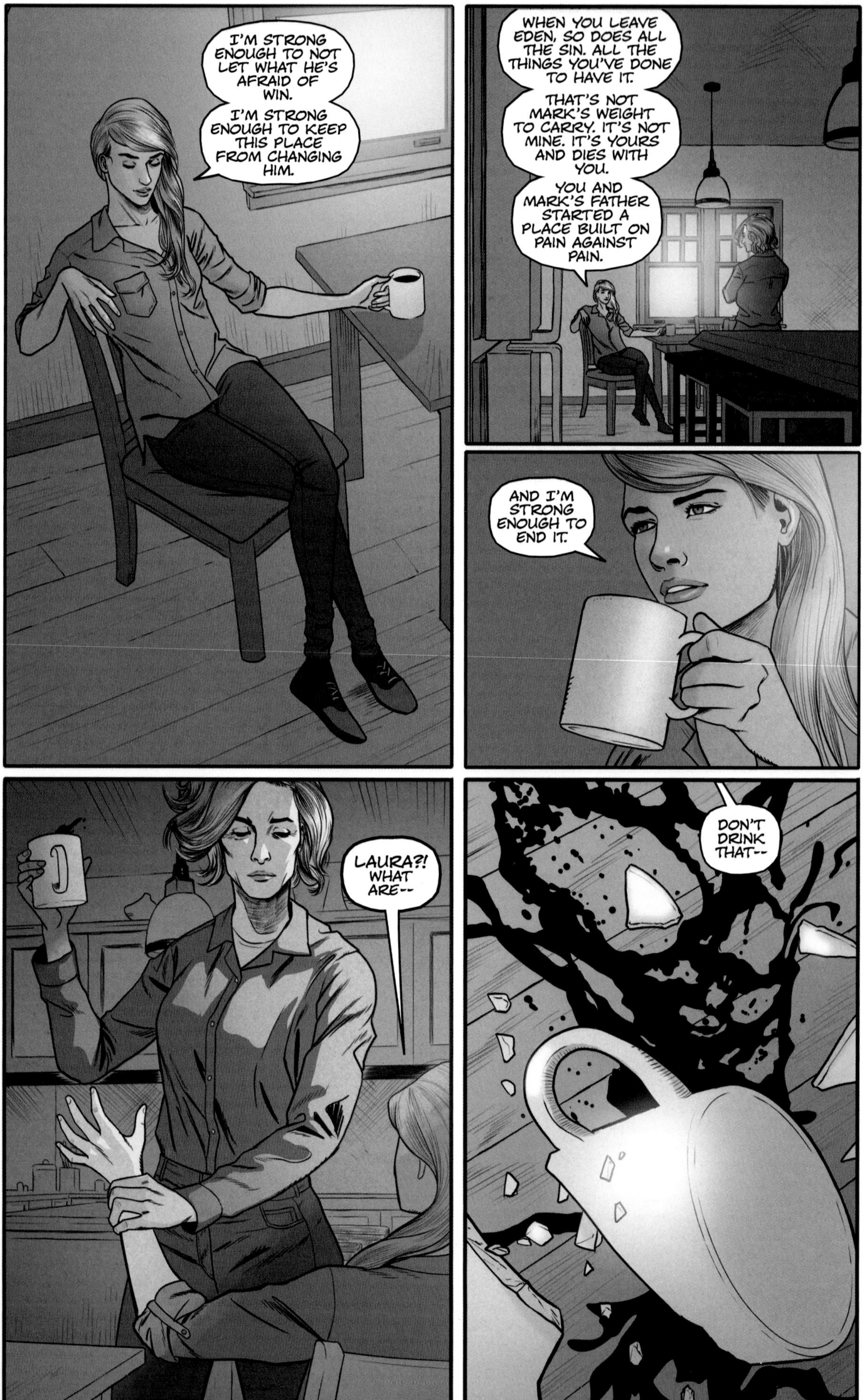
I'M STRONG ENOUGH TO NOT LET WHAT HE'S AFRAID OF WIN.
I'M STRONG ENOUGH TO KEEP THIS PLACE FROM CHANGING HIM.
WHEN YOU LEAVE EDEN, SO DOES ALL THE SIN. ALL THE THINGS YOU'VE DONE TO HAVE IT.
THAT'S NOT MARK'S WEIGHT TO CARRY. IT'S NOT MINE. IT'S YOURS AND DIES WITH YOU.
YOU AND MARK'S FATHER STARTED A PLACE BUILT ON PAIN AGAINST PAIN.
AND I'M STRONG ENOUGH TO END IT.
LAURA?! WHAT ARE--
DON'T DRINK THAT--

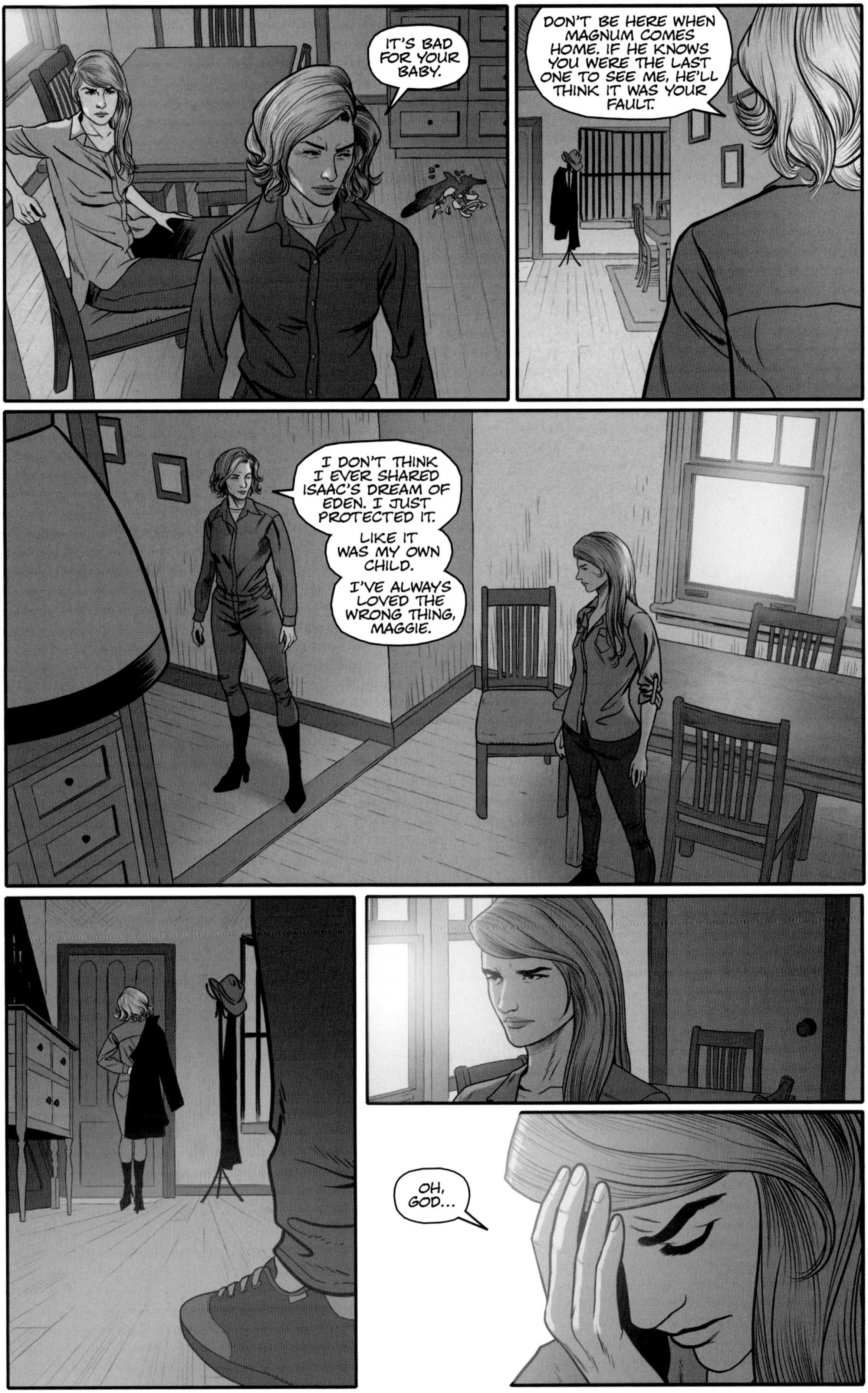
IT'S BAD FOR YOUR BABY.
DON'T BE HERE WHEN MAGNUM COMES HOME. IF HE KNOWS YOU WERE THE LAST ONE TO SEE ME, HE'LL THINK IT WAS YOUR FAULT.
I DON'T THINK I EVER SHARED ISAAC'S DREAM OF EDEN. I JUST PROTECTED IT.
LIKE IT WAS MY OWN CHILD.
I'VE ALWAYS LOVED THE WRONG THING, MAGGIE.
OH, GOD...

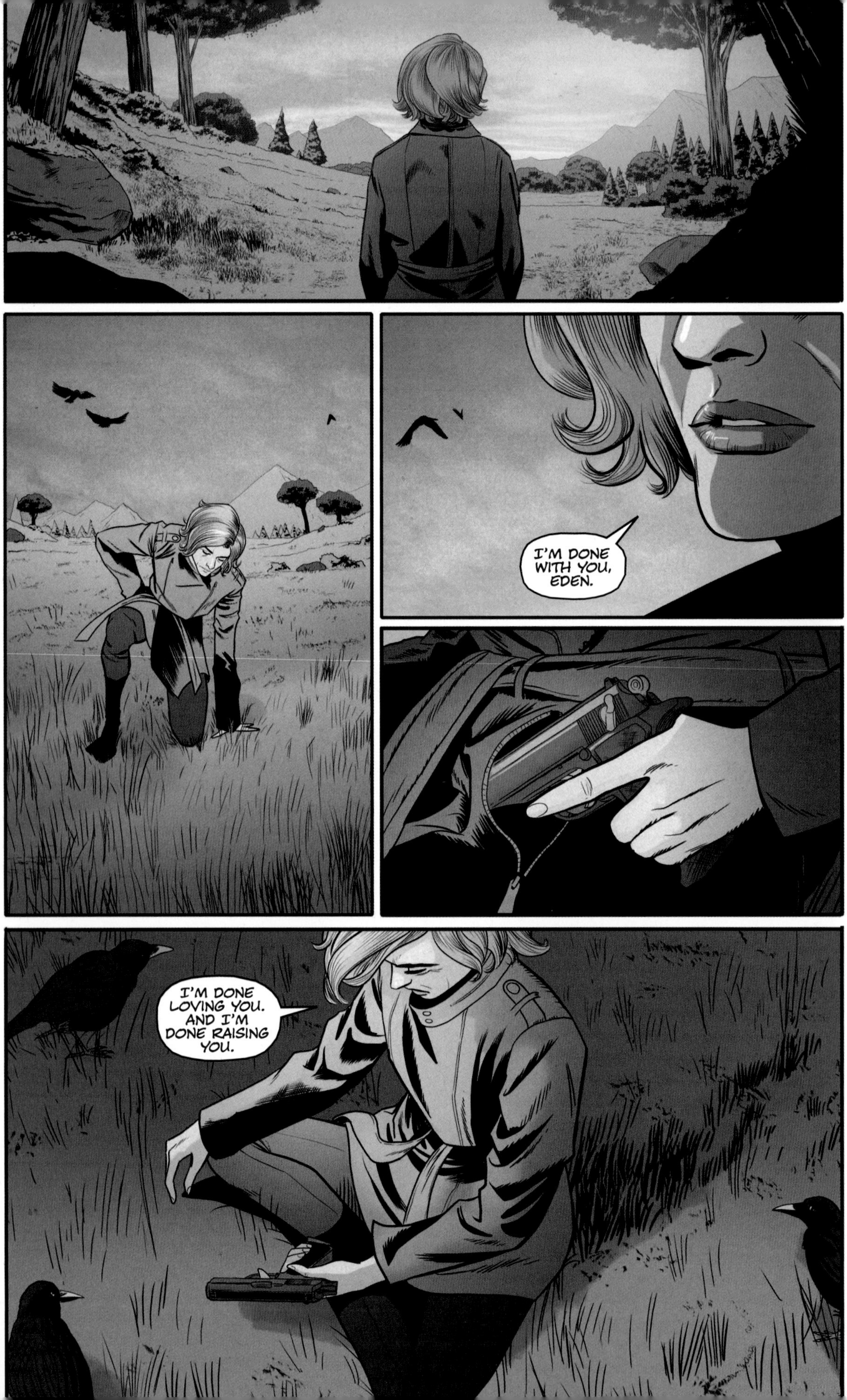
I'M DONE WITH YOU, EDEN.
I'M DONE LOVING YOU. AND I'M DONE RAISING YOU.

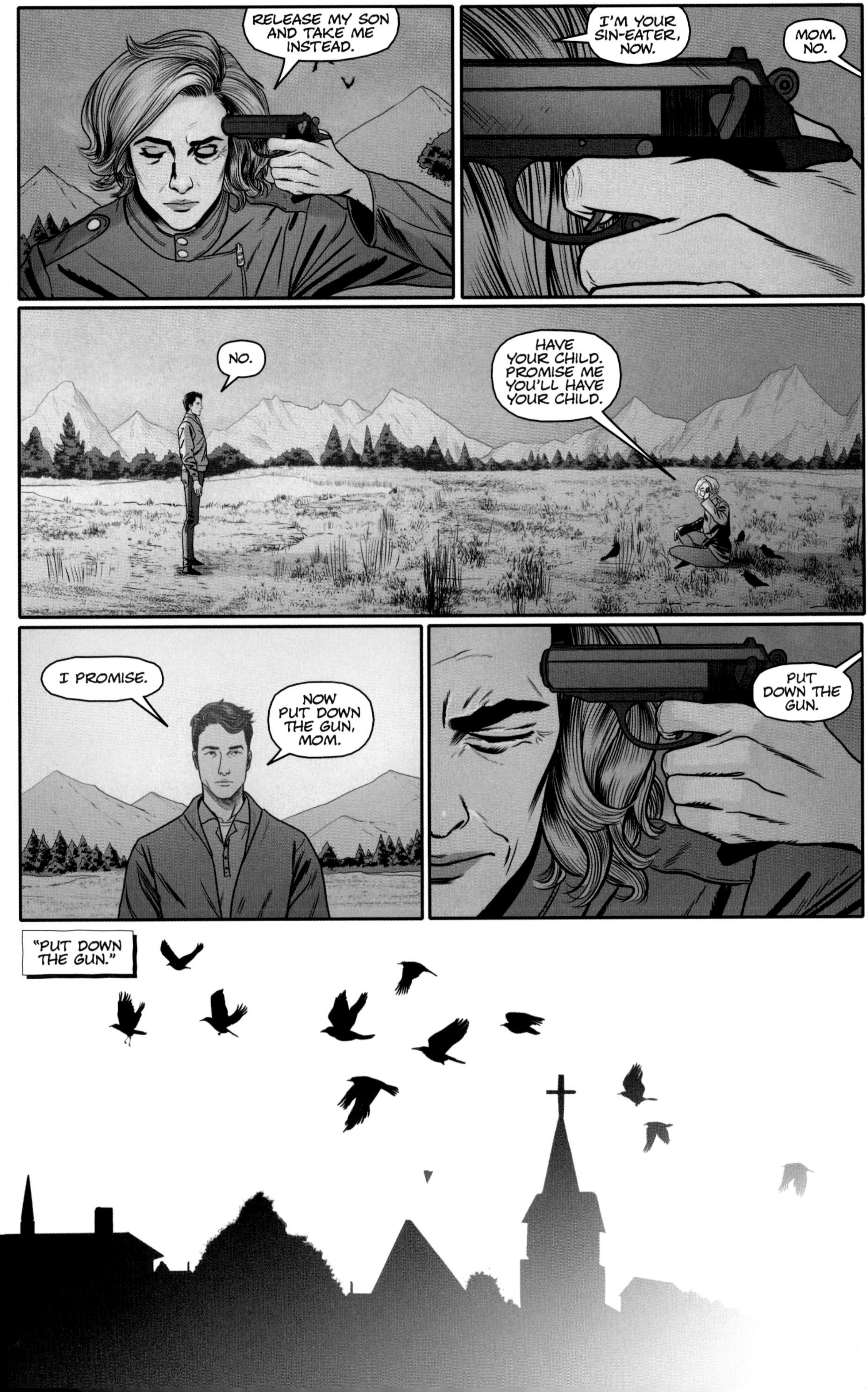
RELEASE MY SON AND TAKE ME INSTEAD.
I'M YOUR SIN-EATER, NOW.
MOM. NO.
NO.
HAVE YOUR CHILD. PROMISE ME YOU'LL HAVE YOUR CHILD.
I PROMISE.
NOW PUT DOWN THE GUN, MOM.
PUT DOWN THE GUN.
"PUT DOWN THE GUN."

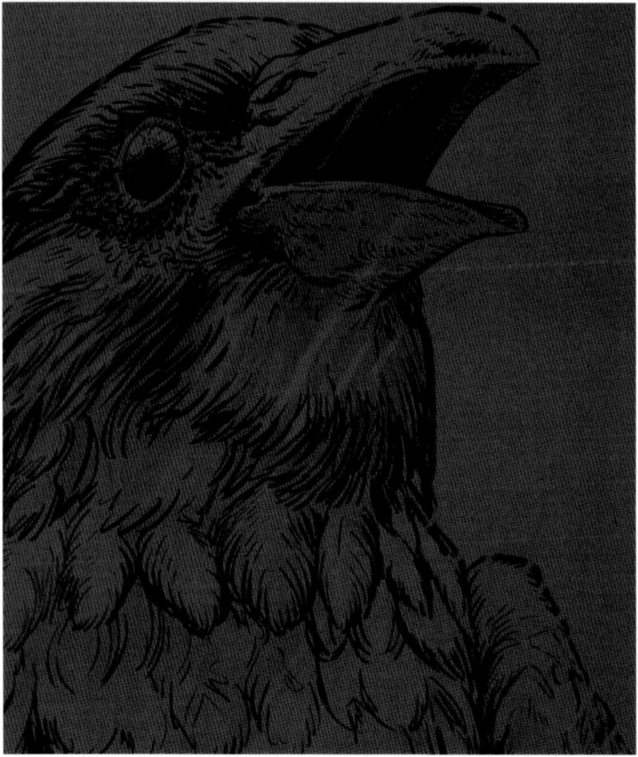

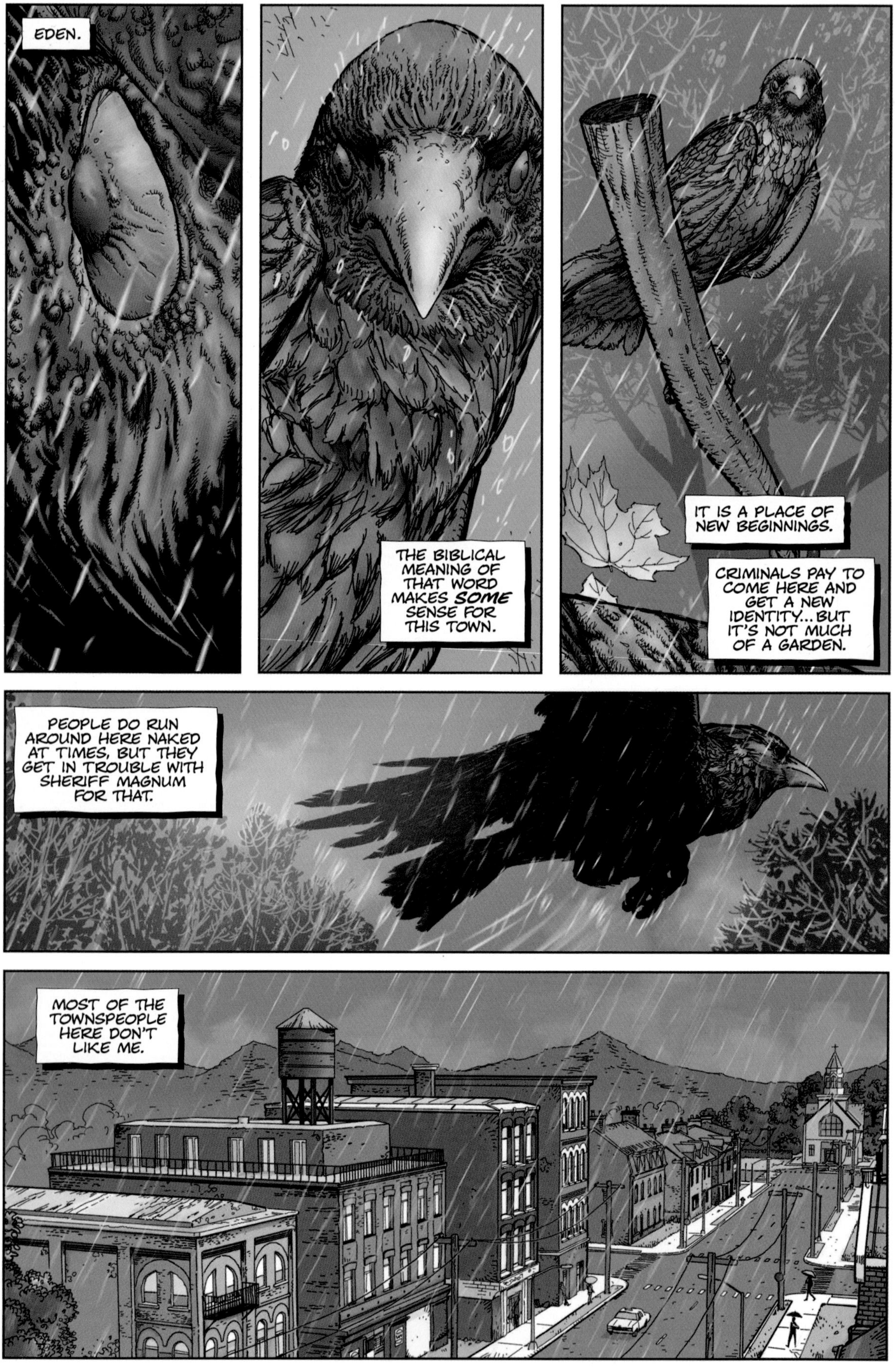
EDEN.
THE BIBLICAL MEANING OF THAT WORD MAKES SOME SENSE FOR THIS TOWN.
IT IS A PLACE OF NEW BEGINNINGS.
CRIMINALS PAY TO COME HERE AND GET A NEW IDENTITY... BUT IT'S NOT MUCH OF A GARDEN.
PEOPLE DO RUN AROUND HERE NAKED AT TIMES, BUT THEY GET IN TROUBLE WITH SHERIFF MAGNUM FOR THAT.
MOST OF THE TOWNSPEOPLE HERE DON'T LIKE ME.

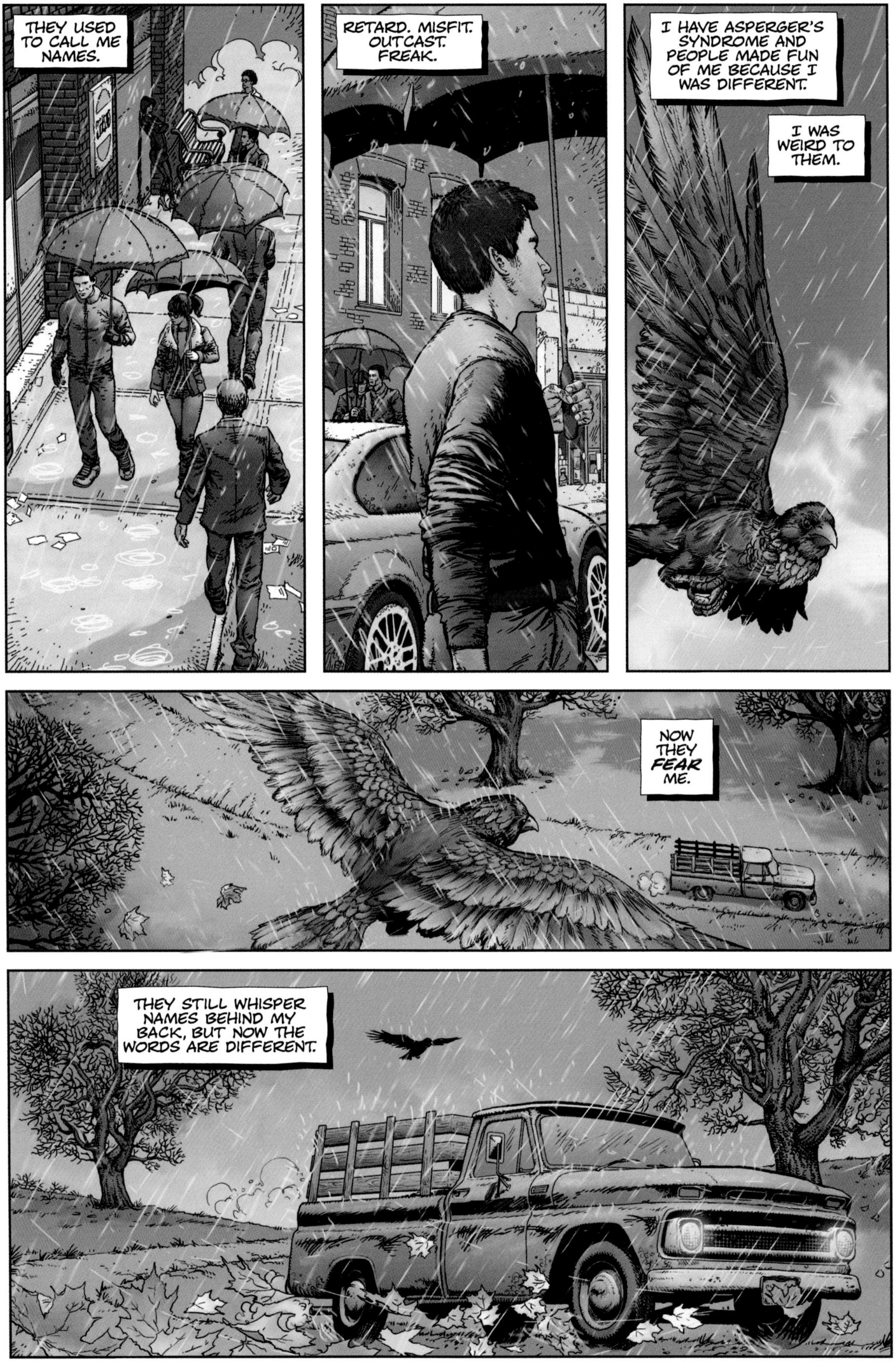
THEY USED TO CALL ME NAMES.
RETARD. MISFIT. OUTCAST. FREAK.
I HAVE ASPERGER'S SYNDROME AND PEOPLE MADE FUN OF ME BECAUSE I WAS DIFFERENT.
I WAS WEIRD TO THEM.
NOW THEY FEAR ME.
THEY STILL WHISPER NAMES BEHIND MY BACK, BUT NOW THE WORDS ARE DIFFERENT.

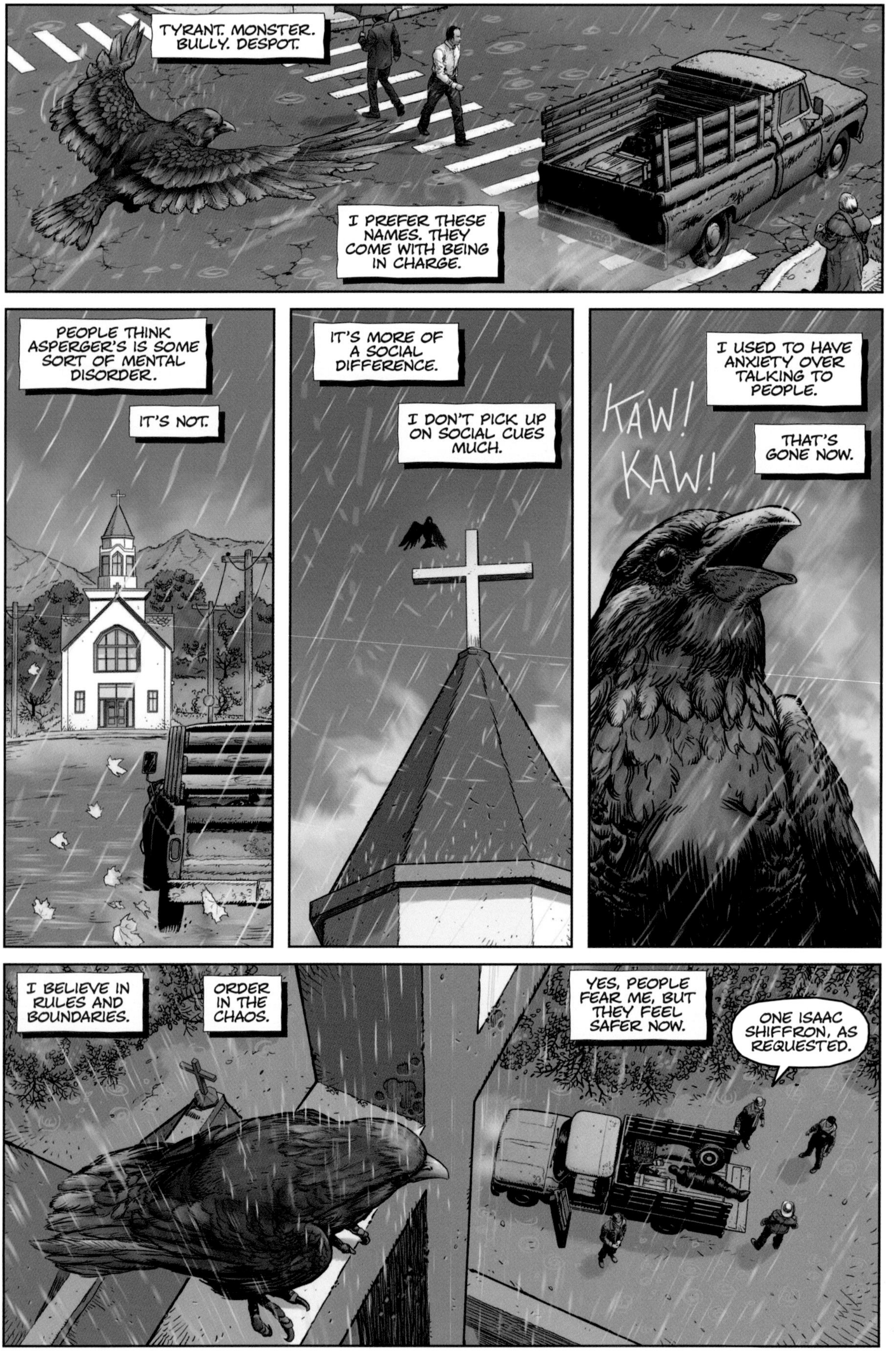
TYRANT. MONSTER. BULLY. DESPOT.
I PREFER THESE NAMES. THEY COME WITH BEING IN CHARGE.
PEOPLE THINK ASPERGER'S IS SOME SORT OF MENTAL DISORDER.
IT'S NOT.
IT'S MORE OF A SOCIAL DIFFERENCE.
I DON'T PICK UP ON SOCIAL CUES MUCH.
KAW! KAW!
I USED TO HAVE ANXIETY OVER TALKING TO PEOPLE.
THAT'S GONE NOW.
I BELIEVE IN RULES AND BOUNDARIES.
ORDER IN THE CHAOS.
YES, PEOPLE FEAR ME, BUT THEY FEEL SAFER NOW.
ONE ISAAC SHIFFRON, AS REQUESTED.

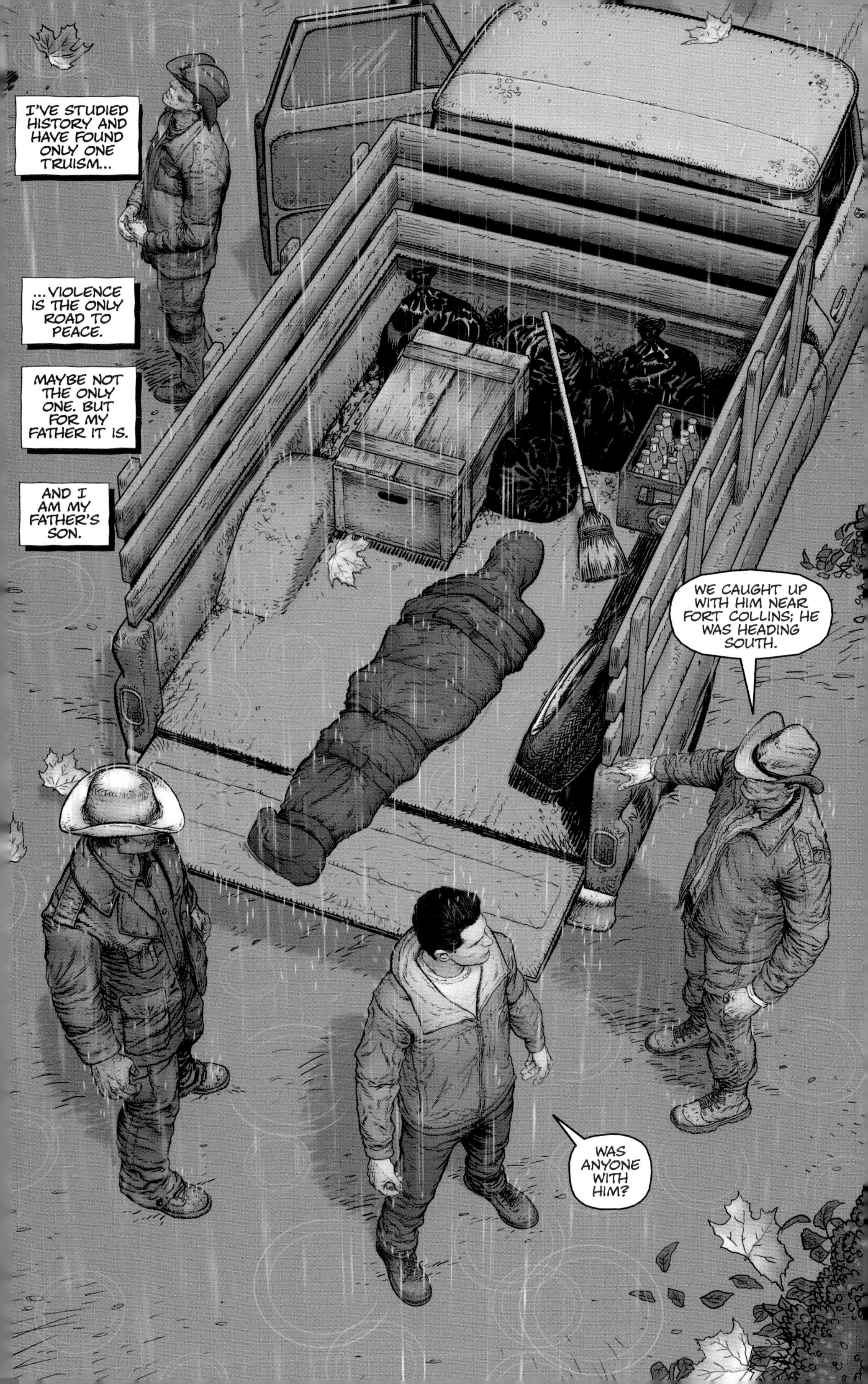
I'VE STUDIED HISTORY AND HAVE FOUND ONLY ONE TRUISM...
...VIOLENCE IS THE ONLY ROAD TO PEACE.
MAYBE NOT THE ONLY ONE. BUT FOR MY FATHER IT IS.
AND I AM MY FATHER'S SON.
WE CAUGHT UP WITH HIM NEAR FORT COLLINS; HE WAS HEADING SOUTH.
WAS ANYONE WITH HIM?

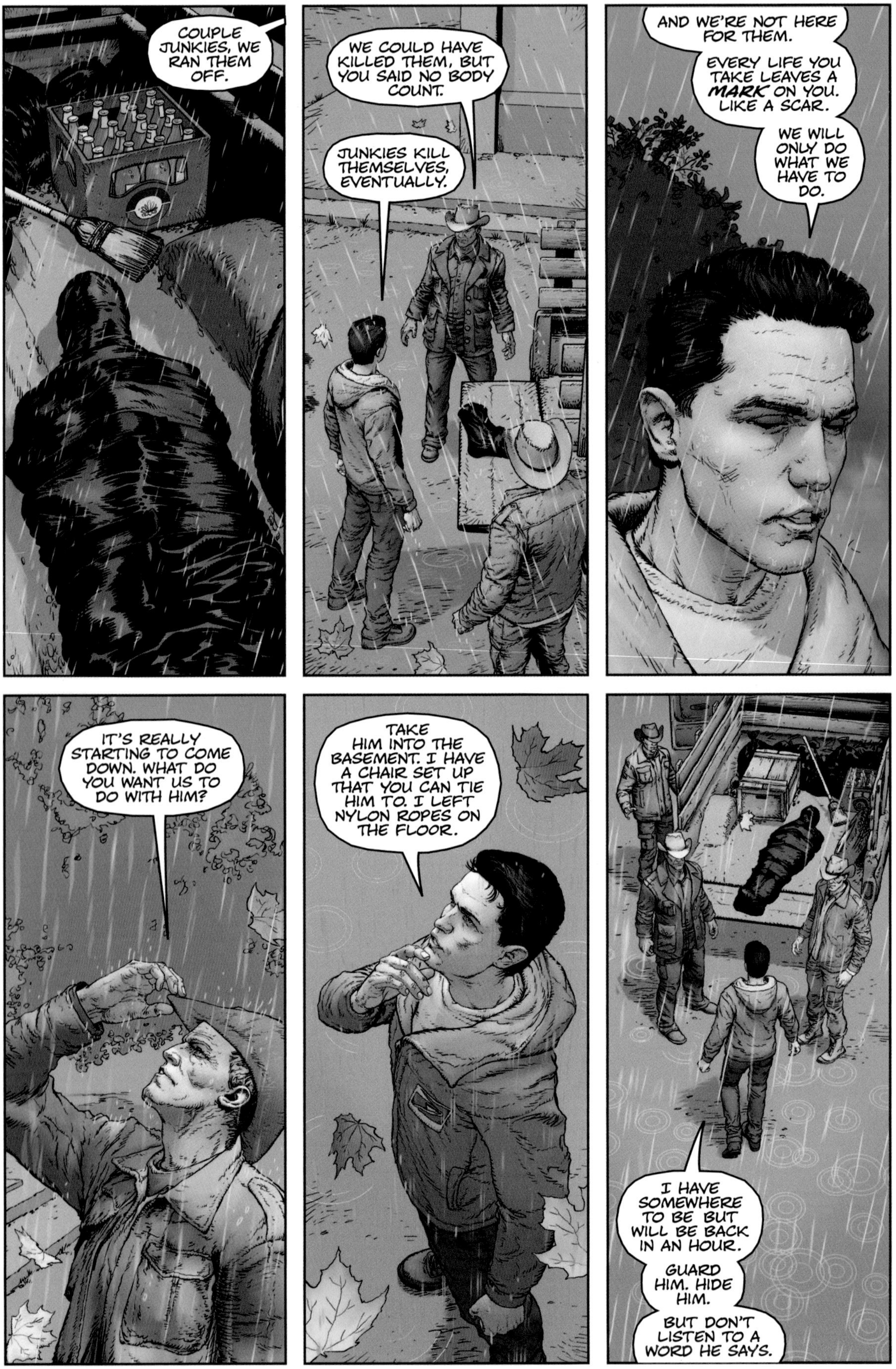
COUPLE JUNKIES, WE RAN THEM OFF.
WE COULD HAVE KILLED THEM, BUT YOU SAID NO BODY COUNT.
JUNKIES KILL THEMSELVES, EVENTUALLY.
AND WE'RE NOT HERE FOR THEM.
EVERY LIFE YOU TAKE LEAVES A MARK ON YOU. LIKE A SCAR.
WE WILL ONLY DO WHAT WE HAVE TO DO.
IT'S REALLY STARTING TO COME DOWN. WHAT DO YOU WANT US TO DO WITH HIM?
TAKE HIM INTO THE BASEMENT. I HAVE A CHAIR SET UP THAT YOU CAN TIE HIM TO. I LEFT NYLON ROPES ON THE FLOOR.
I HAVE SOMEWHERE TO BE BUT WILL BE BACK IN AN HOUR.
GUARD HIM. HIDE HIM.
BUT DON'T LISTEN TO A WORD HE SAYS.

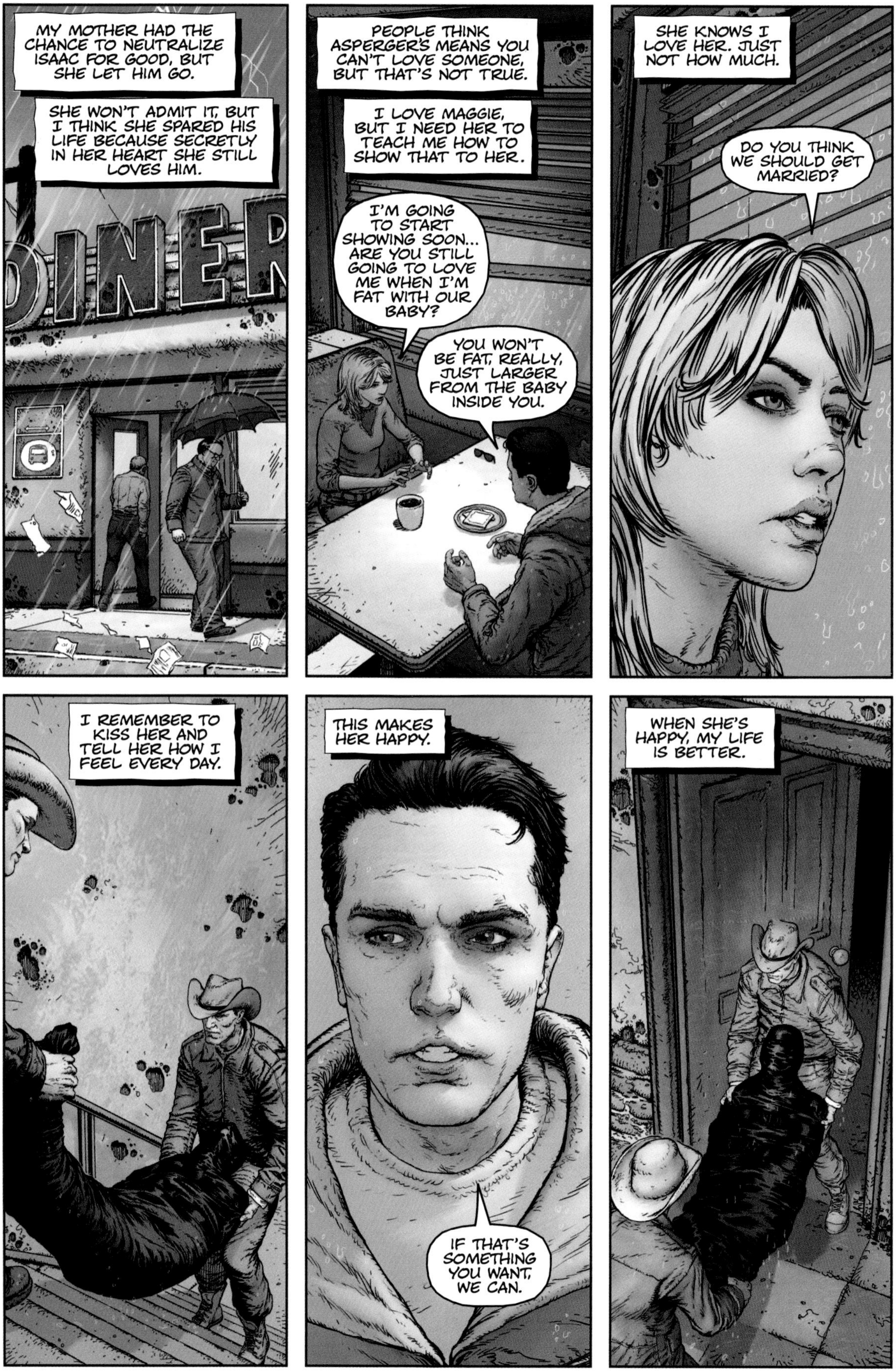
MY MOTHER HAD THE CHANCE TO NEUTRALIZE ISAAC FOR GOOD, BUT SHE LET HIM GO.
SHE WON'T ADMIT IT, BUT I THINK SHE SPARED HIS LIFE BECAUSE SECRETLY IN HER HEART SHE STILL LOVES HIM.
DINER
PEOPLE THINK ASPERGER'S MEANS YOU CAN'T LOVE SOMEONE, BUT THAT'S NOT TRUE.
I LOVE MAGGIE, BUT I NEED HER TO TEACH ME HOW TO SHOW THAT TO HER.
I'M GOING TO START SHOWING SOON... ARE YOU STILL GOING TO LOVE ME WHEN I'M FAT WITH OUR BABY?
YOU WON'T BE FAT, REALLY, JUST LARGER FROM THE BABY INSIDE YOU.
SHE KNOWS I LOVE HER. JUST NOT HOW MUCH.
DO YOU THINK WE SHOULD GET MARRIED?
I REMEMBER TO KISS HER AND TELL HER HOW I FEEL EVERY DAY.
THIS MAKES HER HAPPY.
IF THAT'S SOMETHING YOU WANT, WE CAN.
WHEN SHE'S HAPPY, MY LIFE IS BETTER.

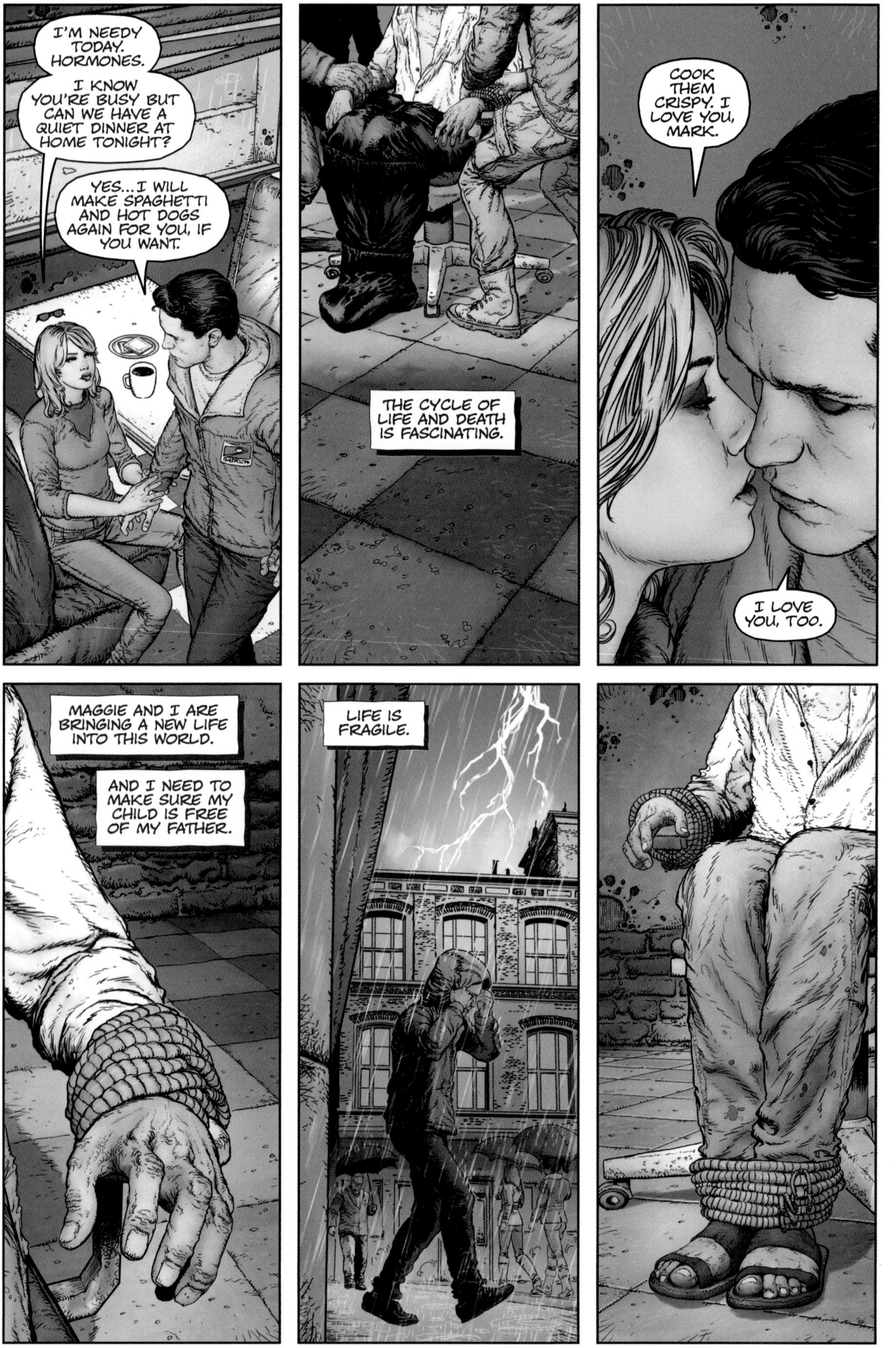
I'M NEEDY TODAY. HORMONES.
I KNOW YOU'RE BUSY BUT CAN WE HAVE A QUIET DINNER AT HOME TONIGHT?
YES...I WILL MAKE SPAGHETTI AND HOT DOGS AGAIN FOR YOU, IF YOU WANT.
THE CYCLE OF LIFE AND DEATH IS FASCINATING.
COOK THEM CRISPY. I LOVE YOU, MARK.
I LOVE YOU, TOO.
MAGGIE AND I ARE BRINGING A NEW LIFE INTO THIS WORLD.
AND I NEED TO MAKE SURE MY CHILD IS FREE OF MY FATHER.
LIFE IS FRAGILE.

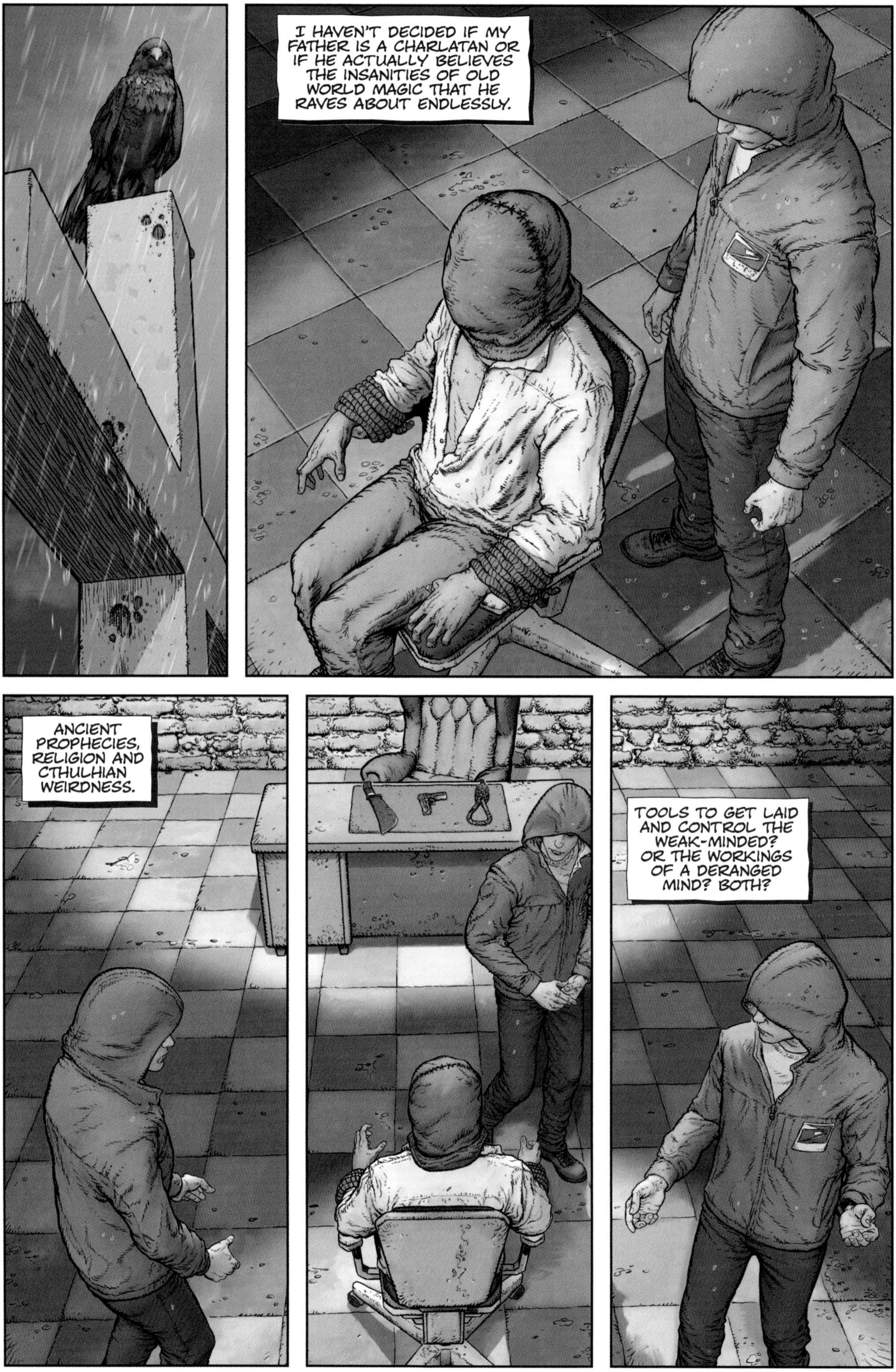
I HAVEN'T DECIDED IF MY FATHER IS A CHARLATAN OR IF HE ACTUALLY BELIEVES THE INSANITIES OF OLD WORLD MAGIC THAT HE RAVES ABOUT ENDLESSLY.
ANCIENT PROPHECIES, RELIGION AND CTHULHIAN WEIRDNESS.
TOOLS TO GET LAID AND CONTROL THE WEAK-MINDED? OR THE WORKINGS OF A DERANGED MIND? BOTH?

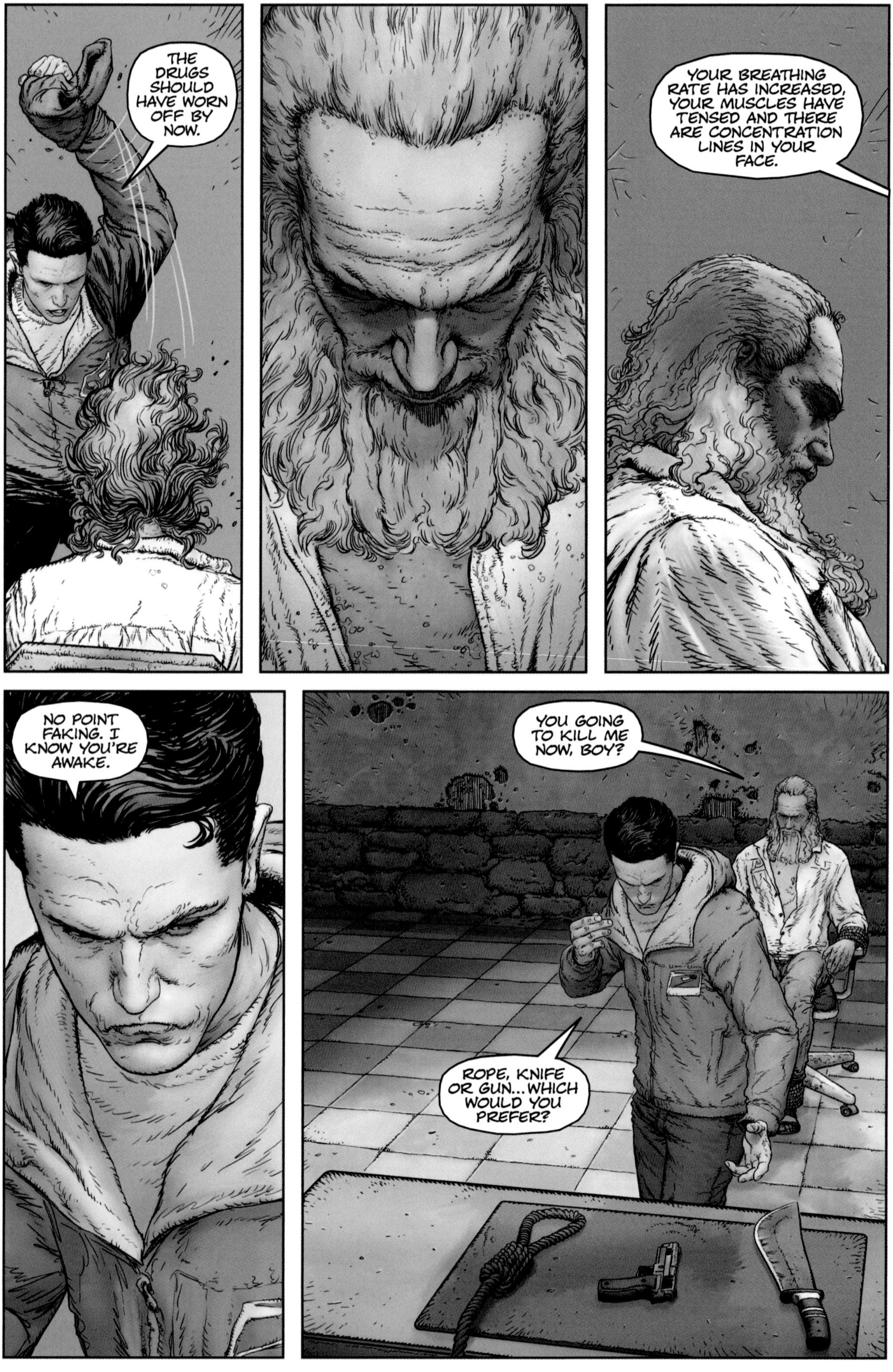
THE DRUGS SHOULD HAVE WORN OFF BY NOW.
YOUR BREATHING RATE HAS INCREASED, YOUR MUSCLES HAVE TENSED AND THERE ARE CONCENTRATION LINES IN YOUR FACE.
NO POINT FAKING. I KNOW YOU'RE AWAKE.
YOU GOING TO KILL ME NOW, BOY?
ROPE, KNIFE OR GUN... WHICH WOULD YOU PREFER?

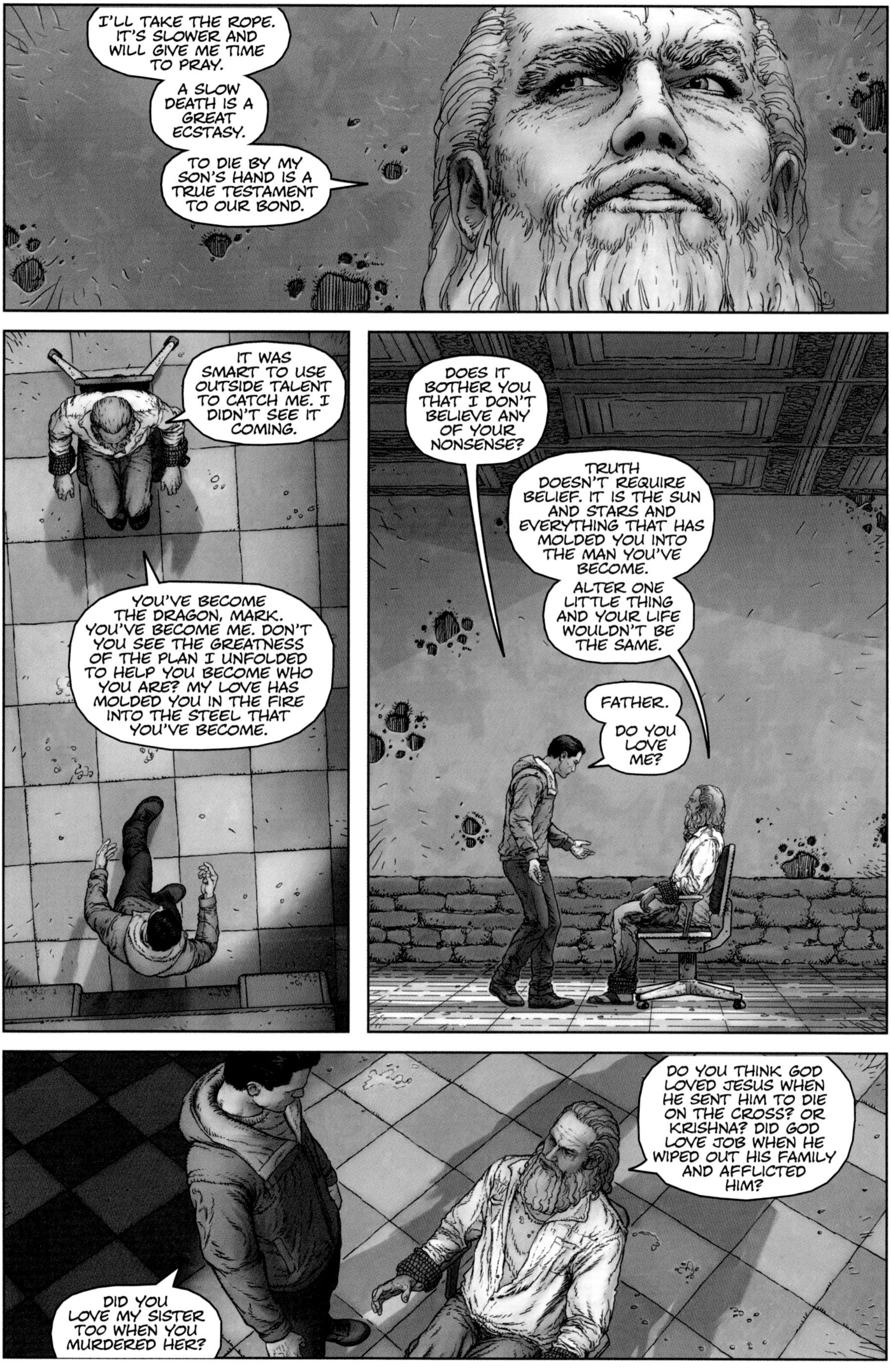
I'LL TAKE THE ROPE. IT'S SLOWER AND WILL GIVE ME TIME TO PRAY.
A SLOW DEATH IS A GREAT ECSTASY.
TO DIE BY MY SON'S HAND IS A TRUE TESTAMENT TO OUR BOND.
IT WAS SMART TO USE OUTSIDE TALENT TO CATCH ME. I DIDN'T SEE IT COMING.
YOU'VE BECOME THE DRAGON, MARK. YOU'VE BECOME ME. DON'T YOU SEE THE GREATNESS OF THE PLAN I UNFOLDED TO HELP YOU BECOME WHO YOU ARE? MY LOVE HAS MOLDED YOU IN THE FIRE INTO THE STEEL THAT YOU'VE BECOME.
DOES IT BOTHER YOU THAT I DON'T BELIEVE ANY OF YOUR NONSENSE?
TRUTH DOESN'T REQUIRE BELIEF. IT IS THE SUN AND STARS AND EVERYTHING THAT HAS MOLDED YOU INTO THE MAN YOU'VE BECOME.
ALTER ONE LITTLE THING AND YOUR LIFE WOULDN'T BE THE SAME.
FATHER.
DO YOU LOVE ME?
DO YOU THINK GOD LOVED JESUS WHEN HE SENT HIM TO DIE ON THE CROSS? OR KRISHNA? DID GOD LOVE JOB WHEN HE WIPED OUT HIS FAMILY AND AFFLICTED HIM?
DID YOU LOVE MY SISTER TOO WHEN YOU MURDERED HER?

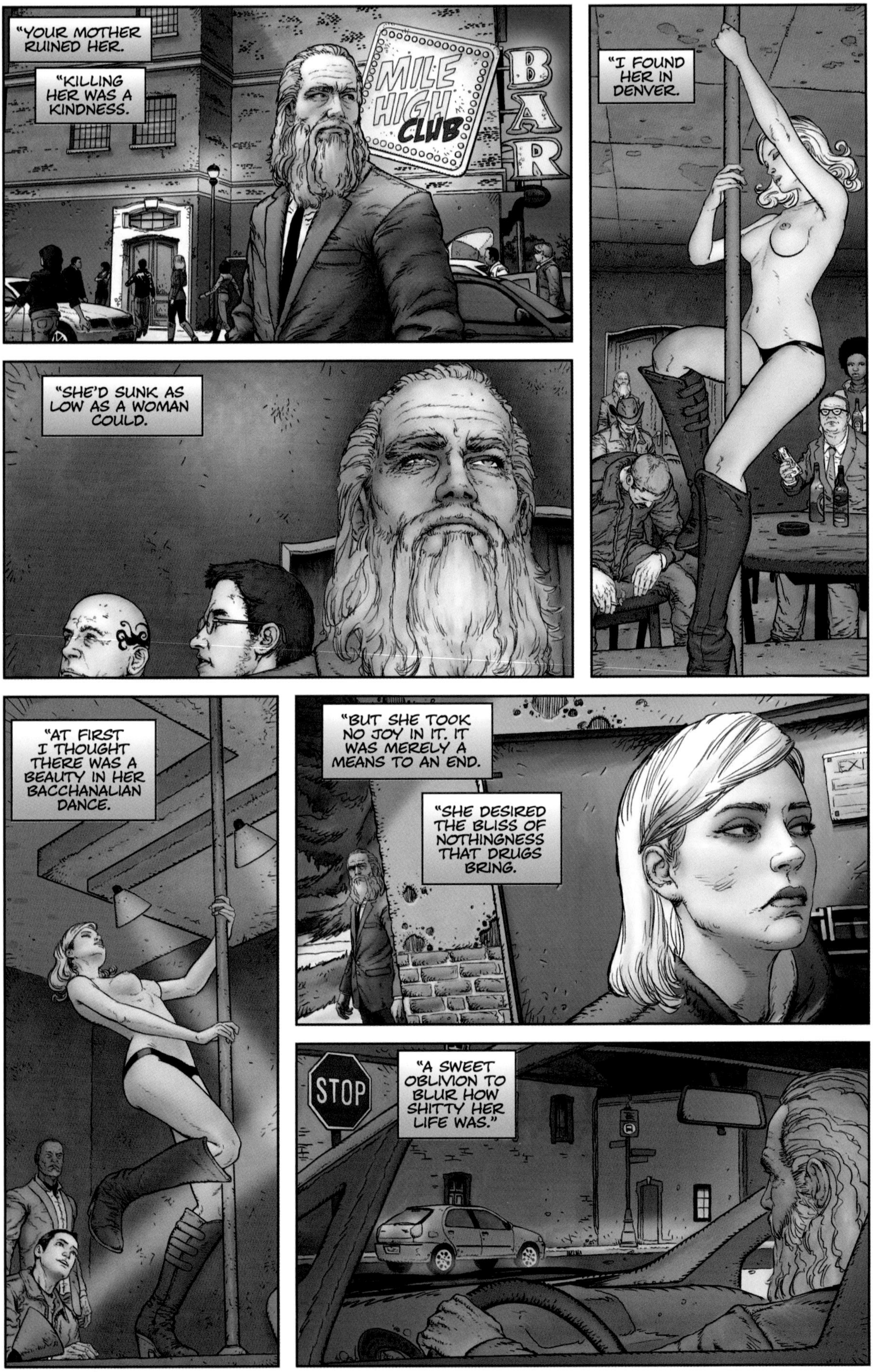
"YOUR MOTHER RUINED HER.
"KILLING HER WAS A KINDNESS.
MILE HIGH CLUB
BAR
"I FOUND HER IN DENVER.
"SHE'D SUNK AS LOW AS A WOMAN COULD.
"AT FIRST I THOUGHT THERE WAS A BEAUTY IN HER BACCHANALIAN DANCE.
"BUT SHE TOOK NO JOY IN IT. IT WAS MERELY A MEANS TO AN END.
"SHE DESIRED THE BLISS OF NOTHINGNESS THAT DRUGS BRING.
STOP
"A SWEET OBLIVION TO BLUR HOW SHITTY HER LIFE WAS."

"SHE SOUGHT TO FORGET HER PAIN.

"IF SHE HAD FELT MORE, SHE MIGHT HAVE EVOLVED.

"HER BOYFRIEND WAS A DRUG DEALER WHO LIKED TO SAMPLE HIS OWN PRODUCT."

WORK WAS DECENT TONIGHT.

"SHE WANTED TO DIE, BUT WAS TOO AFRAID TO KILL HERSELF."

MADE A LITTLE OVER SEVEN HUNDRED. NEW BOUNCER WANTS TO GET SOME E FROM YOU.

"SHE HAD FORGOTTEN A BASIC TRUTH.

"SHE WAS A REFLECTION OF YOUR MOTHER'S WEAKNESS, SO I RETURNED HER TO LAURA. SO SHE COULD SEE WHAT SHE HAD SPAWNED."

"DEATH IS NOT THE GREATEST LOSS IN LIFE. THE GREATEST LOSS IS WHAT DIES INSIDE US WHILE WE LIVE.

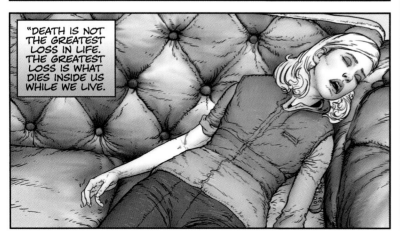

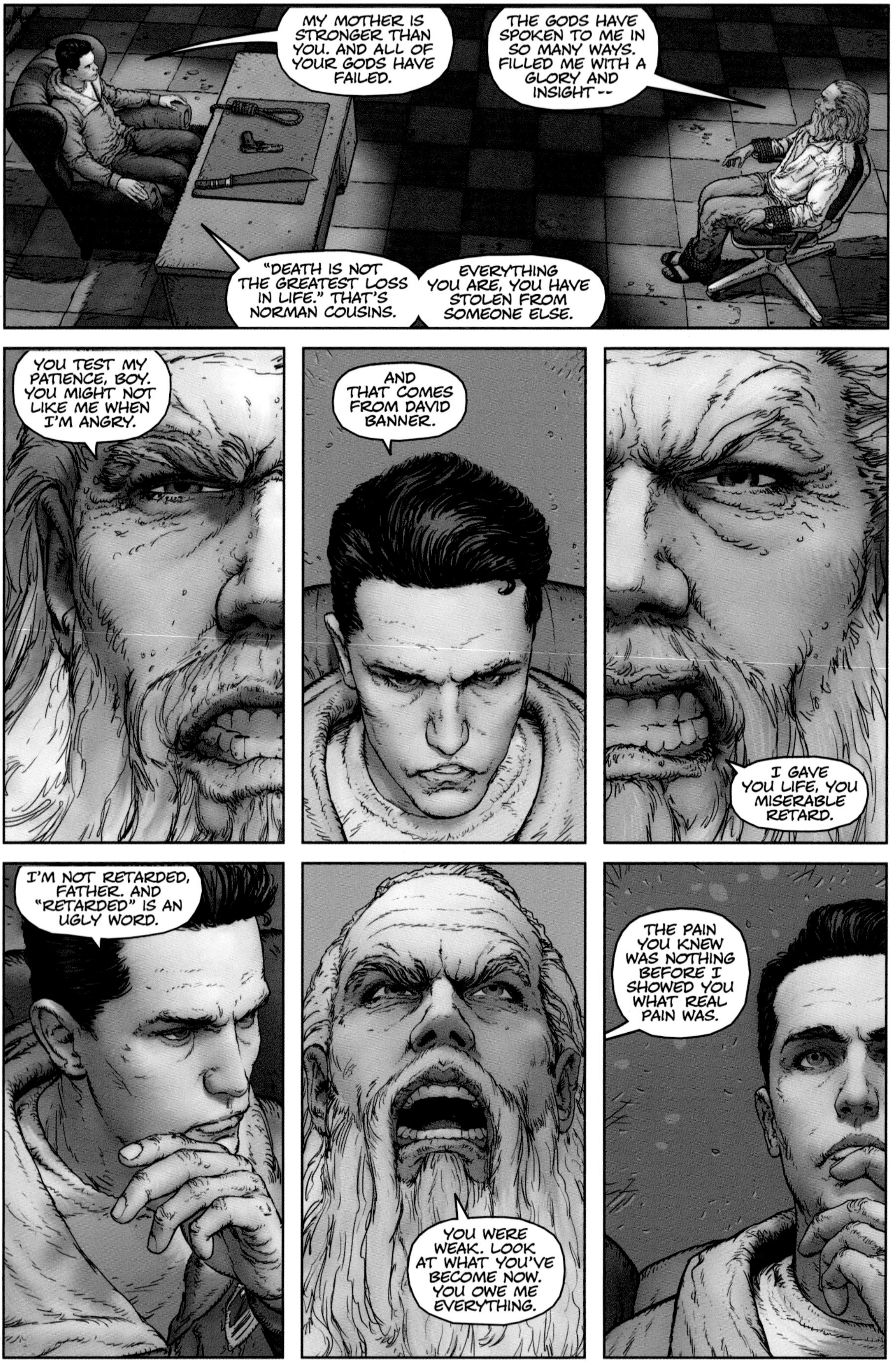
MY MOTHER IS STRONGER THAN YOU. AND ALL OF YOUR GODS HAVE FAILED.
THE GODS HAVE SPOKEN TO ME IN SO MANY WAYS. FILLED ME WITH A GLORY AND INSIGHT --
"DEATH IS NOT THE GREATEST LOSS IN LIFE." THAT'S NORMAN COUSINS.
EVERYTHING YOU ARE, YOU HAVE STOLEN FROM SOMEONE ELSE.
YOU TEST MY PATIENCE, BOY. YOU MIGHT NOT LIKE ME WHEN I'M ANGRY.
AND THAT COMES FROM DAVID BANNER.
I GAVE YOU LIFE, YOU MISERABLE RETARD.
I'M NOT RETARDED, FATHER. AND "RETARDED" IS AN UGLY WORD.
YOU WERE WEAK. LOOK AT WHAT YOU'VE BECOME NOW. YOU OWE ME EVERYTHING.
THE PAIN YOU KNEW WAS NOTHING BEFORE I SHOWED YOU WHAT REAL PAIN WAS.

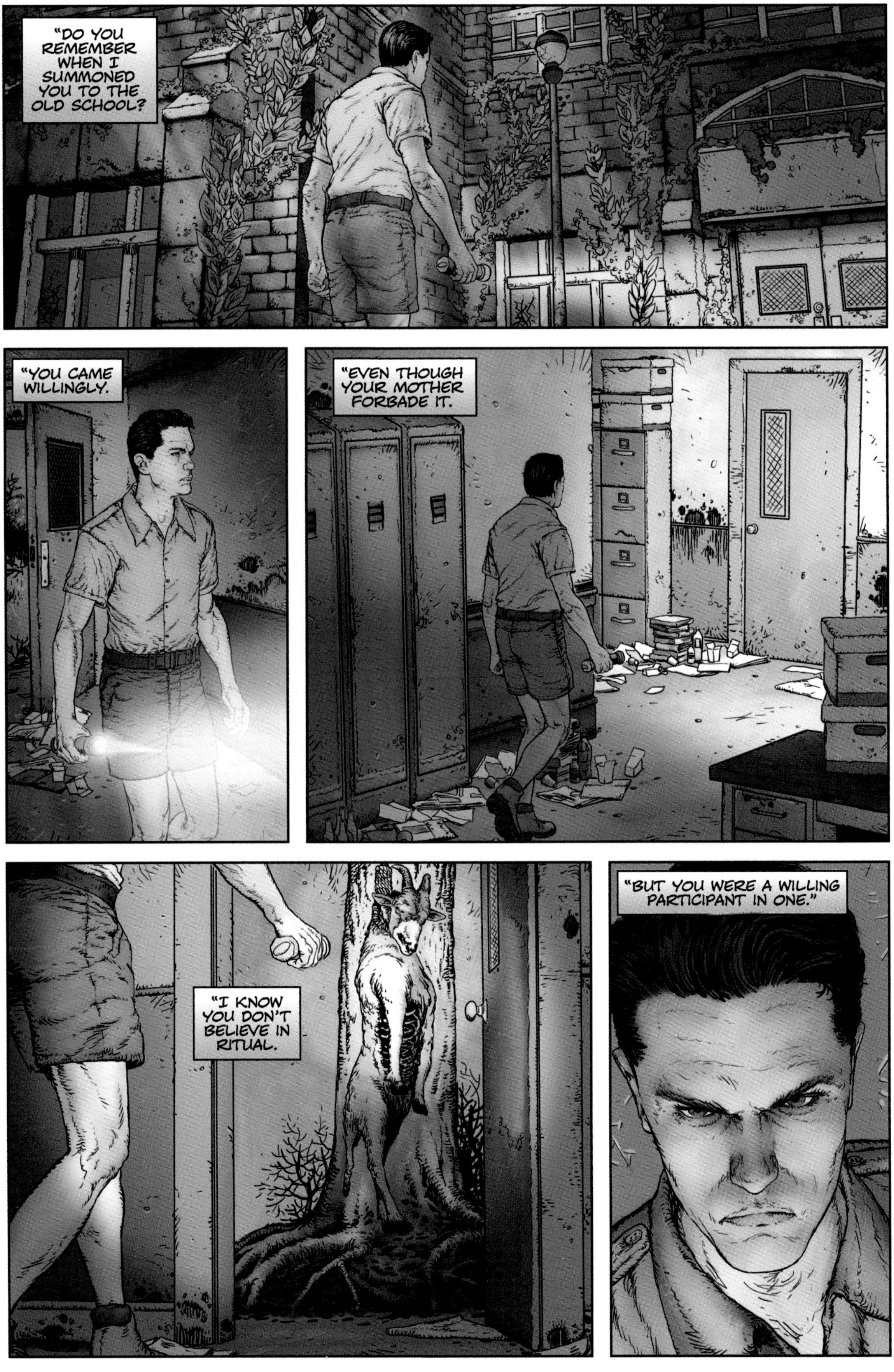
"DO YOU REMEMBER WHEN I SUMMONED YOU TO THE OLD SCHOOL?
"YOU CAME WILLINGLY.
"EVEN THOUGH YOUR MOTHER FORBADE IT.
"I KNOW YOU DON'T BELIEVE IN RITUAL.
"BUT YOU WERE A WILLING PARTICIPANT IN ONE."

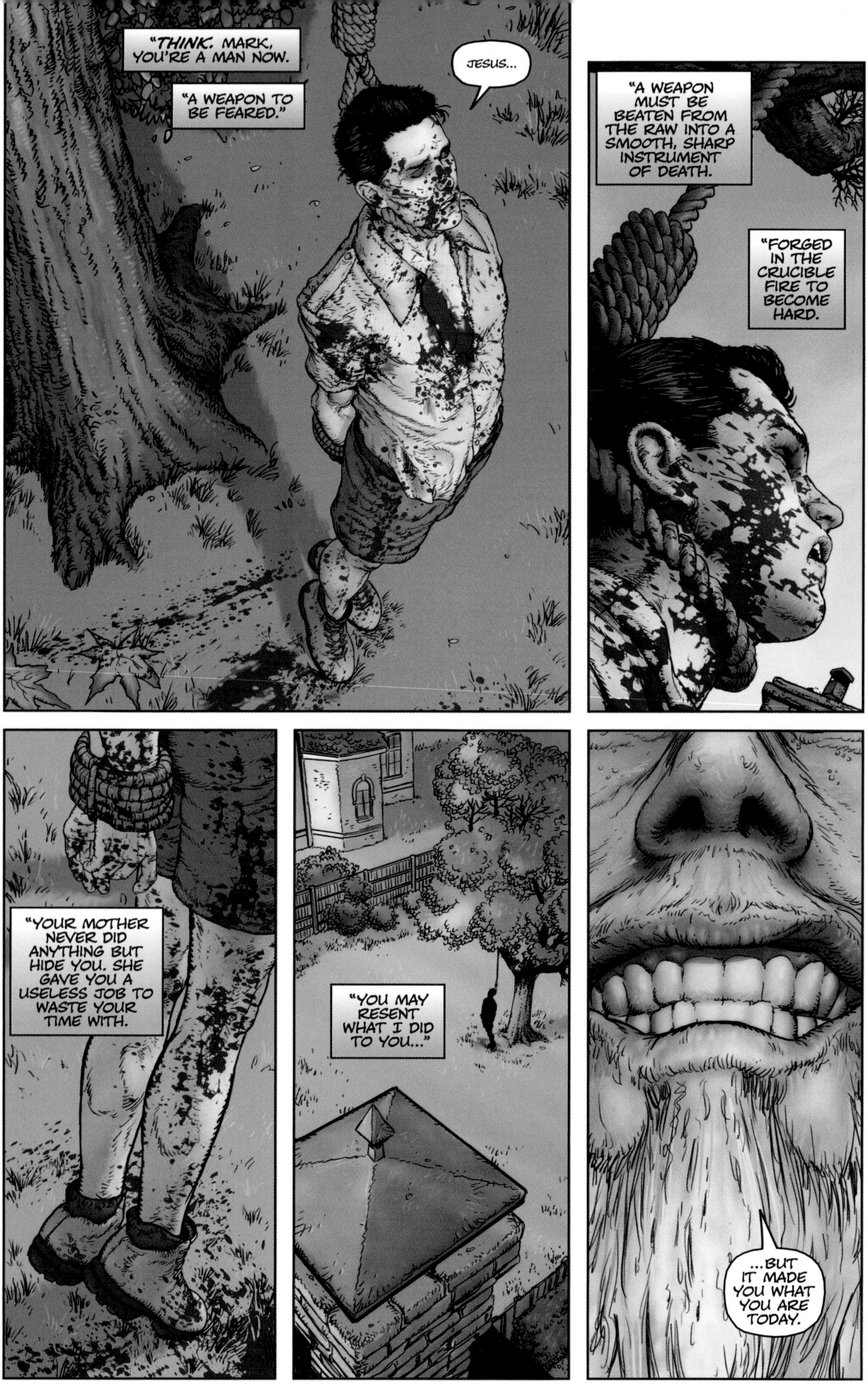
"THINK. MARK, YOU'RE A MAN NOW.
"A WEAPON TO BE FEARED."
JESUS...
"A WEAPON MUST BE BEATEN FROM THE RAW INTO A SMOOTH, SHARP INSTRUMENT OF DEATH.
"FORGED IN THE CRUCIBLE FIRE TO BECOME HARD.
"YOUR MOTHER NEVER DID ANYTHING BUT HIDE YOU. SHE GAVE YOU A USELESS JOB TO WASTE YOUR TIME WITH.
"YOU MAY RESENT WHAT I DID TO YOU..."
...BUT IT MADE YOU WHAT YOU ARE TODAY.

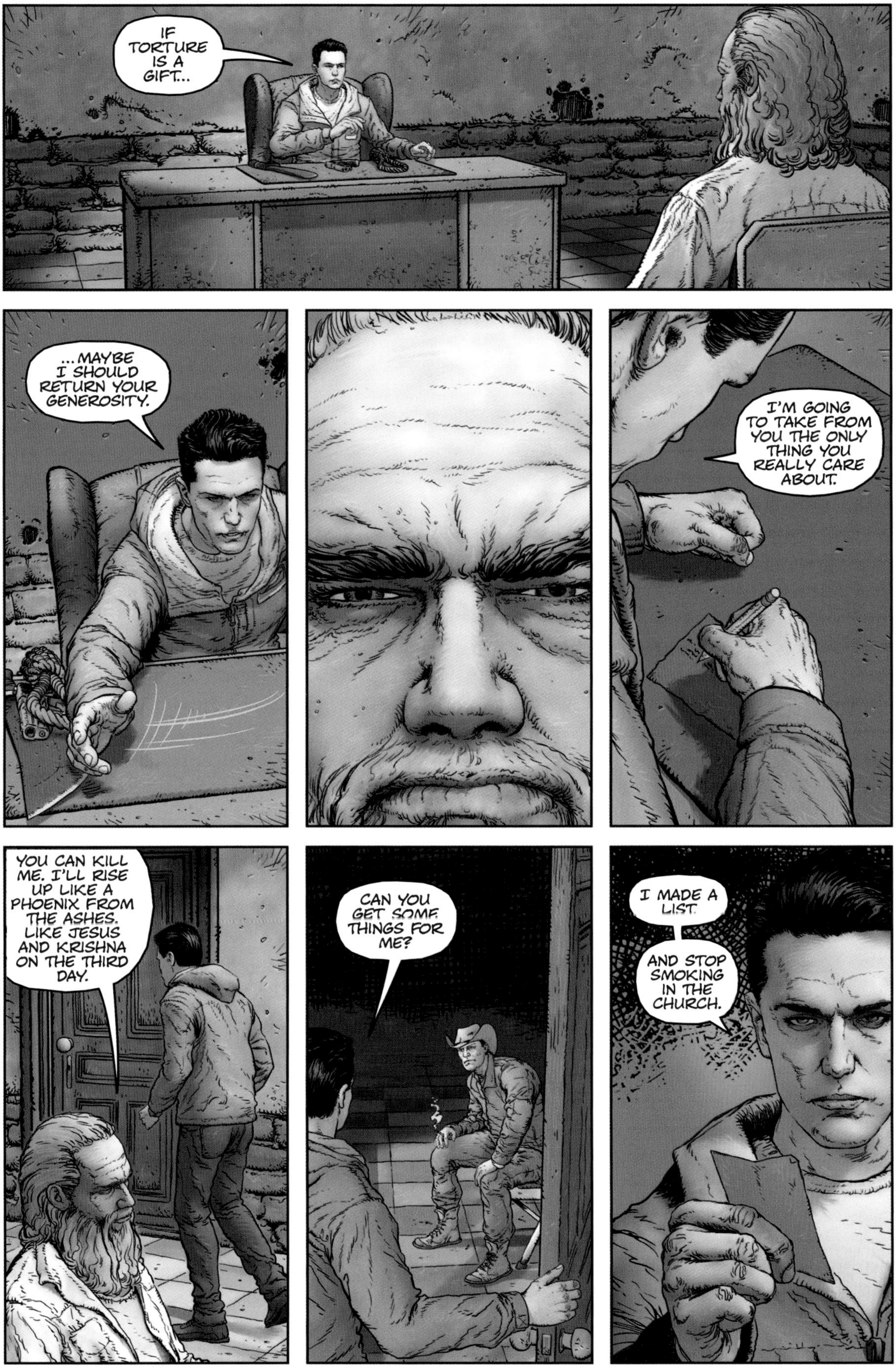
IF TORTURE IS A GIFT...
...MAYBE I SHOULD RETURN YOUR GENEROSITY.
I'M GOING TO TAKE FROM YOU THE ONLY THING YOU REALLY CARE ABOUT.
YOU CAN KILL ME. I'LL RISE UP LIKE A PHOENIX FROM THE ASHES. LIKE JESUS AND KRISHNA ON THE THIRD DAY.
CAN YOU GET SOME THINGS FOR ME?
I MADE A LIST.
AND STOP SMOKING IN THE CHURCH.

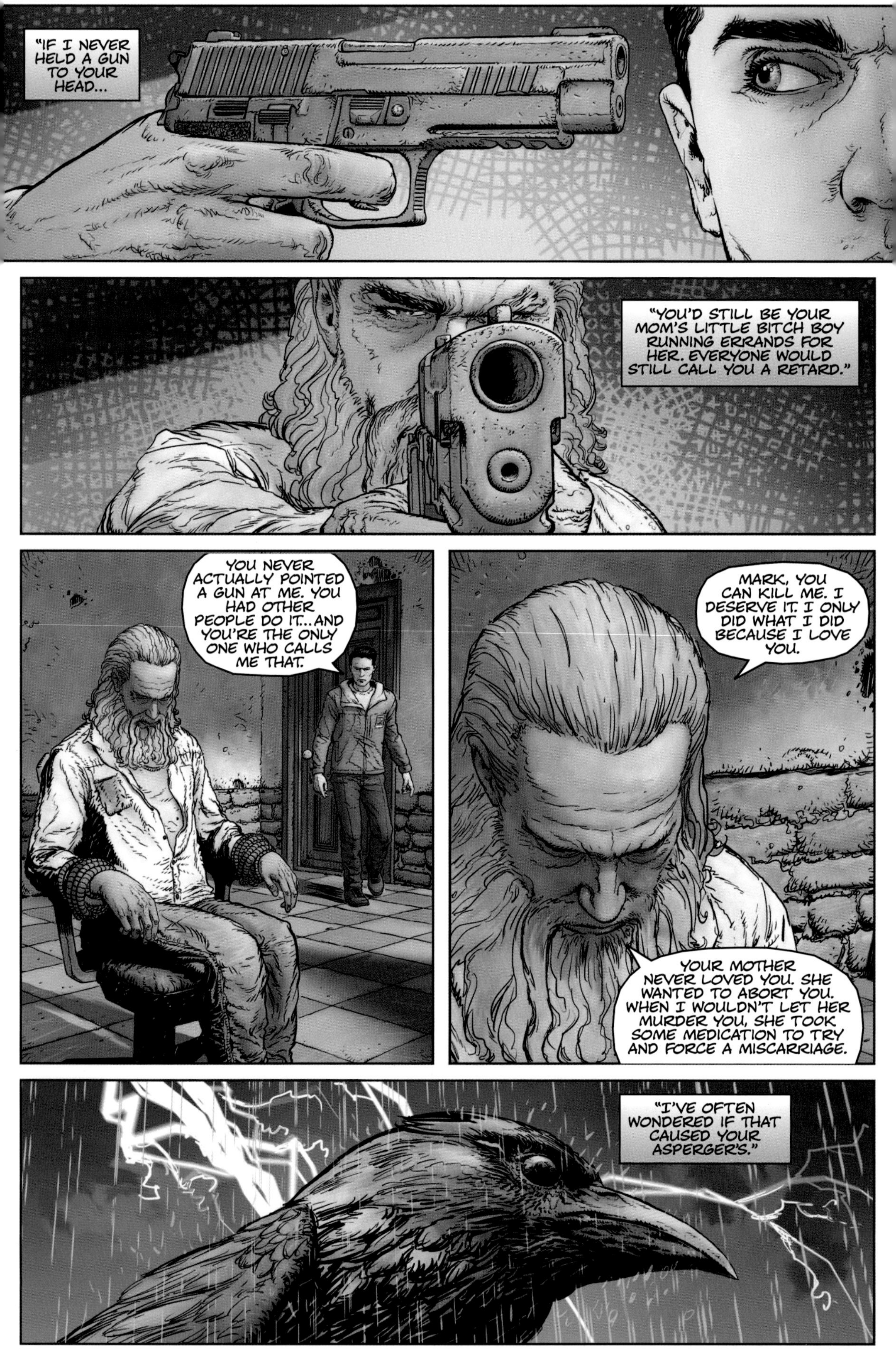
"IF I NEVER HELD A GUN TO YOUR HEAD...
"YOU'D STILL BE YOUR MOM'S LITTLE BITCH BOY RUNNING ERRANDS FOR HER. EVERYONE WOULD STILL CALL YOU A RETARD."
YOU NEVER ACTUALLY POINTED A GUN AT ME. YOU HAD OTHER PEOPLE DO IT...AND YOU'RE THE ONLY ONE WHO CALLS ME THAT.
MARK, YOU CAN KILL ME. I DESERVE IT. I ONLY DID WHAT I DID BECAUSE I LOVE YOU.
YOUR MOTHER NEVER LOVED YOU. SHE WANTED TO ABORT YOU. WHEN I WOULDN'T LET HER MURDER YOU, SHE TOOK SOME MEDICATION TO TRY AND FORCE A MISCARRIAGE.
"I'VE OFTEN WONDERED IF THAT CAUSED YOUR ASPERGER'S."

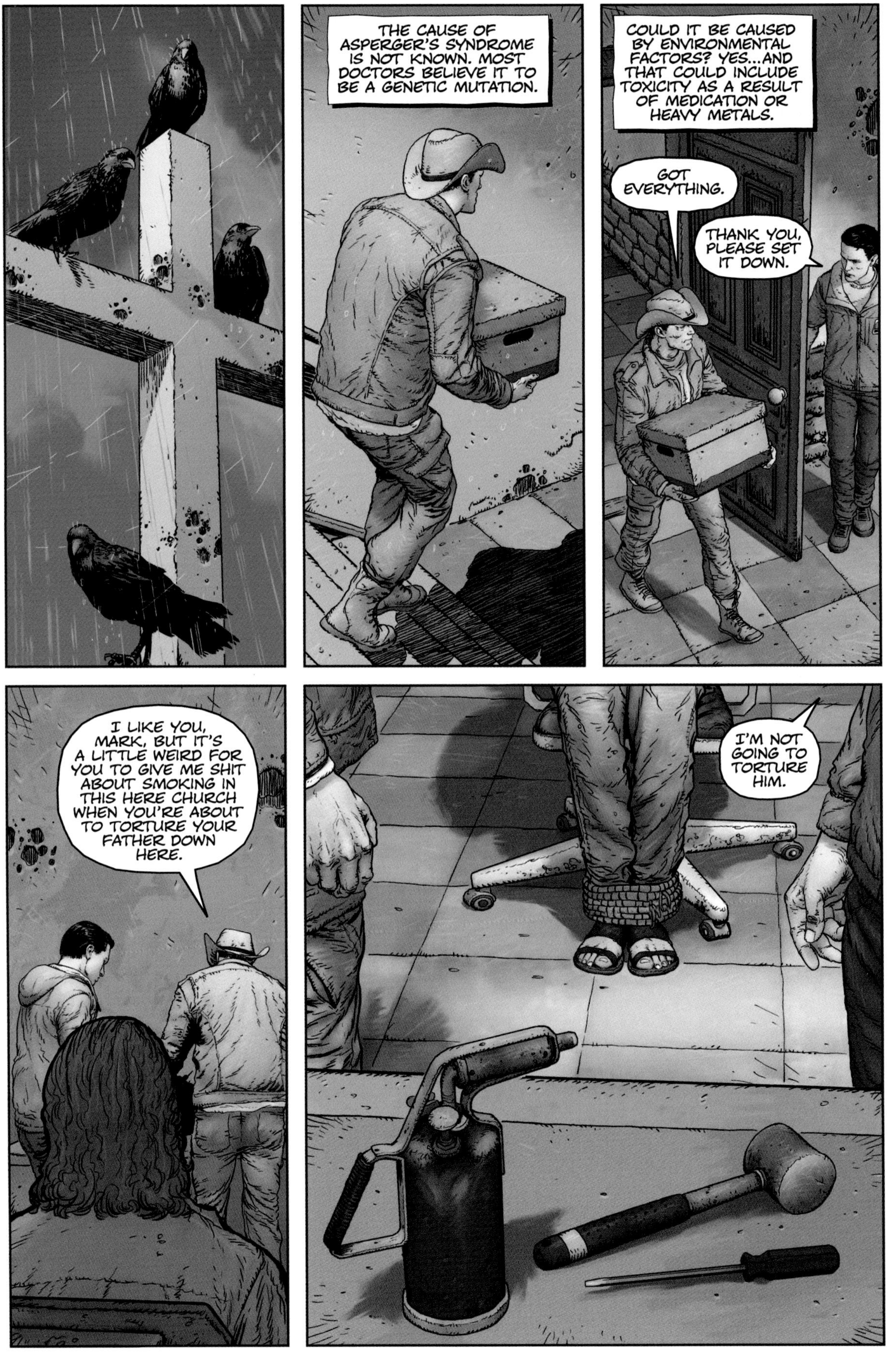
THE CAUSE OF ASPERGER'S SYNDROME IS NOT KNOWN. MOST DOCTORS BELIEVE IT TO BE A GENETIC MUTATION.
COULD IT BE CAUSED BY ENVIRONMENTAL FACTORS? YES...AND THAT COULD INCLUDE TOXICITY AS A RESULT OF MEDICATION OR HEAVY METALS.
GOT EVERYTHING.
THANK YOU, PLEASE SET IT DOWN.
I LIKE YOU, MARK, BUT IT'S A LITTLE WEIRD FOR YOU TO GIVE ME SHIT ABOUT SMOKING IN THIS HERE CHURCH WHEN YOU'RE ABOUT TO TORTURE YOUR FATHER DOWN HERE.
I'M NOT GOING TO TORTURE HIM.

I'M GOING TO FREE HIM.

HOLD HIM STILL.

WAIT...

I KNOW WHAT YOU'RE DOING, PLEASE DON'T DO THIS.

I BEG YOU.

KILL ME, PLEASE, DON'T TAKE MY MIND.

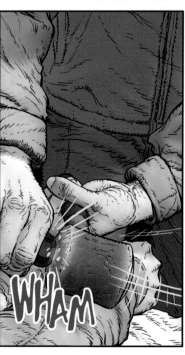

WHAM

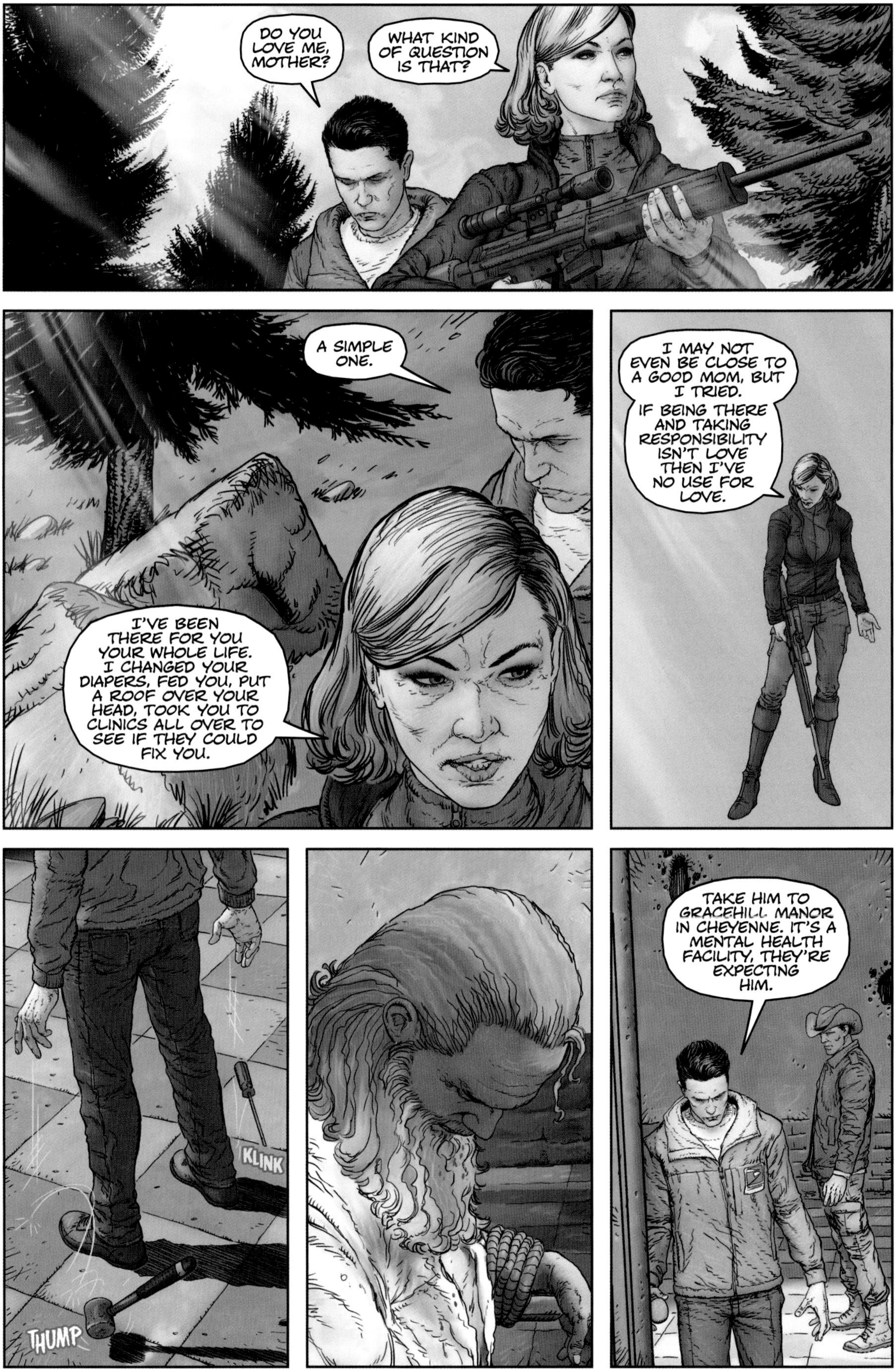
DO YOU LOVE ME, MOTHER?
WHAT KIND OF QUESTION IS THAT?
A SIMPLE ONE.
I'VE BEEN THERE FOR YOU YOUR WHOLE LIFE. I CHANGED YOUR DIAPERS, FED YOU, PUT A ROOF OVER YOUR HEAD, TOOK YOU TO CLINICS ALL OVER TO SEE IF THEY COULD FIX YOU.
I MAY NOT EVEN BE CLOSE TO A GOOD MOM, BUT I TRIED.
IF BEING THERE AND TAKING RESPONSIBILITY ISN'T LOVE THEN I'VE NO USE FOR LOVE.
KLINK
THUMP
TAKE HIM TO GRACEHILL MANOR IN CHEYENNE. IT'S A MENTAL HEALTH FACILITY, THEY'RE EXPECTING HIM.

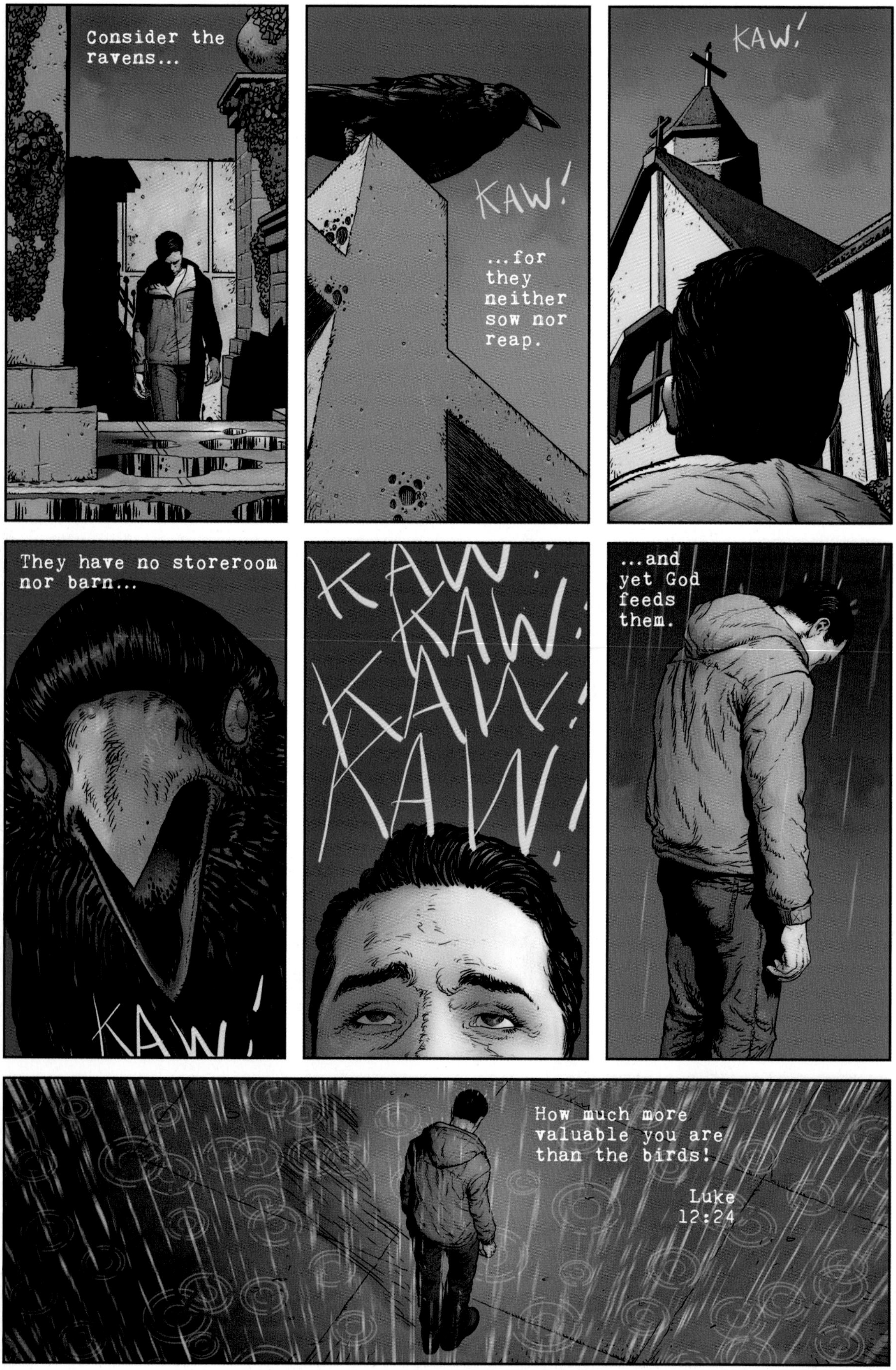
Consider the ravens...
KAW!
...for they neither sow nor reap.
KAW!
They have no storeroom nor barn...
KAW!
KAW! KAW! KAW! KAW!
...and yet God feeds them.
How much more valuable you are than the birds!
Luke 12:24

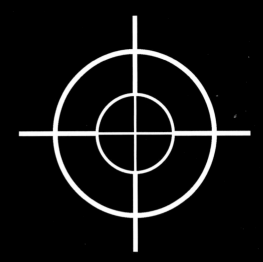

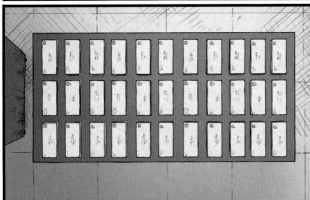

"MARK. WAKE UP.

"MAYORS CAN'T SLEEP IN.

"AND TODAY IS A SPECIAL DAY FOR EDEN."

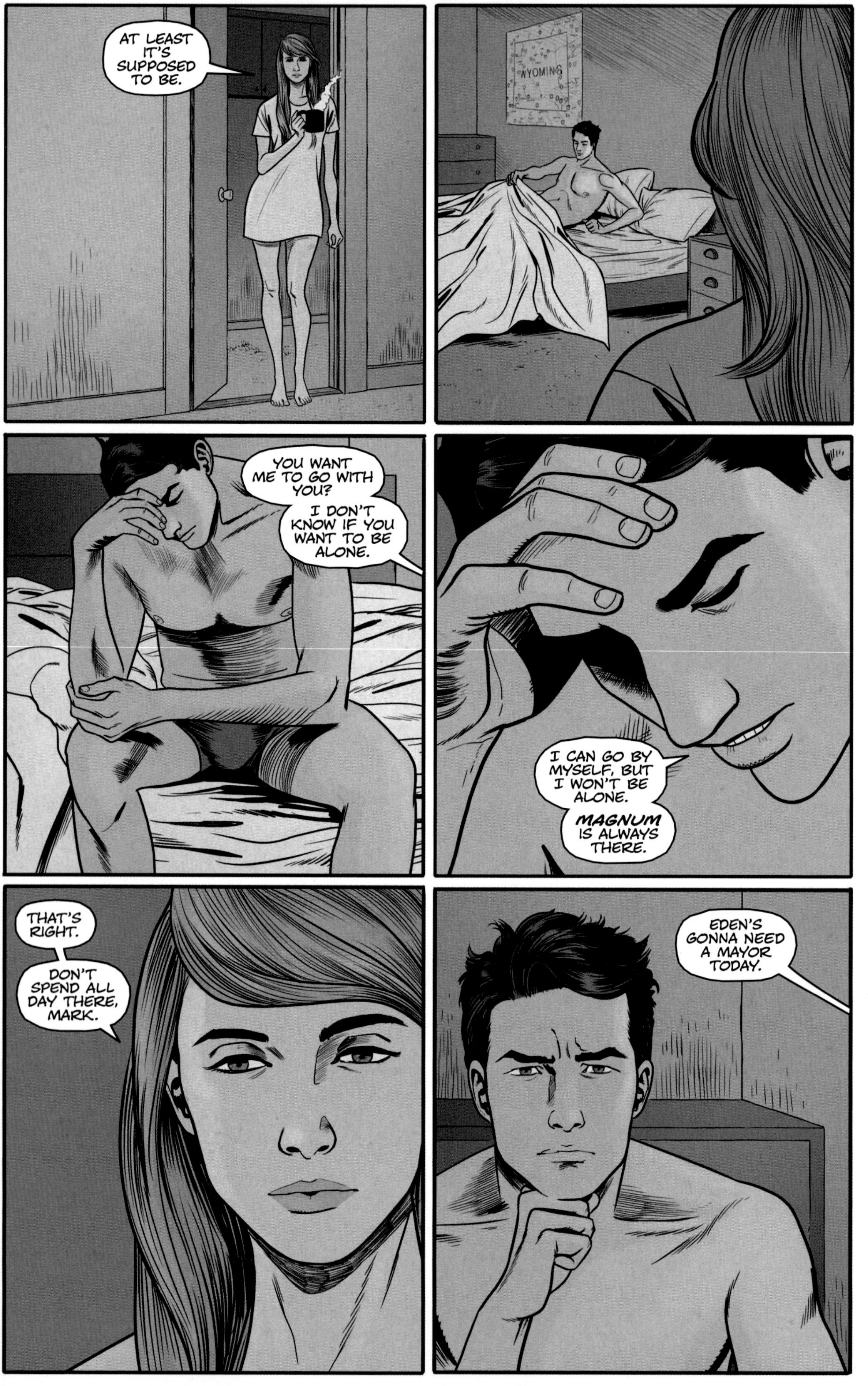
AT LEAST IT'S SUPPOSED TO BE.
WYOMING
YOU WANT ME TO GO WITH YOU?
I DON'T KNOW IF YOU WANT TO BE ALONE.
I CAN GO BY MYSELF, BUT I WON'T BE ALONE.
MAGNUM IS ALWAYS THERE.
THAT'S RIGHT.
DON'T SPEND ALL DAY THERE, MARK.
EDEN'S GONNA NEED A MAYOR TODAY.

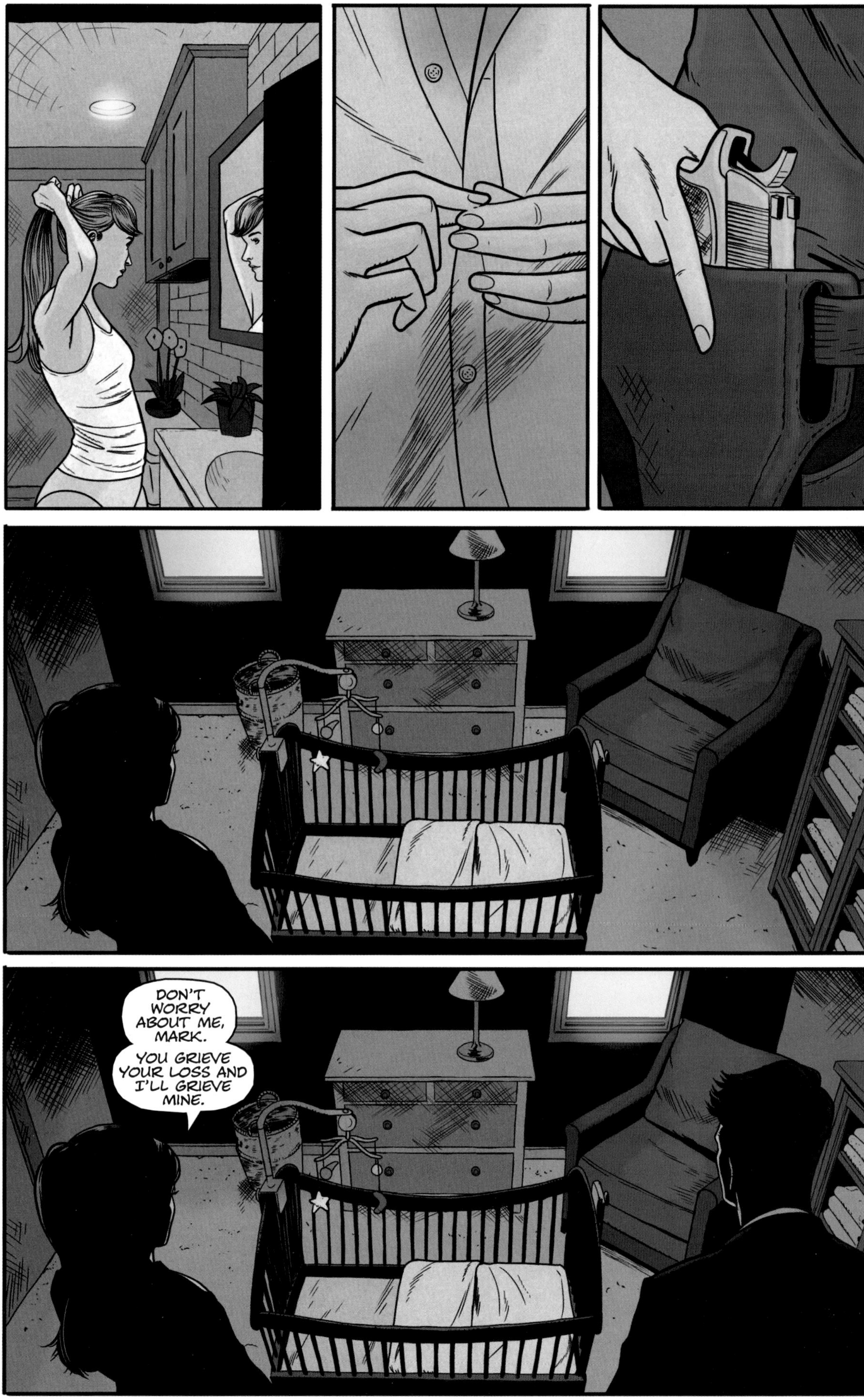
DON'T WORRY ABOUT ME, MARK.
YOU GRIEVE YOUR LOSS AND I'LL GRIEVE MINE.

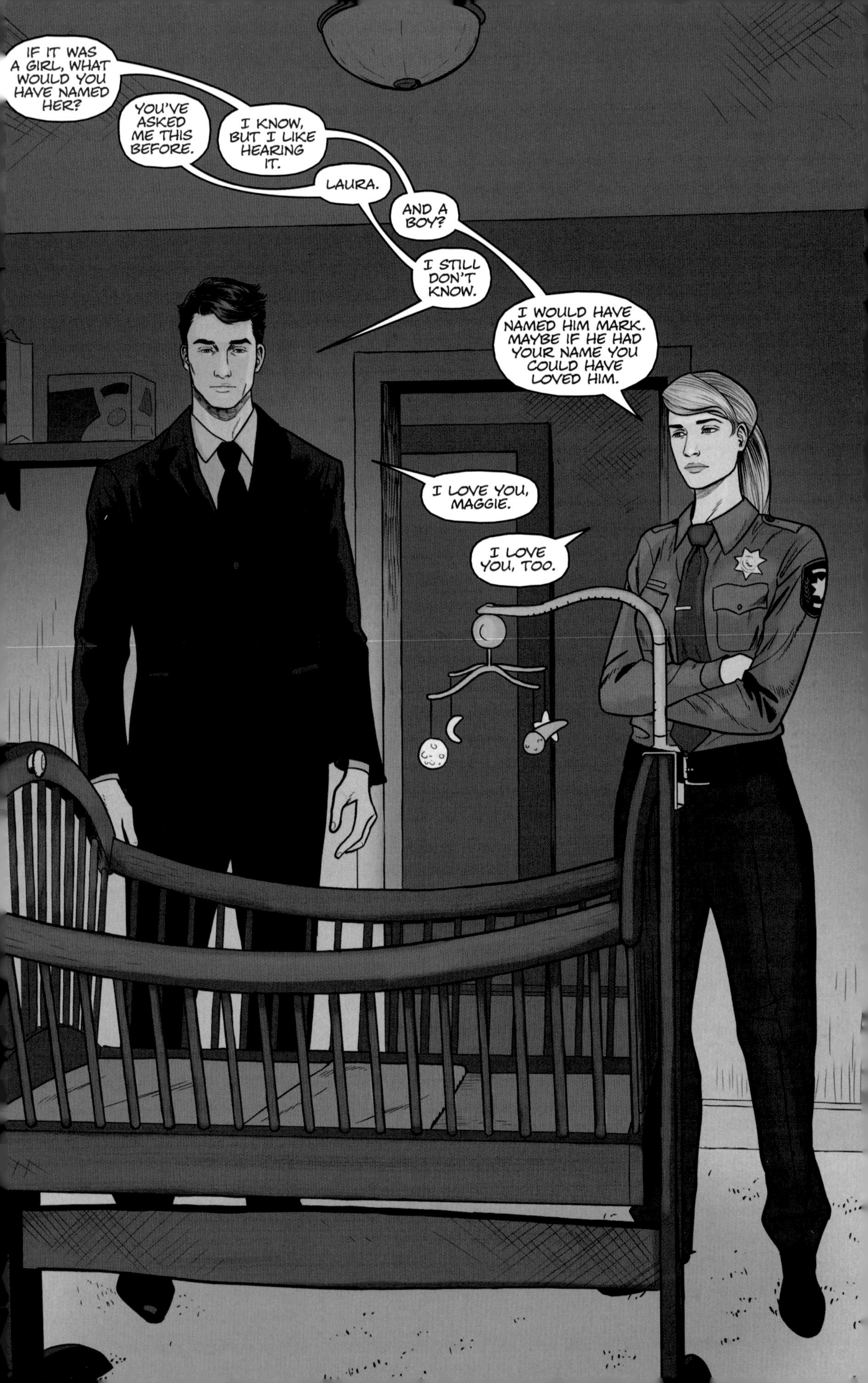

IF IT WAS A GIRL, WHAT WOULD YOU HAVE NAMED HER?
YOU'VE ASKED ME THIS BEFORE.
I KNOW, BUT I LIKE HEARING IT.
LAURA.
AND A BOY?
I STILL DON'T KNOW.
I WOULD HAVE NAMED HIM MARK. MAYBE IF HE HAD YOUR NAME YOU COULD HAVE LOVED HIM.
I LOVE YOU, MAGGIE.
I LOVE YOU, TOO.

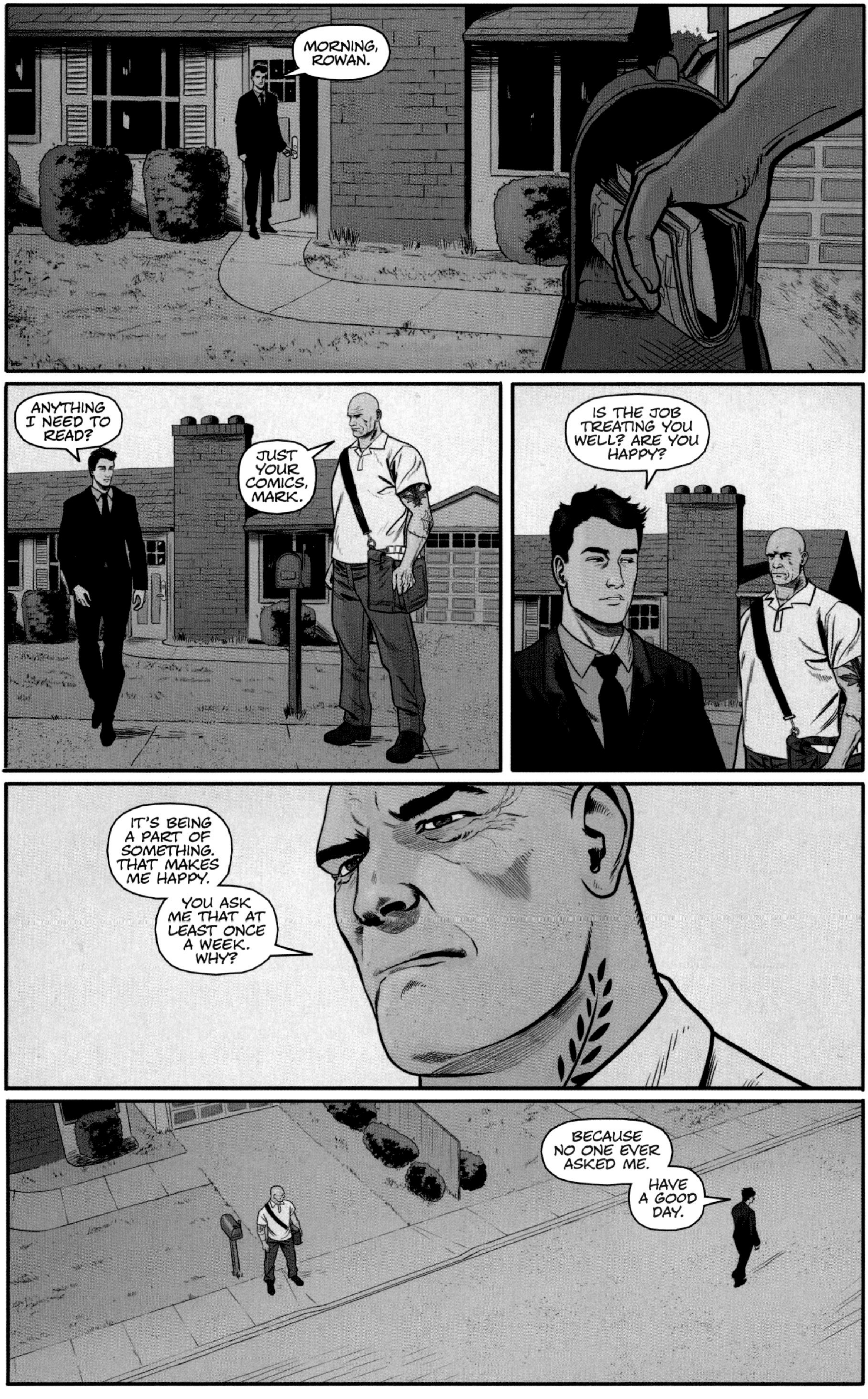
MORNING, ROWAN.
ANYTHING I NEED TO READ?
JUST YOUR COMICS, MARK.
IS THE JOB TREATING YOU WELL? ARE YOU HAPPY?
IT'S BEING A PART OF SOMETHING. THAT MAKES ME HAPPY.
YOU ASK ME THAT AT LEAST ONCE A WEEK. WHY?
BECAUSE NO ONE EVER ASKED ME.
HAVE A GOOD DAY.

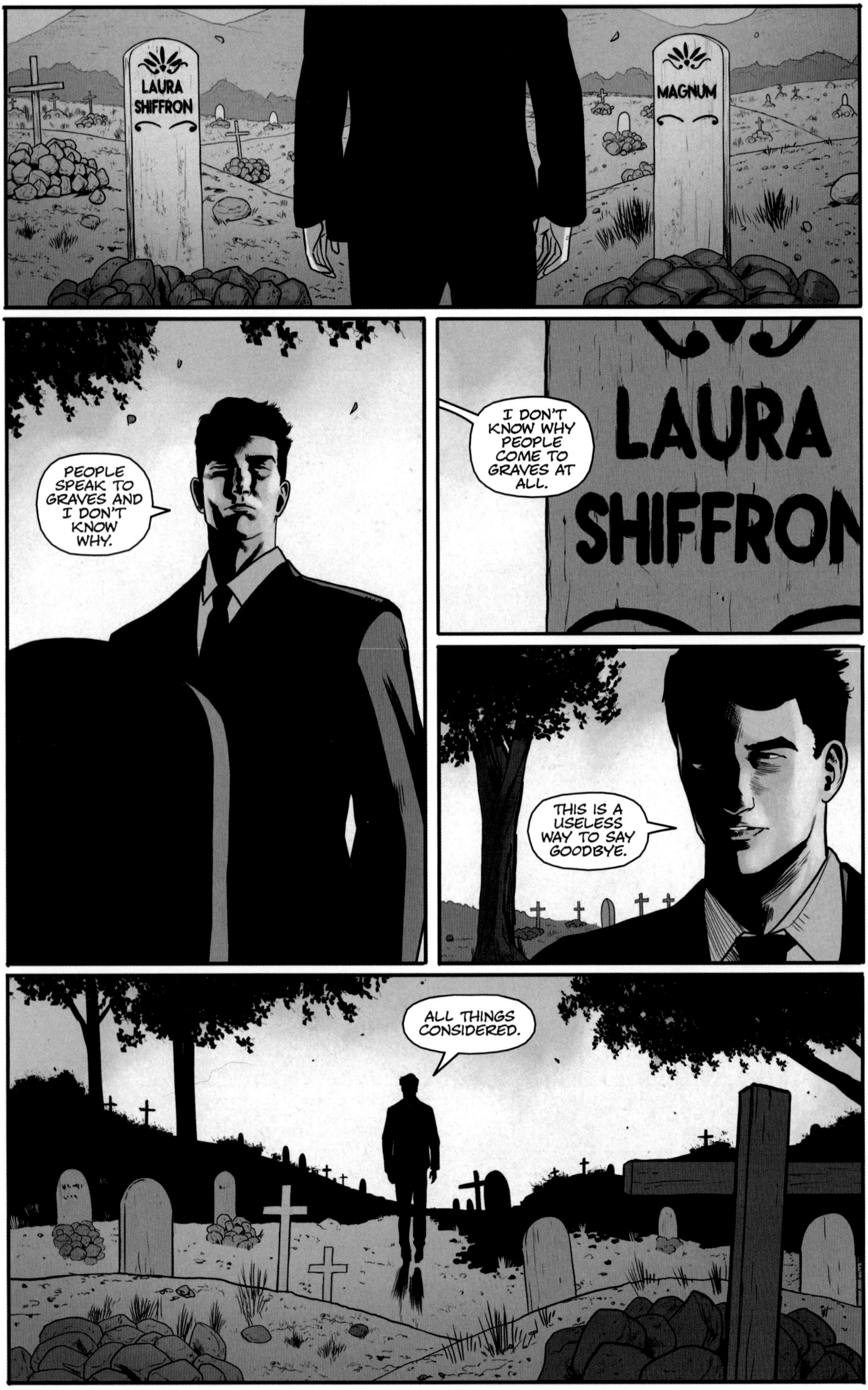

LAURA SHIFFRON
MAGNUM
PEOPLE SPEAK TO GRAVES AND I DON'T KNOW WHY.
I DON'T KNOW WHY PEOPLE COME TO GRAVES AT ALL.
LAURA SHIFFRON
THIS IS A USELESS WAY TO SAY GOODBYE.
ALL THINGS CONSIDERED.

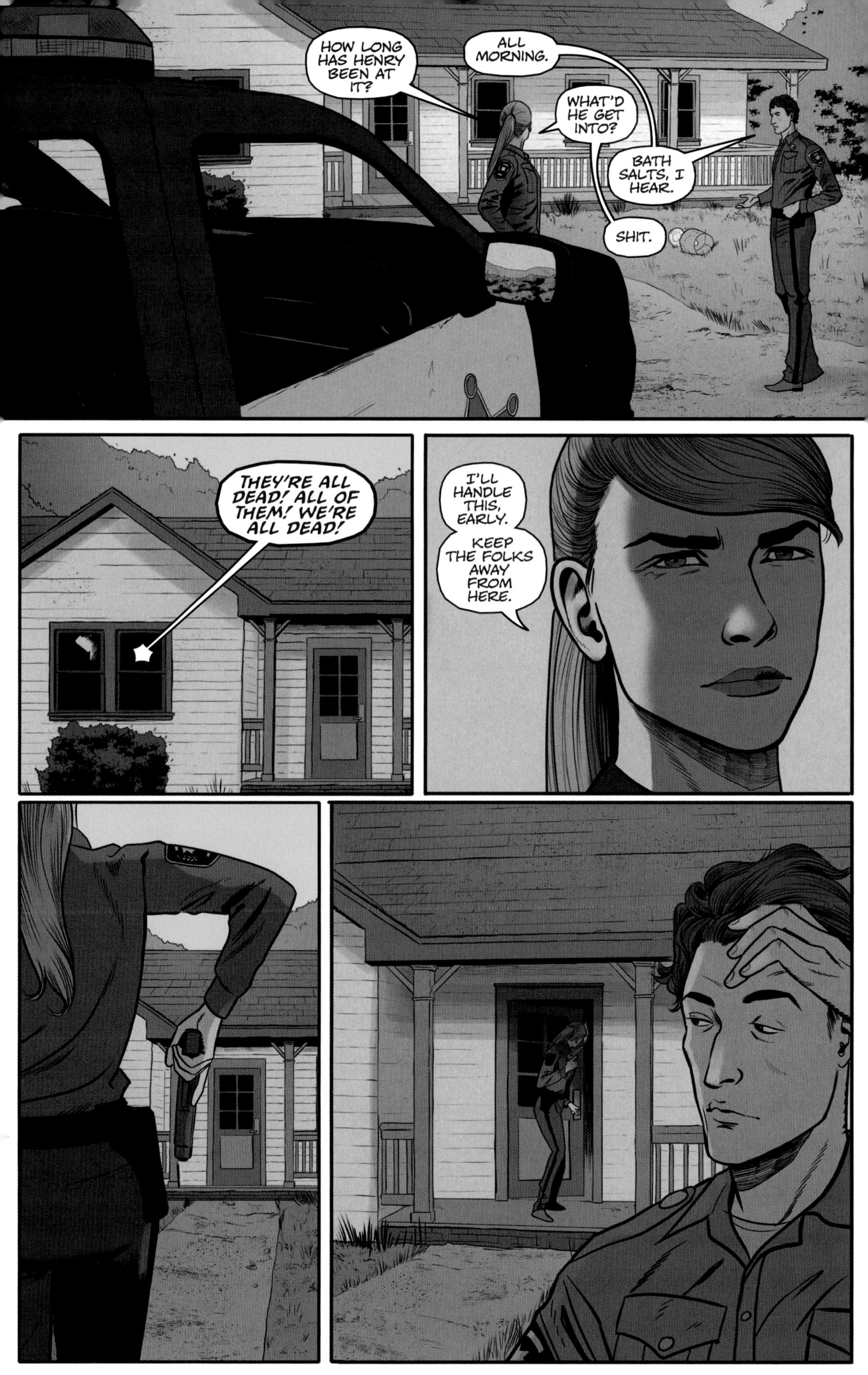
HOW LONG HAS HENRY BEEN AT IT?
ALL MORNING.
WHAT'D HE GET INTO?
BATH SALTS, I HEAR.
SHIT.
THEY'RE ALL DEAD! ALL OF THEM! WE'RE ALL DEAD!
I'LL HANDLE THIS, EARLY.
KEEP THE FOLKS AWAY FROM HERE.

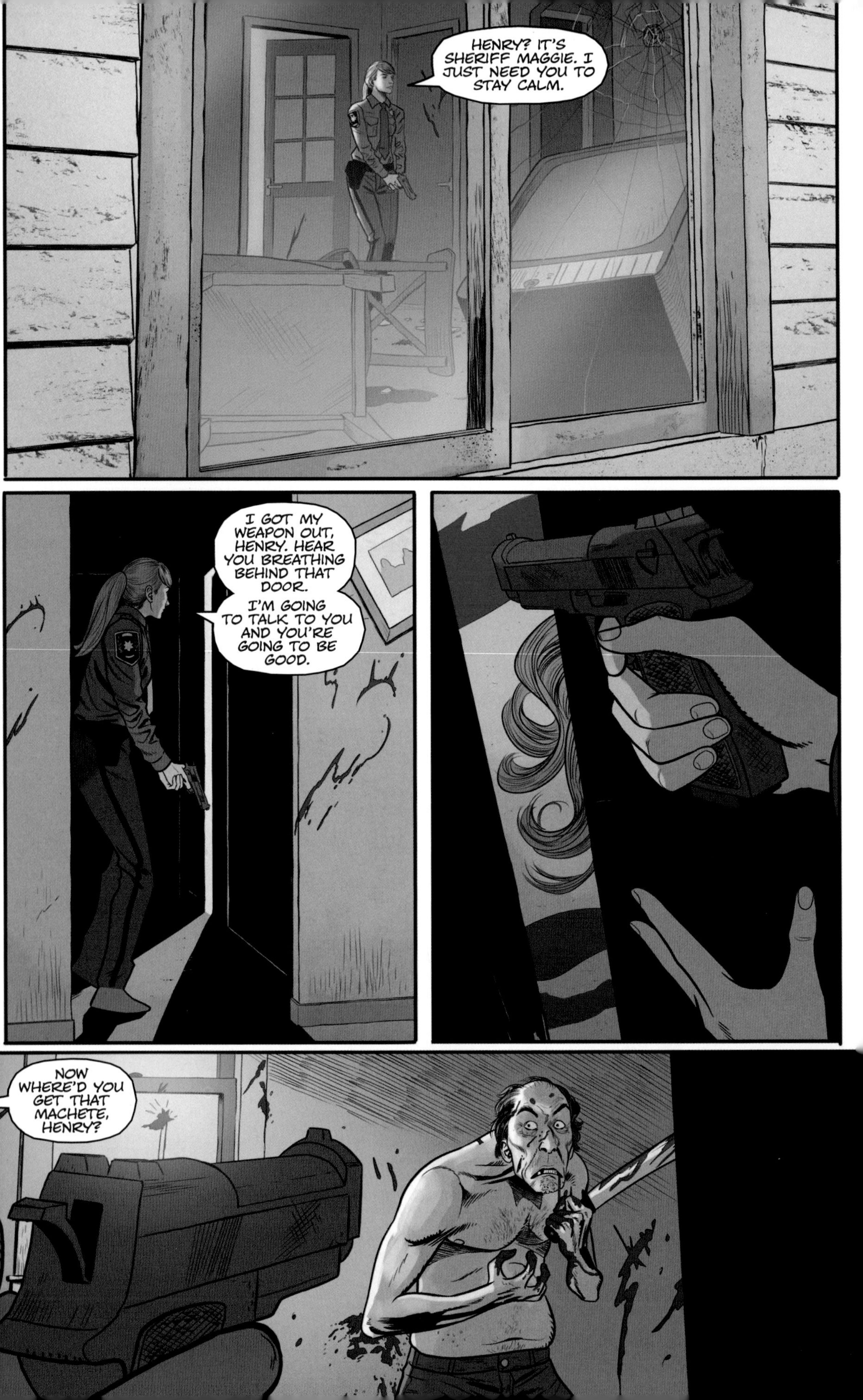
HENRY? IT'S SHERIFF MAGGIE. I JUST NEED YOU TO STAY CALM.
I GOT MY WEAPON OUT, HENRY. HEAR YOU BREATHING BEHIND THAT DOOR.
I'M GOING TO TALK TO YOU AND YOU'RE GOING TO BE GOOD.
NOW WHERE'D YOU GET THAT MACHETE, HENRY?

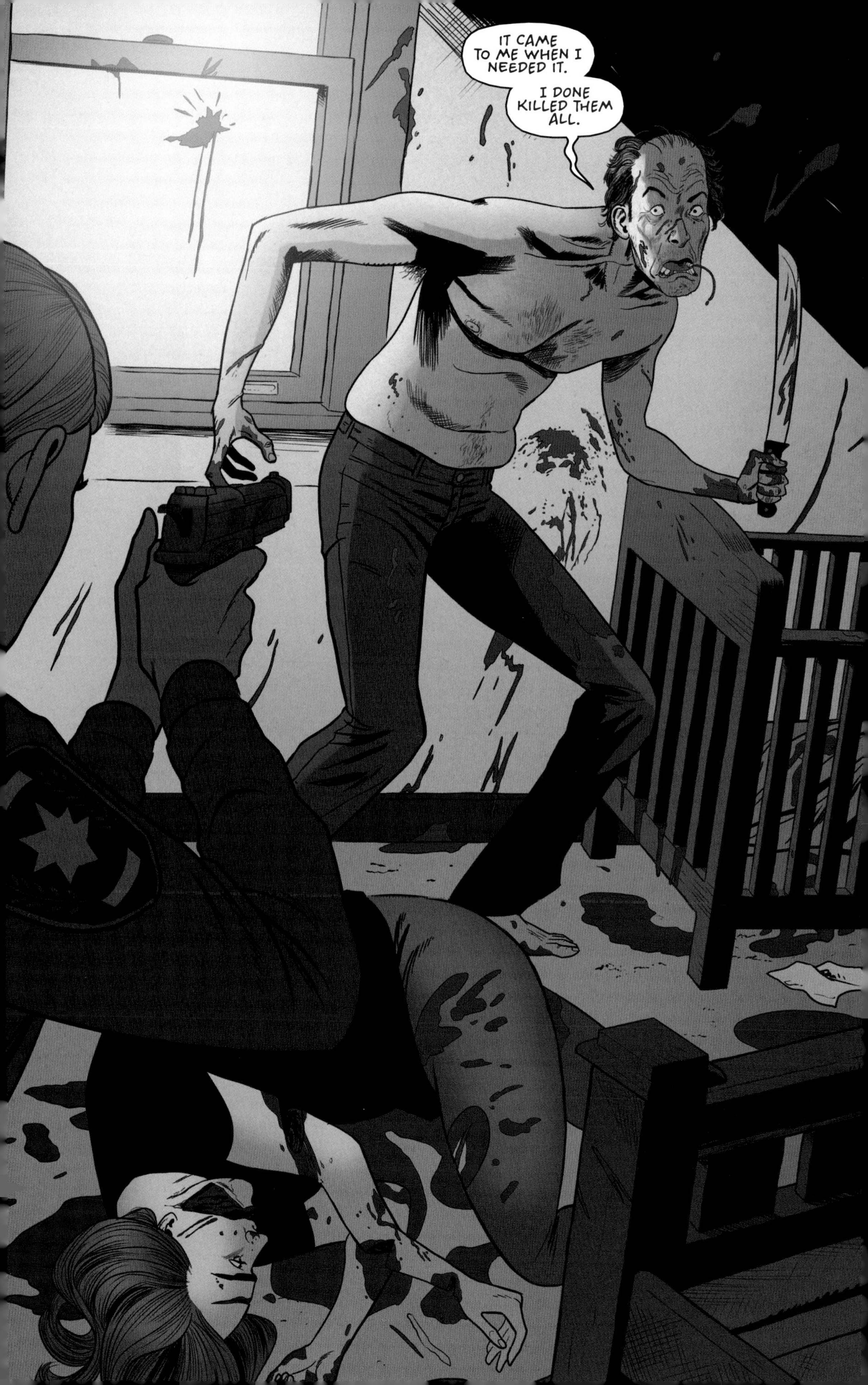
IT CAME TO ME WHEN I NEEDED IT.
I DONE KILLED THEM ALL.

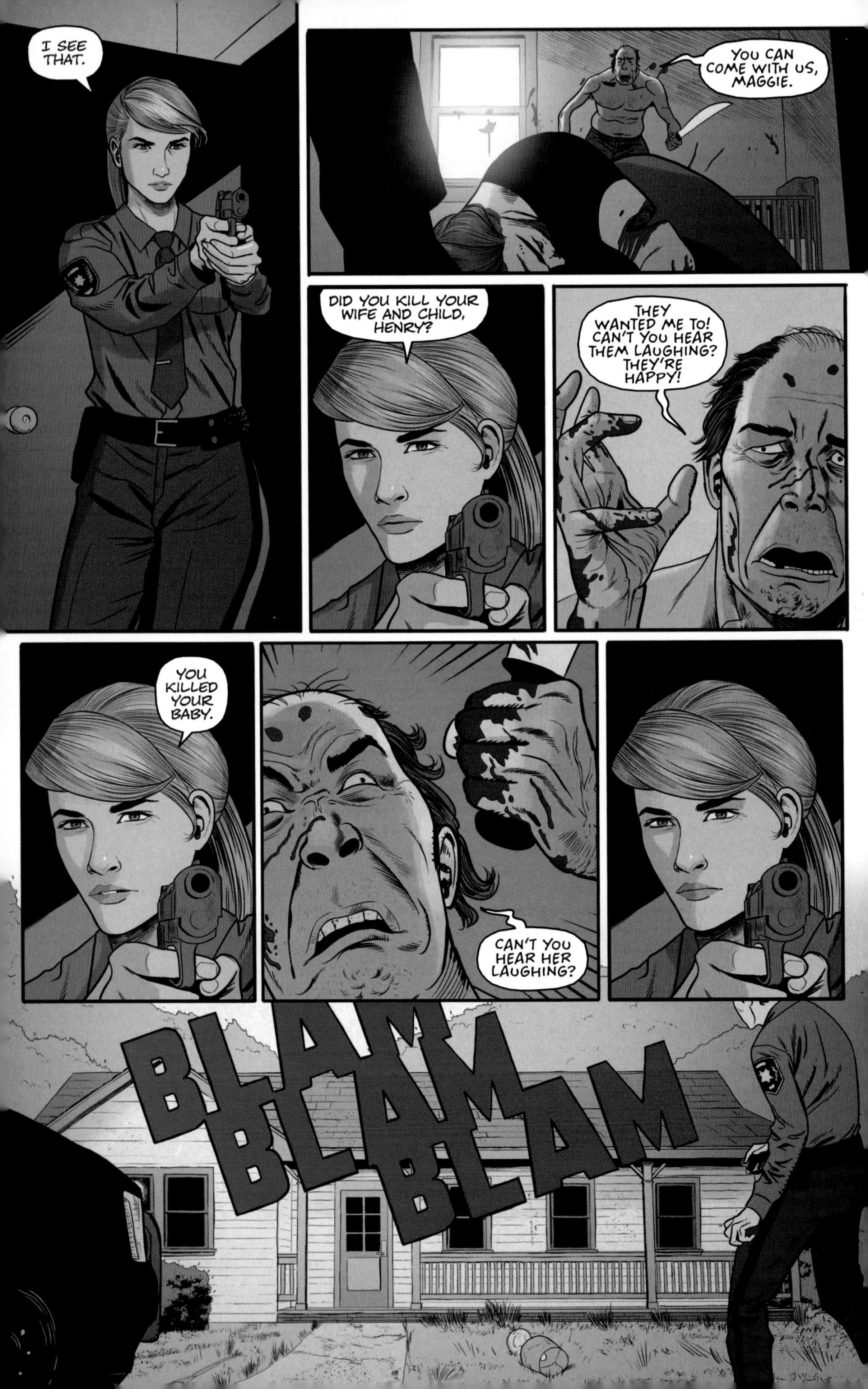
I SEE THAT.
YOU CAN COME WITH US, MAGGIE.
DID YOU KILL YOUR WIFE AND CHILD, HENRY?
THEY WANTED ME TO! CAN'T YOU HEAR THEM LAUGHING? THEY'RE HAPPY!
YOU KILLED YOUR BABY.
CAN'T YOU HEAR HER LAUGHING?
BLAM
BLAM
BLAM

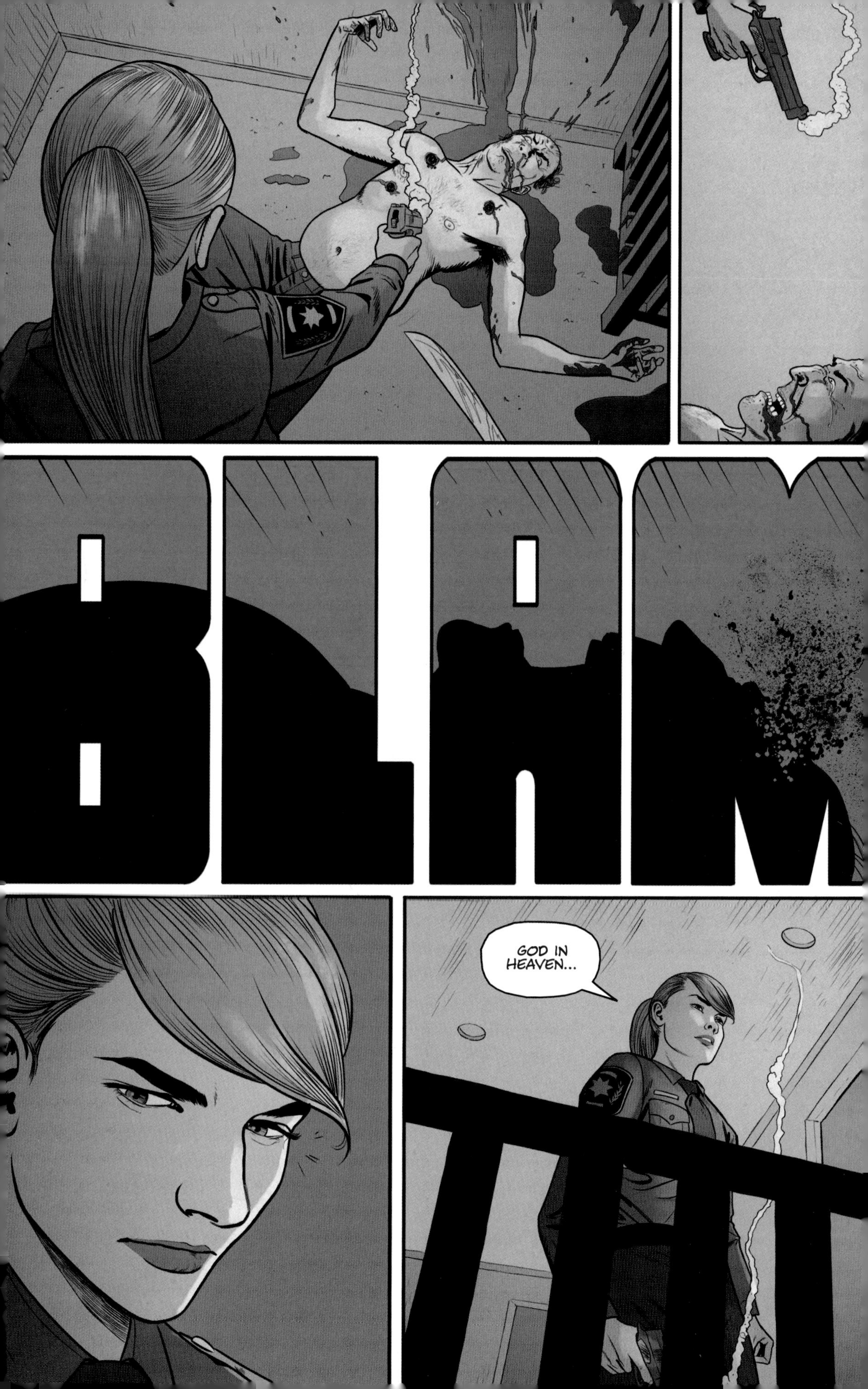
BLAM
GOD IN HEAVEN...

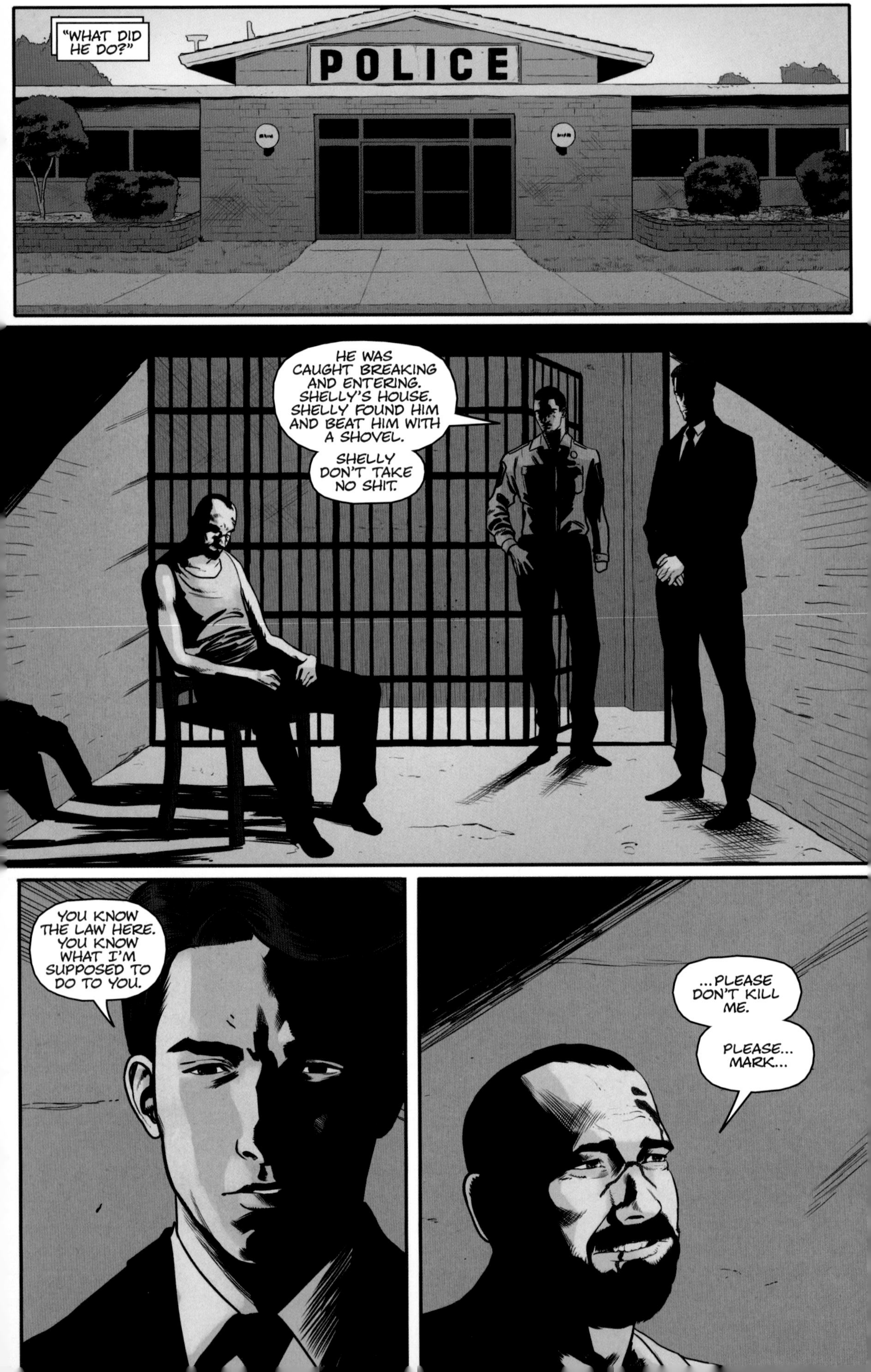
"WHAT DID HE DO?"
POLICE
HE WAS CAUGHT BREAKING AND ENTERING. SHELLY'S HOUSE. SHELLY FOUND HIM AND BEAT HIM WITH A SHOVEL.
SHELLY DON'T TAKE NO SHIT.
YOU KNOW THE LAW HERE. YOU KNOW WHAT I'M SUPPOSED TO DO TO YOU.
...PLEASE DON'T KILL ME.
PLEASE... MARK...

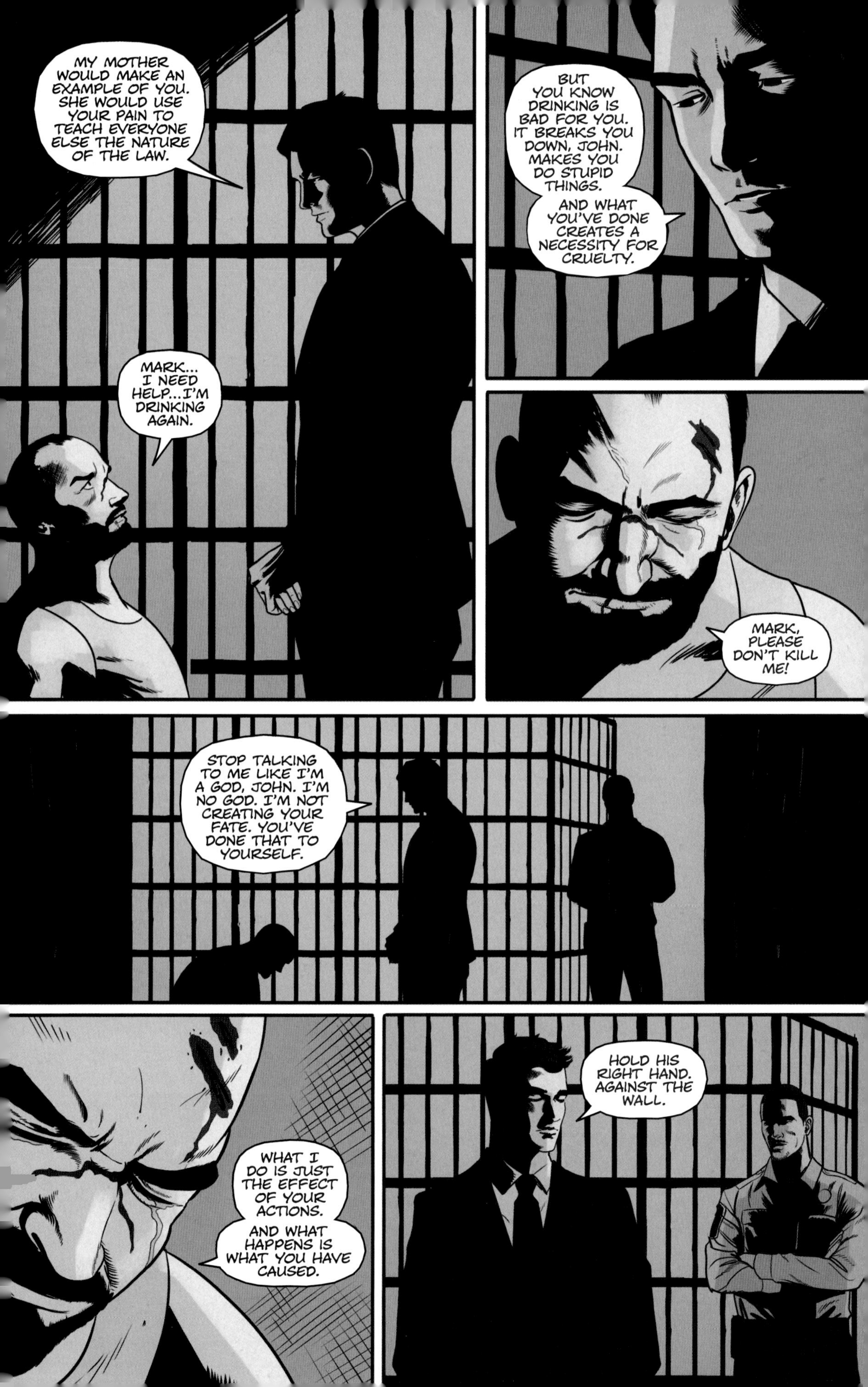
MY MOTHER WOULD MAKE AN EXAMPLE OF YOU. SHE WOULD USE YOUR PAIN TO TEACH EVERYONE ELSE THE NATURE OF THE LAW.
MARK... I NEED HELP...I'M DRINKING AGAIN.
BUT YOU KNOW DRINKING IS BAD FOR YOU. IT BREAKS YOU DOWN, JOHN. MAKES YOU DO STUPID THINGS.
AND WHAT YOU'VE DONE CREATES A NECESSITY FOR CRUELTY.
MARK, PLEASE DON'T KILL ME!
STOP TALKING TO ME LIKE I'M A GOD, JOHN. I'M NO GOD. I'M NOT CREATING YOUR FATE. YOU'VE DONE THAT TO YOURSELF.
WHAT I DO IS JUST THE EFFECT OF YOUR ACTIONS.
AND WHAT HAPPENS IS WHAT YOU HAVE CAUSED.
HOLD HIS RIGHT HAND. AGAINST THE WALL.

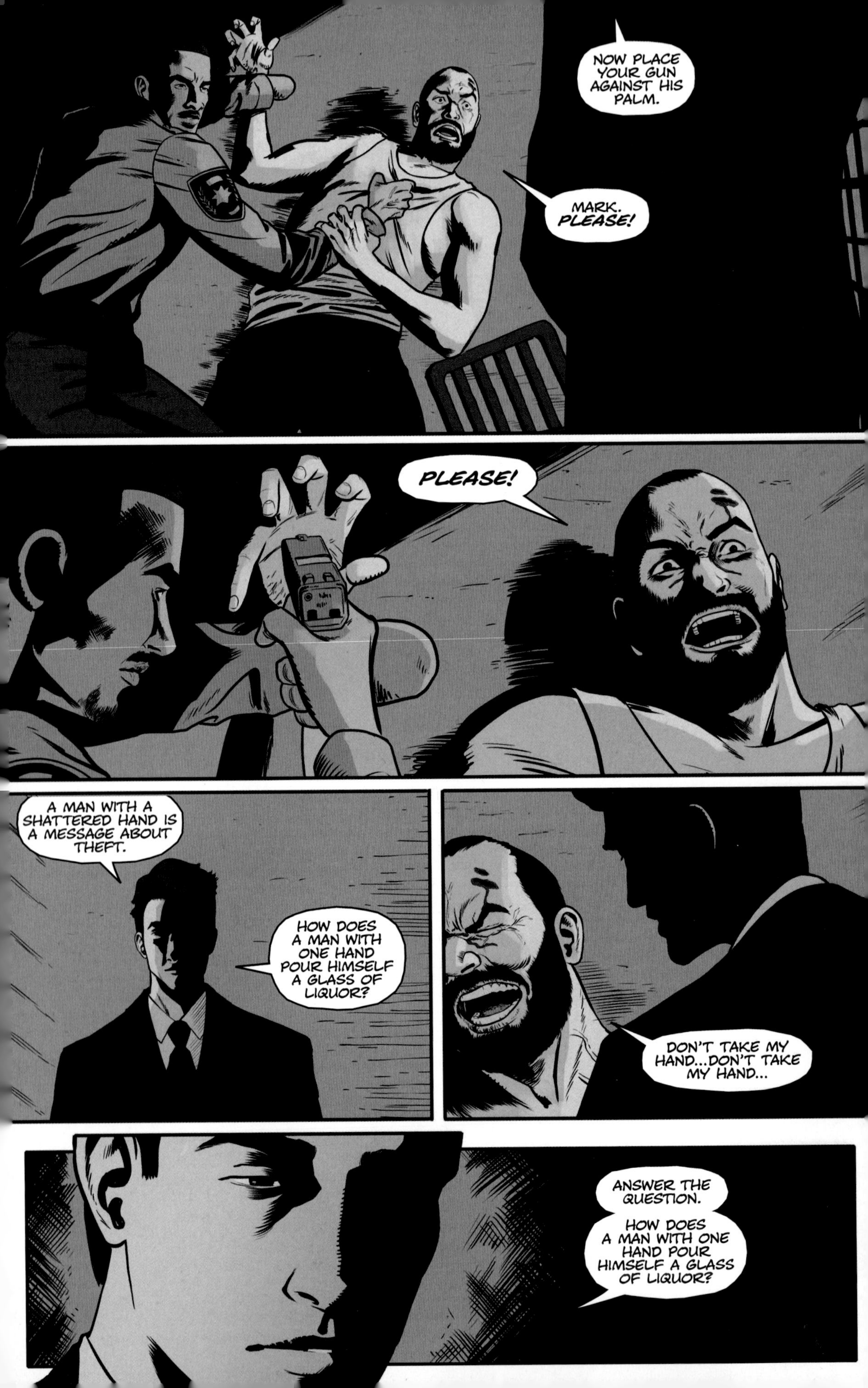
NOW PLACE YOUR GUN AGAINST HIS PALM.
MARK. PLEASE!
PLEASE!
A MAN WITH A SHATTERED HAND IS A MESSAGE ABOUT THEFT.
HOW DOES A MAN WITH ONE HAND POUR HIMSELF A GLASS OF LIQUOR?
DON'T TAKE MY HAND...DON'T TAKE MY HAND...
ANSWER THE QUESTION.
HOW DOES A MAN WITH ONE HAND POUR HIMSELF A GLASS OF LIQUOR?

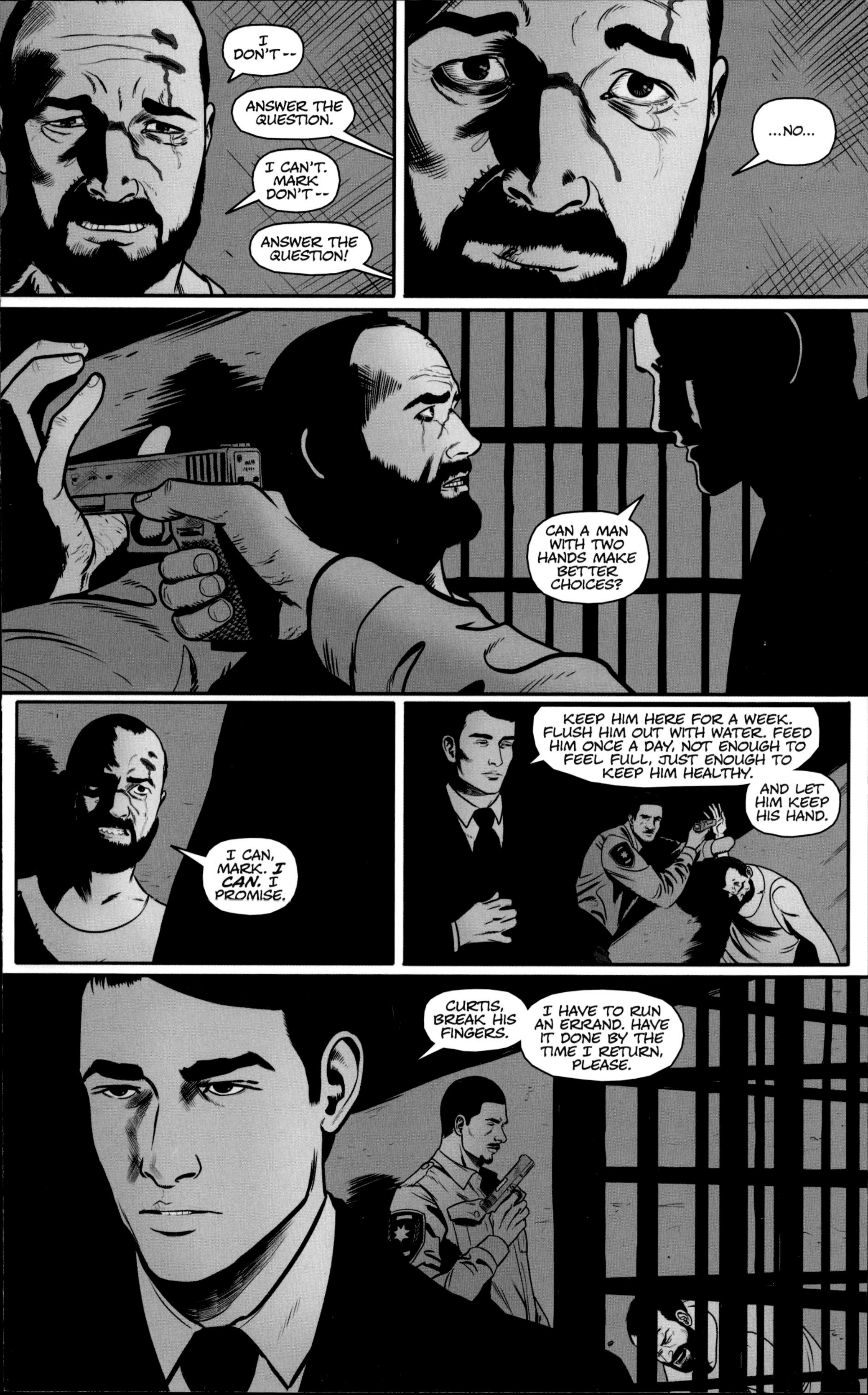
I DON'T --
ANSWER THE QUESTION.
I CAN'T. MARK DON'T --
ANSWER THE QUESTION!
...NO...
CAN A MAN WITH TWO HANDS MAKE BETTER CHOICES?
I CAN, MARK. *I CAN.* I PROMISE.
KEEP HIM HERE FOR A WEEK. FLUSH HIM OUT WITH WATER. FEED HIM ONCE A DAY, NOT ENOUGH TO FEEL FULL, JUST ENOUGH TO KEEP HIM HEALTHY.
AND LET HIM KEEP HIS HAND.
CURTIS, BREAK HIS FINGERS.
I HAVE TO RUN AN ERRAND. HAVE IT DONE BY THE TIME I RETURN, PLEASE.

THE QUESTIONS THAT WILL TORMENT YOU WILL BE POISONED WITH "HOW?" AND "WHY?"

"HOW AM I IN CONTROL OF ALL THESE LIVES?"

"WHY DID THIS HAPPEN TO ME?"

GOTTA PUT ALL THAT AWAY AND JUST DO THE JOB, MARK.

JUST DO THE JOB.

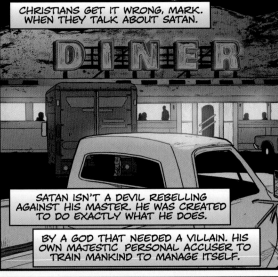

CHRISTIANS GET IT WRONG, MARK. WHEN THEY TALK ABOUT SATAN.

SATAN ISN'T A DEVIL REBELLING AGAINST HIS MASTER. HE WAS CREATED TO DO EXACTLY WHAT HE DOES.

BY A GOD THAT NEEDED A VILLAIN. HIS OWN MAJESTIC PERSONAL ACCUSER TO TRAIN MANKIND TO MANAGE ITSELF.

SO YOU BE THE SATAN THEY NEED.

WHEN THEY NEED IT.

ACCUSE THEM OF ALL THEIR FLAWS.

LET THEM OVERCOME YOU. LET THEM BE PROUD THEY ENDURED WHAT YOU PUT THEM THROUGH.

PARADISE IS BUILT ON PUNISHMENT. THAT'S WHY GOD NEEDED HELL.

WITHOUT IT, THERE'S NOTHING TO COMPARE TO HEAVEN.

THAT'S WHERE YOUR FATHER LOST HIS WAY. MEN DON'T NEED YOU TO PLAY GOD. THEY NEED A DEVIL.

THEN THEY'LL FIND GOD ALL ON THEIR OWN.

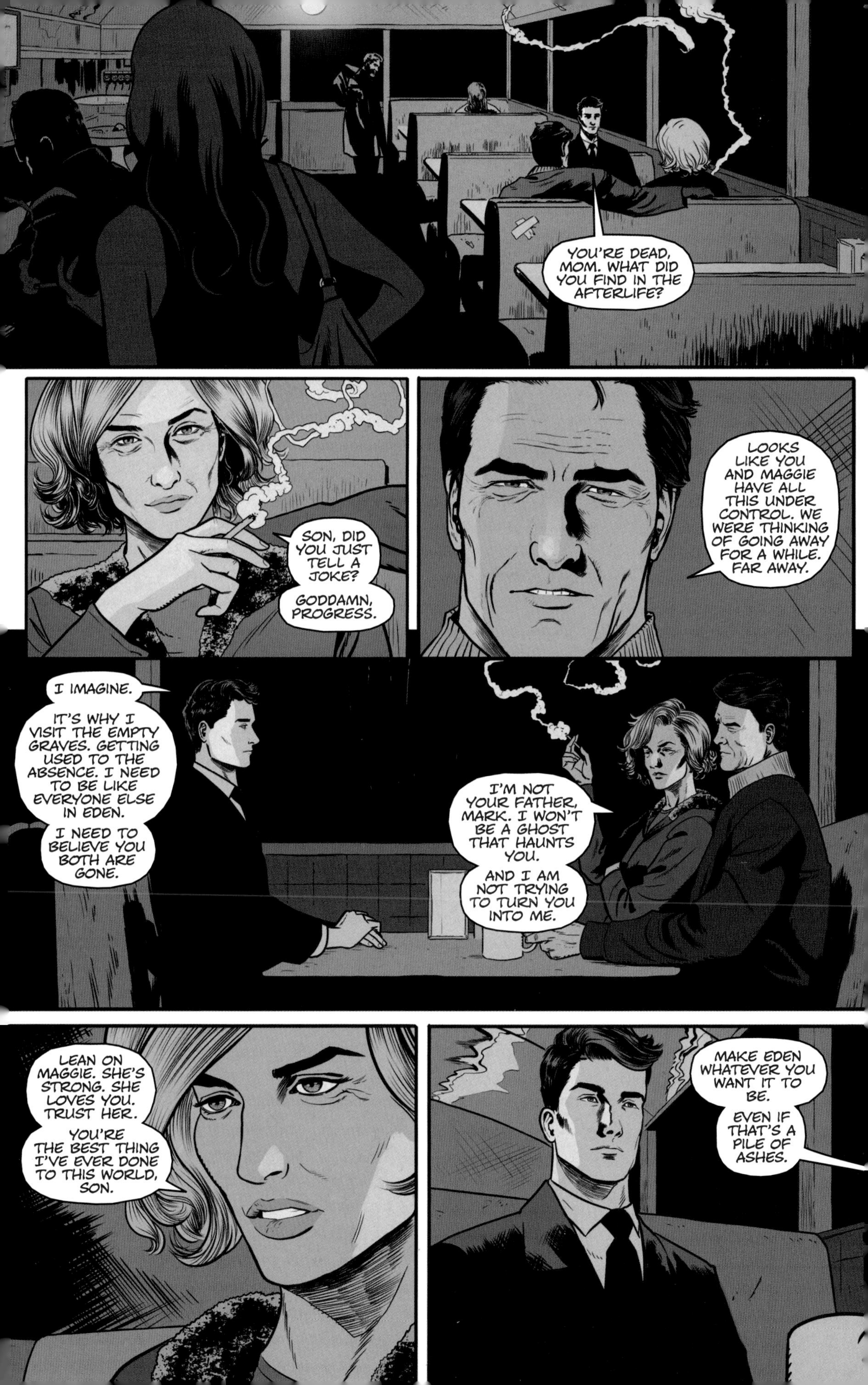
YOU'RE DEAD, MOM. WHAT DID YOU FIND IN THE AFTERLIFE?
SON, DID YOU JUST TELL A JOKE?
GODDAMN, PROGRESS.
LOOKS LIKE YOU AND MAGGIE HAVE ALL THIS UNDER CONTROL. WE WERE THINKING OF GOING AWAY FOR A WHILE. FAR AWAY.
I IMAGINE.
IT'S WHY I VISIT THE EMPTY GRAVES. GETTING USED TO THE ABSENCE. I NEED TO BE LIKE EVERYONE ELSE IN EDEN.
I NEED TO BELIEVE YOU BOTH ARE GONE.
I'M NOT YOUR FATHER, MARK. I WON'T BE A GHOST THAT HAUNTS YOU.
AND I AM NOT TRYING TO TURN YOU INTO ME.
LEAN ON MAGGIE. SHE'S STRONG. SHE LOVES YOU. TRUST HER.
YOU'RE THE BEST THING I'VE EVER DONE TO THIS WORLD, SON.
MAKE EDEN WHATEVER YOU WANT IT TO BE.
EVEN IF THAT'S A PILE OF ASHES.

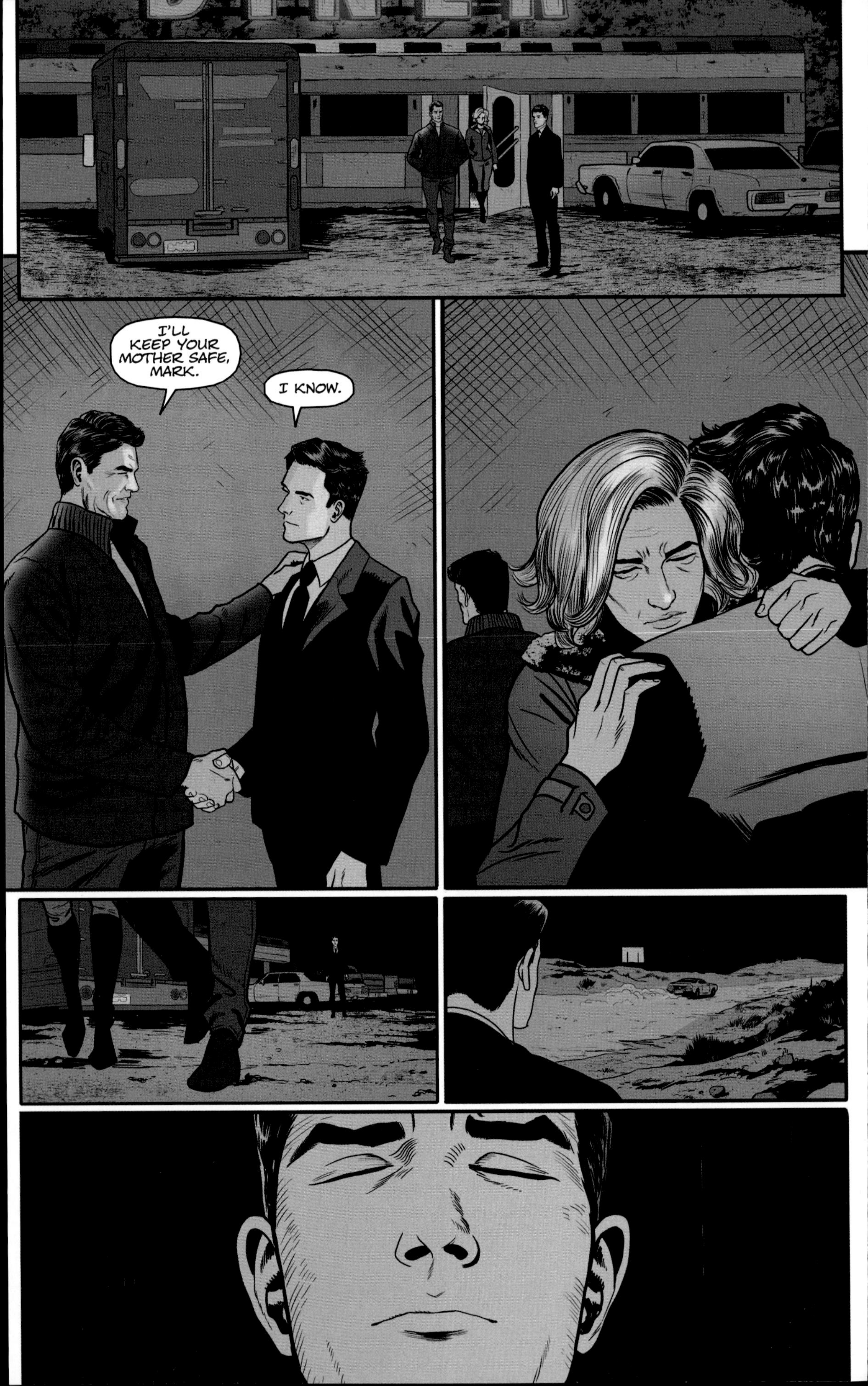
I'LL KEEP YOUR MOTHER SAFE, MARK.
I KNOW.

I'M NOT ASHAMED TO TELL YOU I WANT THIS. AND IF I CAN'T HAVE IT, THEN I'LL ACCEPT IT. BUT I MIGHT NOT FORGIVE YOU FOR IT.

IF I SAID NO, WOULD YOU LEAVE ME?

NO. I JUST WOULDN'T FORGIVE YOU.

SHE'S NOT YOUR BLOOD, MARK. NO LEGACY. SHE'S JUST A CHILD I FOUND IN THE MIDDLE OF HELL.

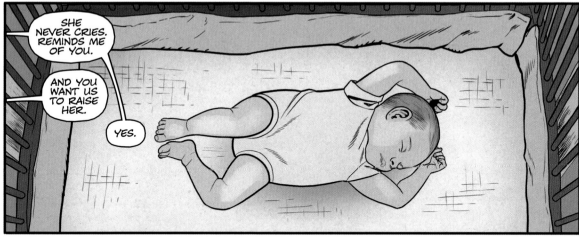

SHE NEVER CRIES. REMINDS ME OF YOU.

AND YOU WANT US TO RAISE HER.

YES.

OKAY, BUT WE NAME HER "LAURA."

AND WE CAN'T RAISE HER TO BE LIKE US.

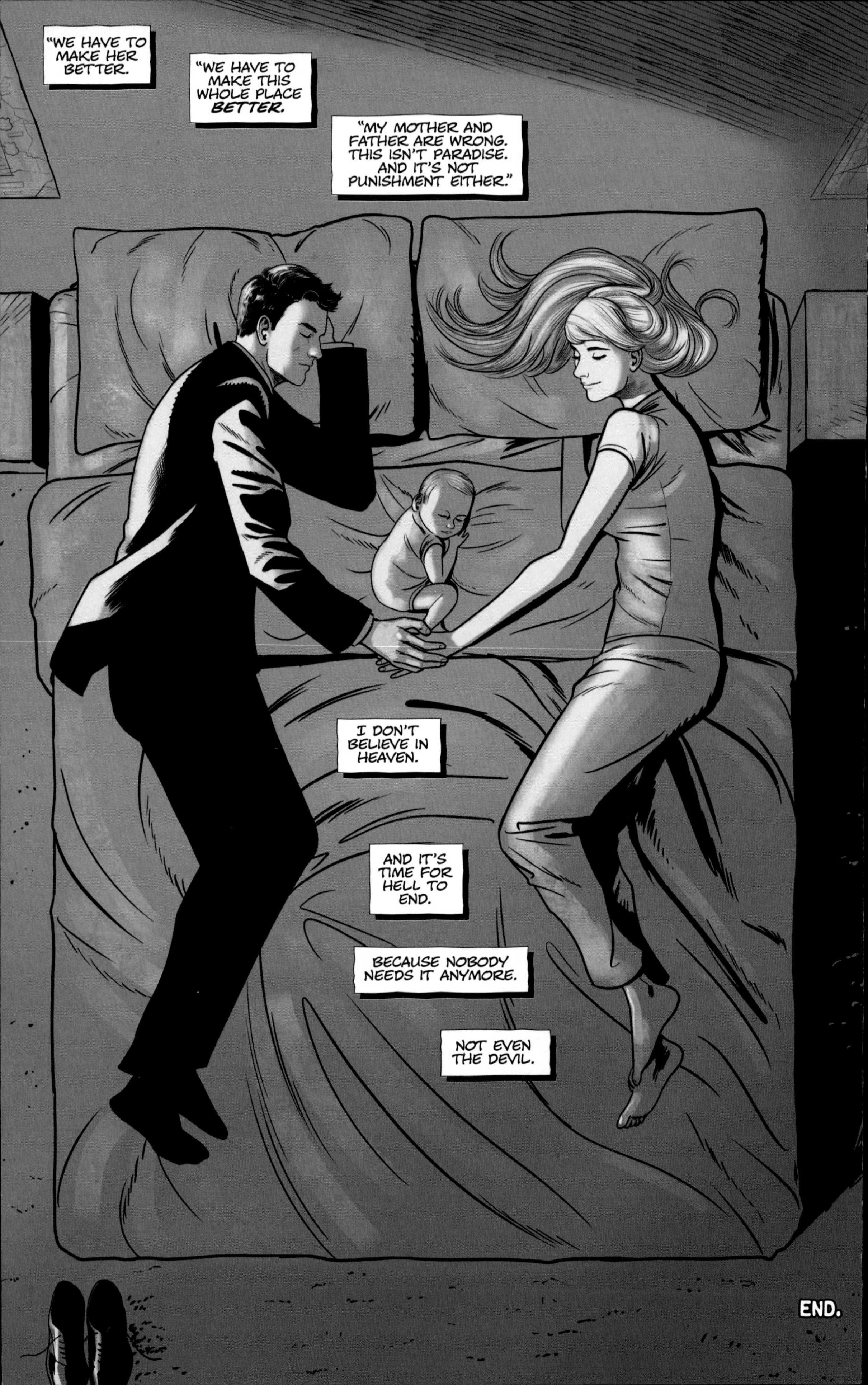
"WE HAVE TO MAKE HER BETTER.
"WE HAVE TO MAKE THIS WHOLE PLACE *BETTER.*
"MY MOTHER AND FATHER ARE WRONG. THIS ISN'T PARADISE. AND IT'S NOT PUNISHMENT EITHER."
I DON'T BELIEVE IN HEAVEN.
AND IT'S TIME FOR HELL TO END.
BECAUSE NOBODY NEEDS IT ANYMORE.
NOT EVEN THE DEVIL.
END.

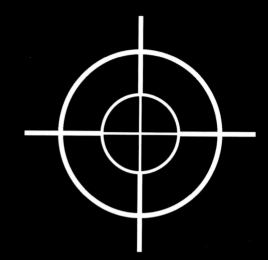

Postal #25
Isaac Goodhart

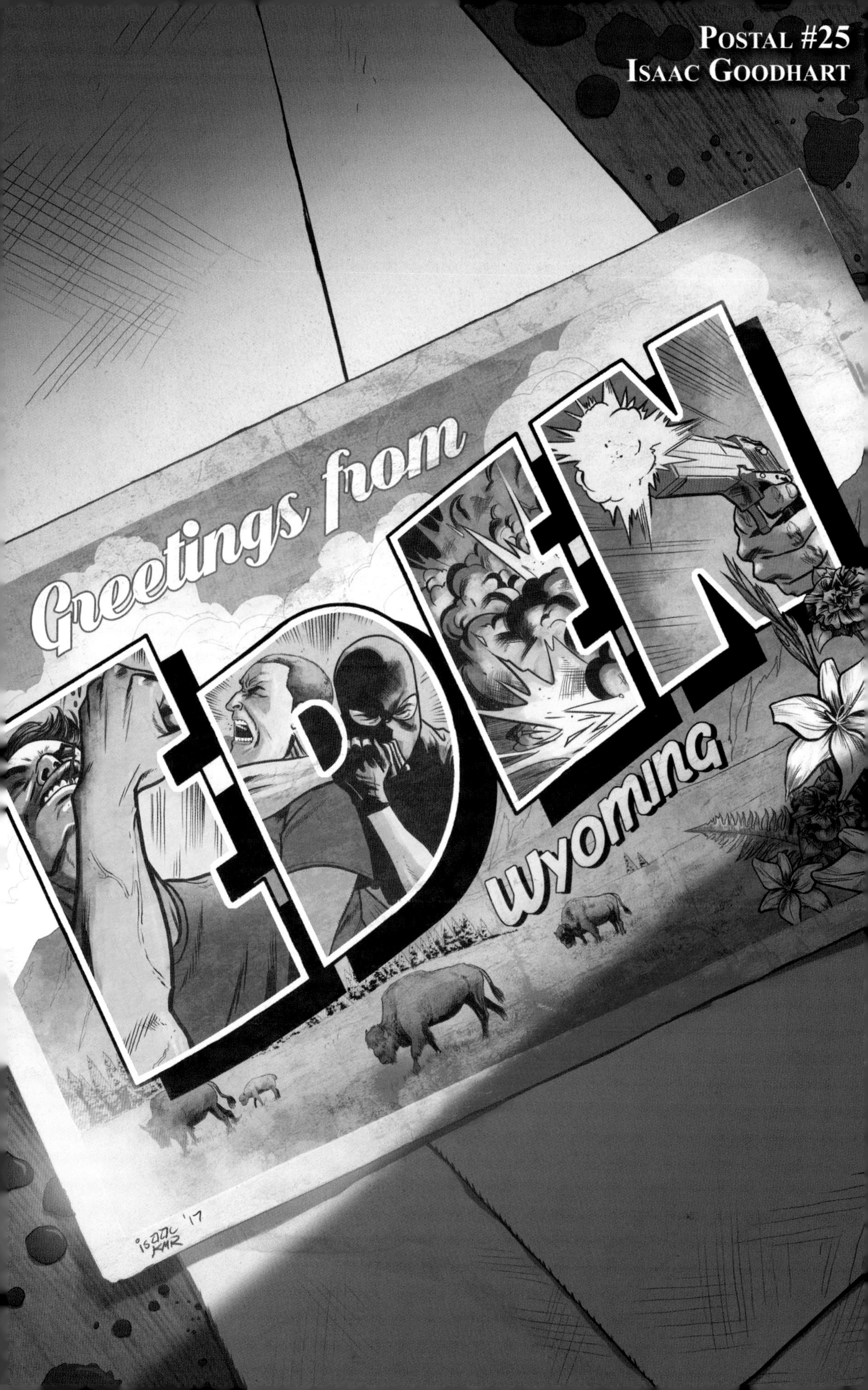
Greetings from
EDEN
Wyoming
isaac '17
KMR

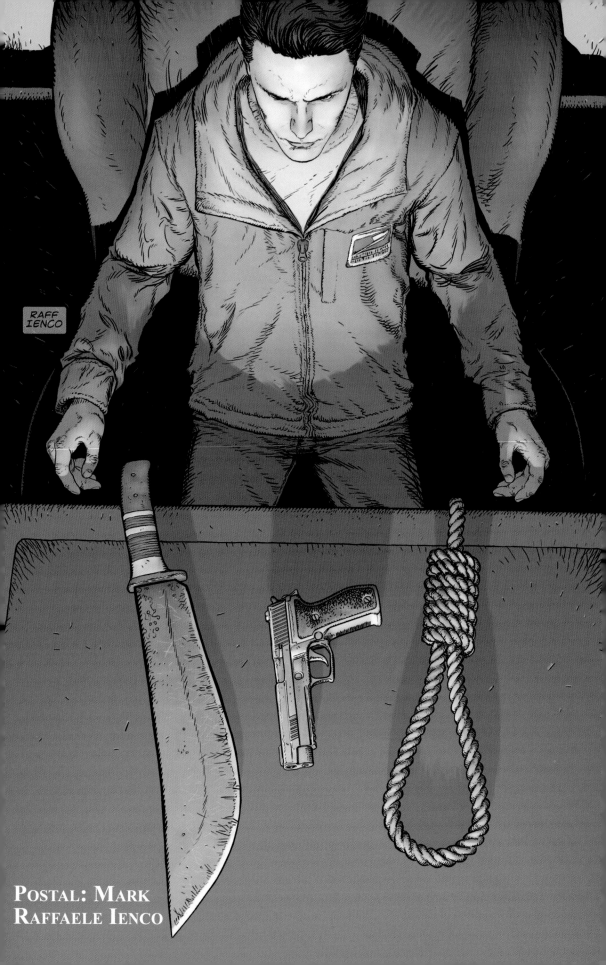

POSTAL: MARK
RAFFAELE IENCO

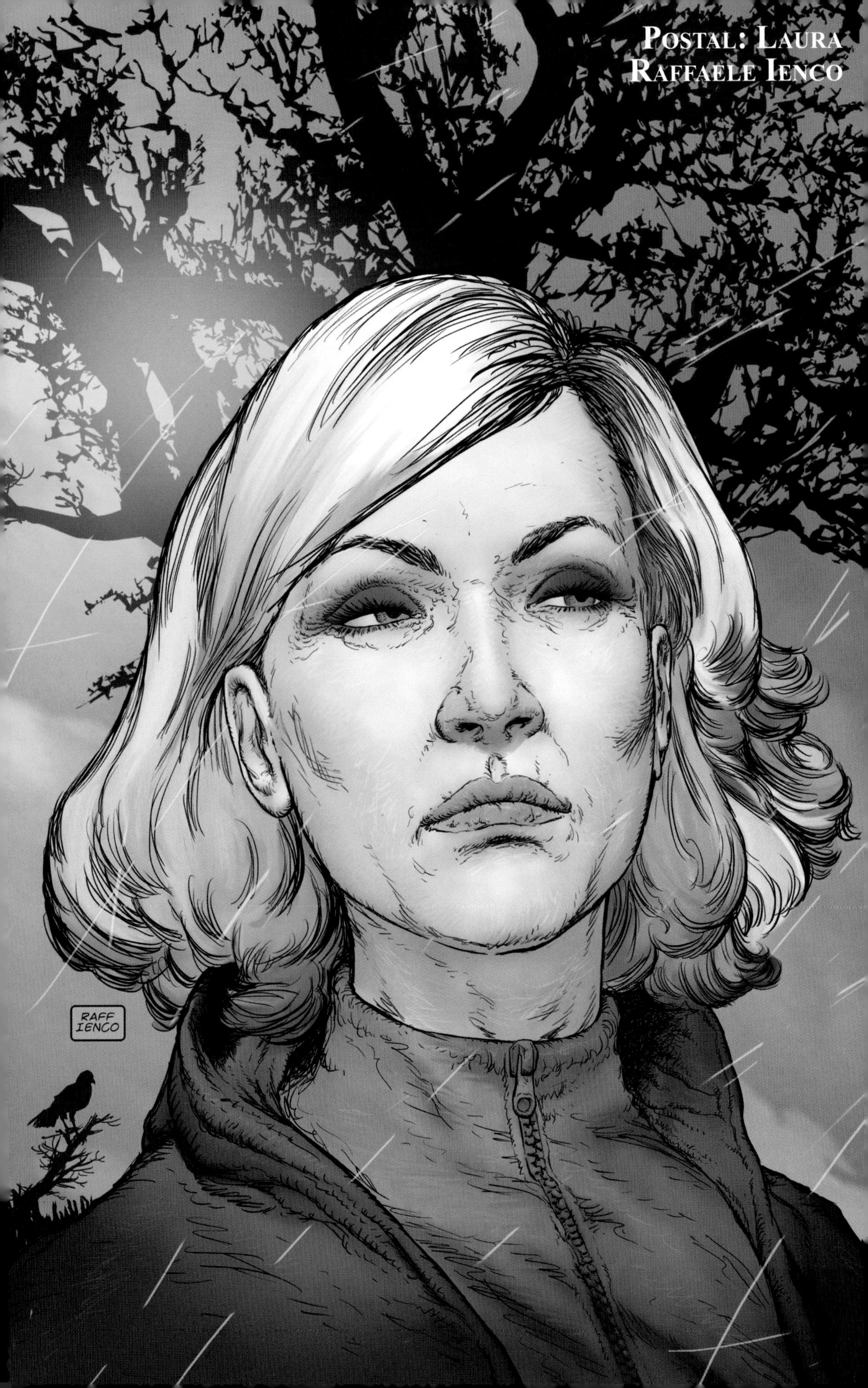
RAFF IENCO
Postal: Laura
Raffaele Ienco

## SCIENCE CLASS (SPECIAL *POSTAL* EDITION)

Thank you for reading this book! When we first started *Postal* I told Bryan Hill and Isaac Goodhart that I wanted them to both commit to a twenty-five issue run. I then brazenly went out and publicly said we're going to do that. I would have looked pretty stupid if we cancelled it after four issues because no one cared, I've seen this happen before. Fortunately, it had not happened to me when I proudly declared it! I've certainly cancelled series earlier than I wanted to, but that's how it goes. With *Postal*, when we laid out the outline for the long arc, we knew the beginning and end of the story, but not the middle. That's pretty common in story development. When we got to issue twenty-one and were planning for the end, the end felt unfinished. So, Bryan and I decided to add two one-shot issues focusing on the aftermath of Mark and Laura to round it out. And this isn't the end of *Postal*. I think we'll take a year or so off and then come back to it, in the meantime please tell your friends about it!

## ASPERGER'S SYNDROME

Mark is near and dear to my heart and is why I wanted to write this one shot. I haven't written an issue of *Postal* in a long time, so it felt good to come back to it. I based a lot of Mark on a guy I knew from college who had Asperger's. I knew him well from about 88-94 and then he went to work for Raytheon. Flash forward a couple decades and he's still there building amazing things that protect us all. So what is Asperger's?

*"Asperger Syndrome (AS) is a neurobiological disorder on the higher-functioning end of the autism spectrum. An individual's symptoms can range from mild to severe. While sharing many of the same characteristics as other Autism Spectrum Disorders (ASD's) including Pervasive Developmental Disorder – Not Otherwise Specified (PDD-NOS) and High-Functioning Autism (HFA), AS has been recognized as a distinct medical diagnosis in Europe for almost 60 years, but has only been included in the U.S. medical diagnostic manual since 1994 ("Asperger Disorder" in the DSM-IV).*

*Individuals with AS and related disorders exhibit serious deficiencies in social and communication skills. Their IQ's are typically in the normal to very superior range. They are usually educated in the mainstream, but most require special education services. Because of their naivete, those with AS are often viewed by their peers as "odd" and are frequently a target for bullying and teasing.*

*They desire to fit in socially and have friends, but have a great deal of difficulty making effective social connections. Many of them are at risk for developing mood disorders, such as anxiety or depression, especially in adolescence. Diagnosis of autistic spectrum disorders should be made by a medical expert to rule out other possible diagnoses and to discuss interventions."*

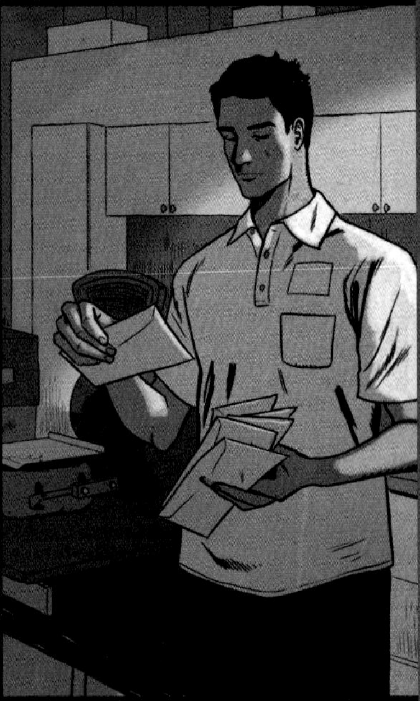

That's from this link: **https://aspennj.org/what-is-asperger-syndrome**
That page also lists out a ton of typical characteristics of someone with AS.

## WHAT CAUSES ASPERGER'S SYNDROME?

So here's the kicker, we don't really know. We know there's some sort of genetic mutation, but the cause of that mutation is still being investigated. There are rumors about vaccines causing Autism and Asperger's Syndrome but there's zero proof this is reality. I've heard rumors that the Earth is flat too. Could it be caused by environmental factors? Are there epigenetic factors to parents that when passed on to the child it manifests? That's certainly possible. There's been a ton of research on it and the below two links I've found to be the most readable by people without medical degrees.

» **http://www.kennethrobersonphd.com/what-causes-aspergers-syndrome/**

» **http://www.autism-help.org/aspergers-syndrome-cause.html**

If you want a more science-heavy explanation, go here:

» **http://www.autisme.com/autism/explanatory-theories-on-asd.html**

» **https://www.scientificamerican.com/article/broken-mirrors-a-theory-of-autism-2007-06/**

**WHAT DOES HAVING ASPERGER'S FEEL LIKE?**
Having known a man with Asperger's for three decades now, I've had many conversations with him about it. His most succinct answer is he feels like he's not the same species as the rest of us. They don't think the same way...and not in a sociopathic way. Imagine not understanding why someone smiles at you. Or that you're expected to respond to people when they talk to you. They have to learn how to make the rest of us not feel uncomfortable around them. When I reflect on that... it's baffling. I've found most Aspies to be smarter than the average human. They care about different things and have interests that we might not get...but isn't that everyone really? They're just people, slightly different. Trying to make their way in this world like the rest of us and find some happiness.

» **https://www.psychologytoday.com/blog/after-party-chat/201405/what-does-it-feel-have-aspergers**

» **https://www.autismspeaks.org/blog/2015/08/25/12-things-you-should-never-say-someone-autism**

What's it like to date if you have Asperger's?

» **https://www.vice.com/en_nz/article/wjjnkw/what-its-like-to-date-when-youre-on-the-autism-spectrum**

» **https://psychcentral.com/lib/romance-love-and-asperger-syndrome/**

**LOBOTOMY**
This was a regularly practiced procedure all the way into the early 20th century. It was used to treat mental disorders and other things. A lobotomy effectively ends your mind. It's not clear if it ends consciousness. I hope it did, can you imagine living and knowing everything but being unable to do anything? How horrifying would that be? Mark decided to remove Isaac's mind because he knew that would be a fitting punishment.

Transorbital Lobotomy Procedure
©2010 HowStuffWorks
Frontal Lobe
Orbitoclast

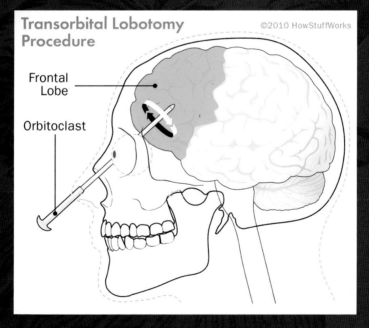

» **http://www.weirdworm.com/lobotomy-victims-and-their-life-afterward/**

That's it for *Postal: Mark*! Thanks again for reading and let me know on my social media feeds what you thought of this book.

**Carpe Diem.**

**Matt Hawkins**
**Twitter: @topcowmatt**
**http://www.facebook.com/selfloathingnarcissist**

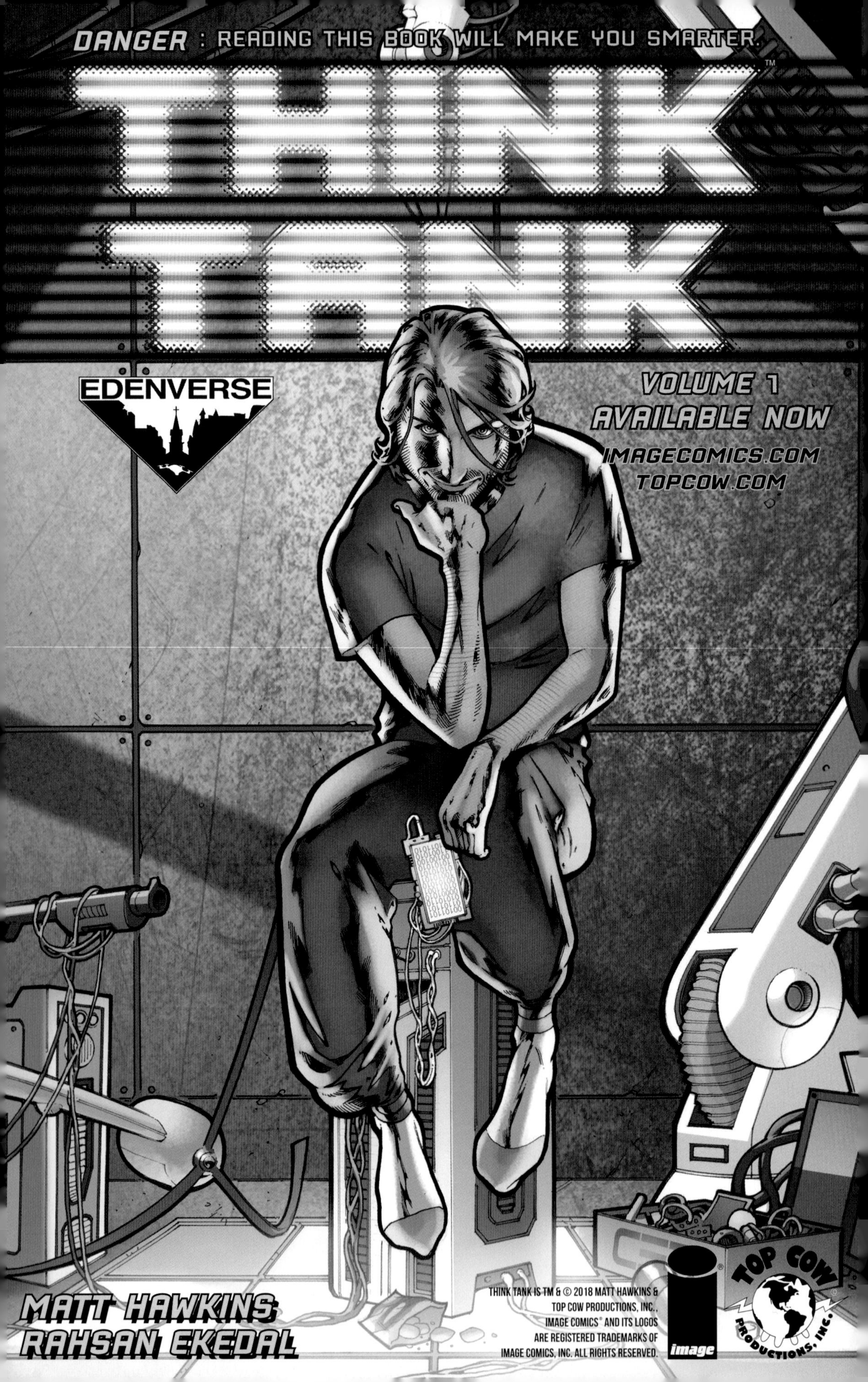

DANGER : READING THIS BOOK WILL MAKE YOU SMARTER.
THINK TANK™
EDENVERSE
VOLUME 1
AVAILABLE NOW
IMAGECOMICS.COM
TOPCOW.COM
MATT HAWKINS
RAHSAN EKEDAL
THINK TANK IS TM & © 2018 MATT HAWKINS & TOP COW PRODUCTIONS, INC., IMAGE COMICS® AND ITS LOGOS ARE REGISTERED TRADEMARKS OF IMAGE COMICS, INC. ALL RIGHTS RESERVED.
image
TOP COW PRODUCTIONS, INC.

$$\oint \vec{E} \cdot d\vec{A} = \frac{1}{\varepsilon_0} q_{in} \qquad \oint \vec{B} \cdot d\vec{A} = 0 \qquad \oint \vec{E} \cdot d\vec{l} = -\frac{d}{dt} \int \vec{B} \cdot d\vec{A}$$

$$\oint \vec{B} \cdot d\vec{l} = \mu_0 I_{in} \qquad \vec{F} = q(\vec{v} \times \vec{B} + \vec{E}) \qquad i = \frac{dq}{dt}$$

point charge $\quad E = \dfrac{1}{4\pi\varepsilon_0} \dfrac{q}{r^2} \qquad V = \dfrac{1}{4\pi\varepsilon_0}\dfrac{q}{r} \qquad\qquad p = qd$

$$V_f - V_i = -\int_i^f \vec{E} \cdot d\vec{s} \qquad E_x = -\frac{\partial V}{\partial x} \qquad\qquad \vec{\tau} = \vec{p} \times \vec{E}$$

$$C = \frac{Q}{V} \qquad U_E = \frac{1}{2}QV = \frac{1}{2}CV^2 = \frac{1}{2}\frac{Q^2}{C} \qquad\qquad C = \varepsilon_0 \frac{A}{d}$$

$$R = \frac{V}{i} \qquad P = Vi \qquad P = i^2 R = \frac{V^2}{R} \qquad R = \rho\frac{L}{A}$$

$$R_{eq} = R_1 + R_2 + \cdots$$

$$\frac{1}{R_{eq}} = \frac{1}{R_1} + \frac{1}{R_2} + \cdots \qquad\qquad \frac{1}{C_{eq}} = \frac{1}{C_1} + \frac{1}{C_2} + \cdots$$

$$d\vec{B} = \frac{\mu_0}{4\pi} \frac{i\, d\vec{s} \times \hat{r}}{r^2} \qquad B = \frac{\mu_0}{2\pi}\frac{i}{r} \qquad B = \mu_0 n i \qquad \vec{\tau} = \vec{\mu} \times$$

$$\mathcal{E} = -\frac{d\Phi}{dt} \qquad \mathcal{E} = -N\frac{d\Phi}{dt} \qquad L = \frac{|\mathcal{E}|}{\left|\frac{di}{dt}\right|} = \frac{N\Phi}{i}$$

$$u_E = \frac{1}{2}\varepsilon_0 E^2 \qquad u_B = \frac{1}{2}\frac{B^2}{\mu_0} \qquad U_B = \frac{1}{2}Li^2$$

$$= q_0 e^{-t/\tau_c} \qquad q = C\mathcal{E}(1 - e^{-t/\tau_c}) \qquad i = i_0 e^{-t/\tau_L} \qquad i = \frac{\mathcal{E}}{R}(1 - e^{-t/\tau_L})$$

$$= \frac{L}{R} \qquad \tau_c = RC \qquad \mu = NiA \qquad \frac{1}{4\pi\varepsilon_0} = 9 \times 10^9 \qquad \frac{\mu_0}{4\pi} = 10^{-7}$$

1 means $10^6 \qquad \mu$ means $10^{-6}$

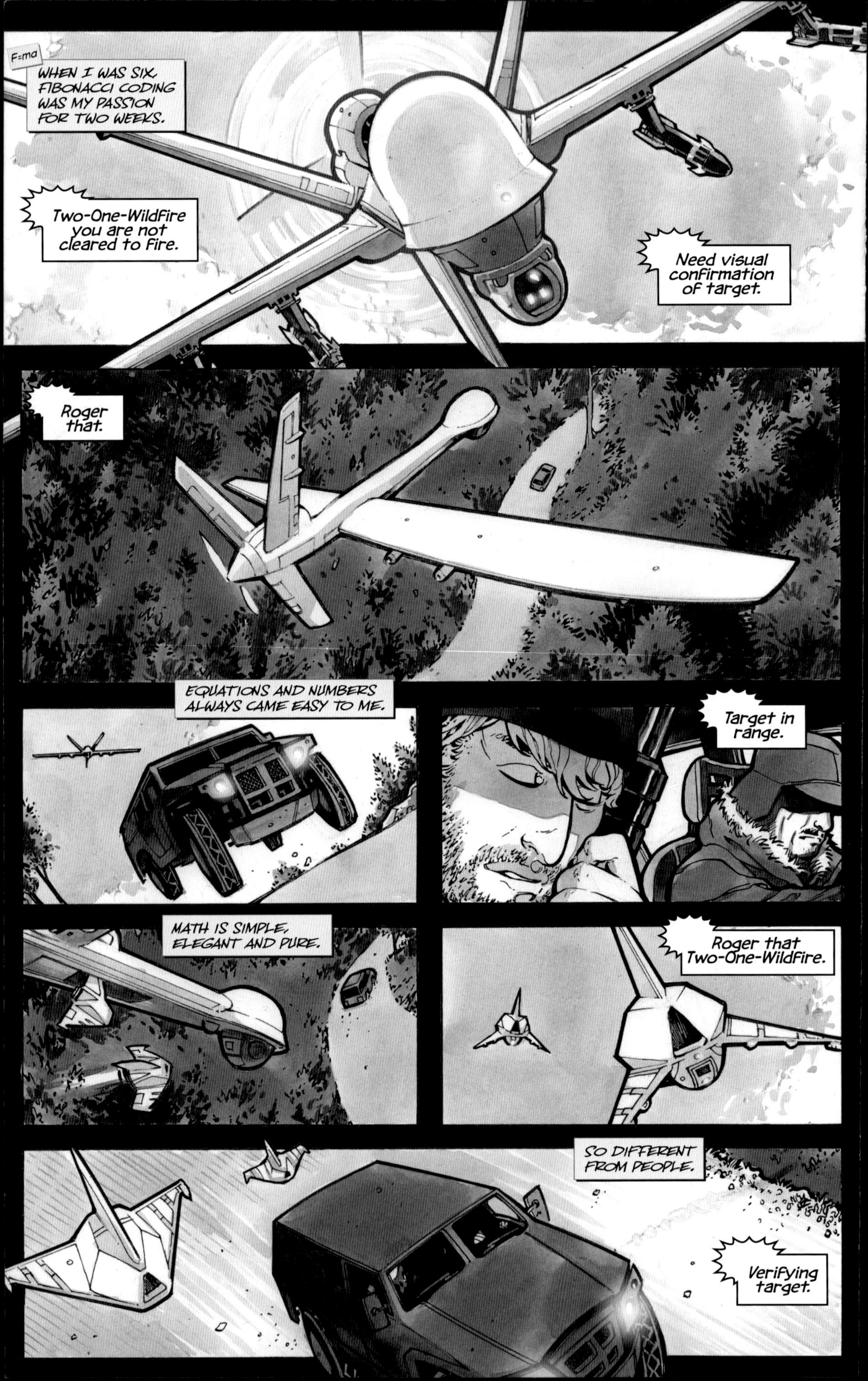
F=ma
WHEN I WAS SIX, FIBONACCI CODING WAS MY PASSION FOR TWO WEEKS.
Two-One-Wildfire you are not cleared to fire.
Need visual confirmation of target.
Roger that.
EQUATIONS AND NUMBERS ALWAYS CAME EASY TO ME.
Target in range.
MATH IS SIMPLE, ELEGANT AND PURE.
Roger that Two-One-Wildfire.
SO DIFFERENT FROM PEOPLE.
Verifying target.

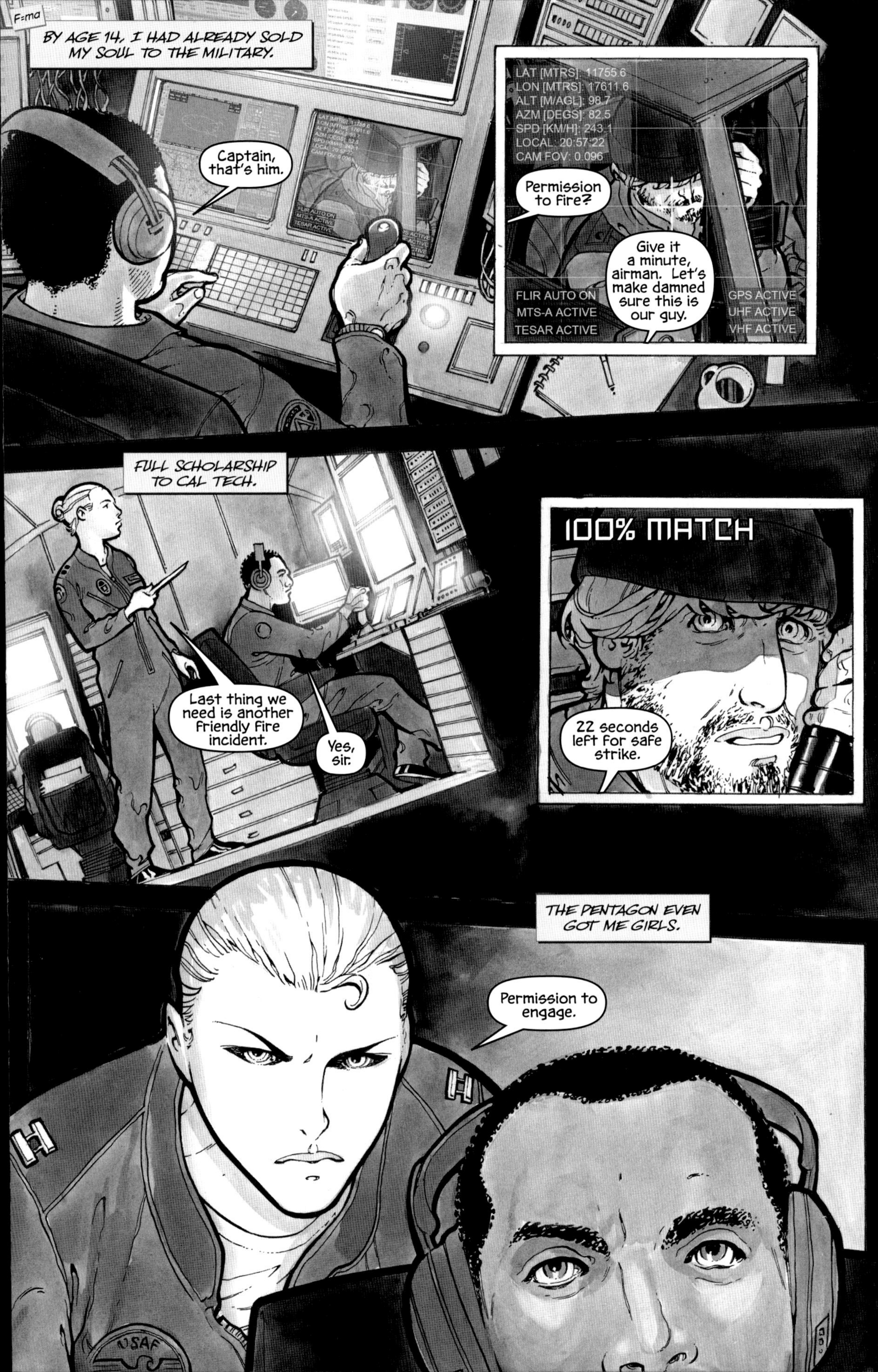
F=ma
BY AGE 14, I HAD ALREADY SOLD MY SOUL TO THE MILITARY.
Captain, that's him.
LAT [MTRS]: 11755.6
LON [MTRS]: 17611.6
ALT [M/AGL]: 98.7
AZM [DEGS]: 82.5
SPD [KM/H]: 243.1
LOCAL: 20:57:22
CAM FOV: 0.096
Permission to fire?
Give it a minute, airman. Let's make damned sure this is our guy.
FLIR AUTO ON
MTS-A ACTIVE
TESAR ACTIVE
GPS ACTIVE
UHF ACTIVE
VHF ACTIVE
FULL SCHOLARSHIP TO CAL TECH.
Last thing we need is another friendly fire incident.
Yes, sir.
100% MATCH
22 seconds left for safe strike.
THE PENTAGON EVEN GOT ME GIRLS.
Permission to engage.
USAF

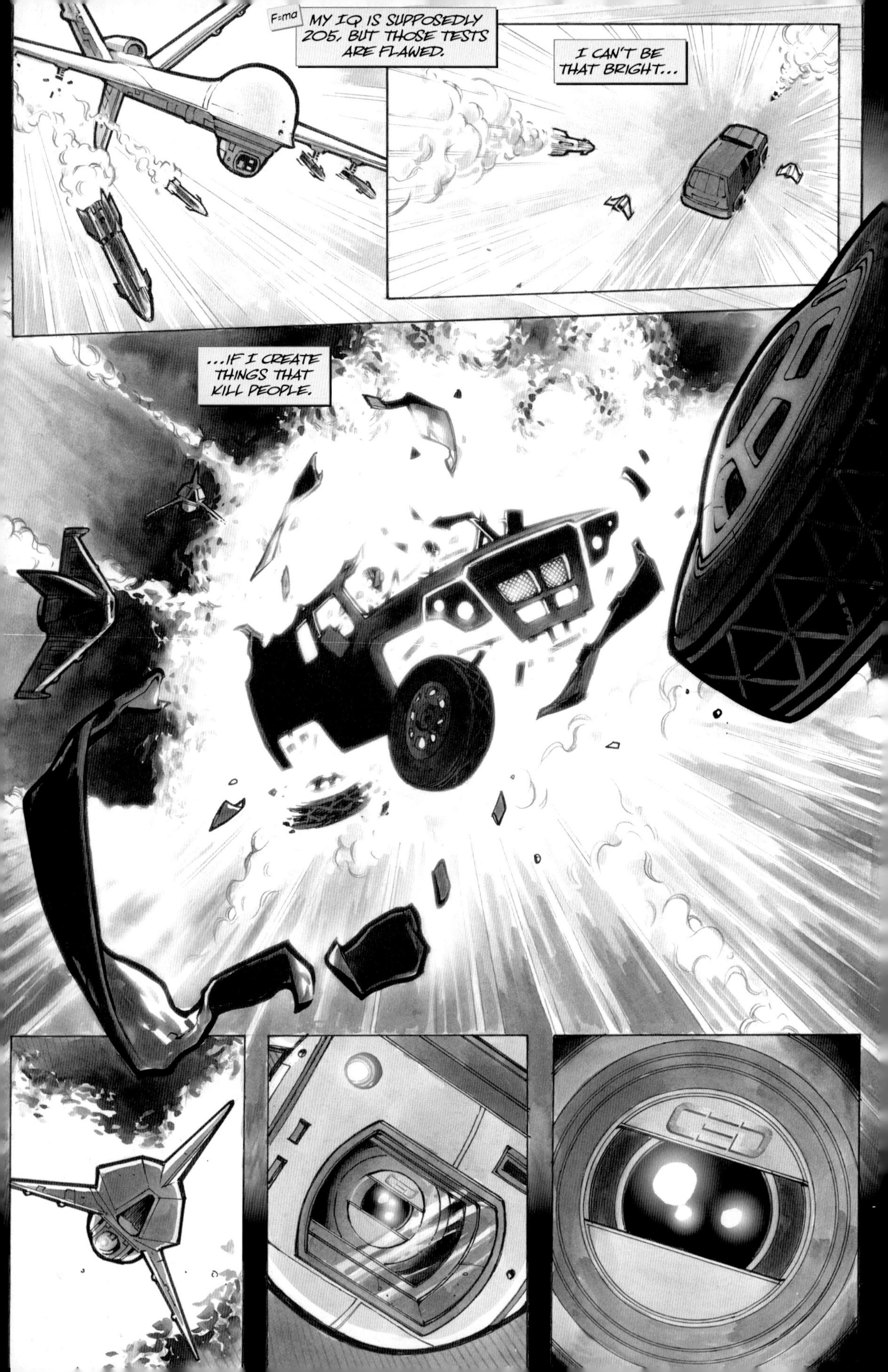
F=ma
MY IQ IS SUPPOSEDLY 205, BUT THOSE TESTS ARE FLAWED.
I CAN'T BE THAT BRIGHT...
...IF I CREATE THINGS THAT KILL PEOPLE.

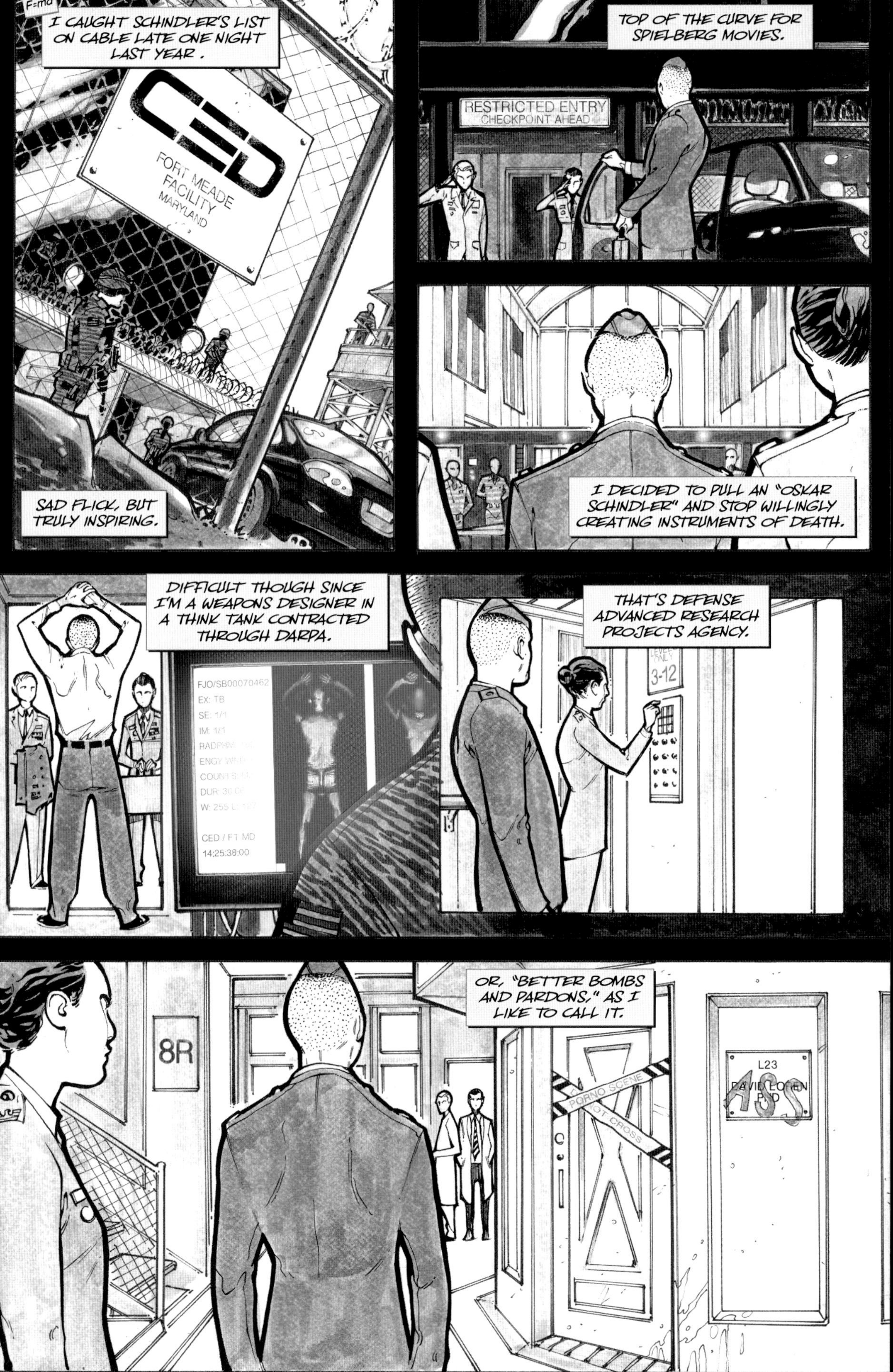
F=ma
I CAUGHT SCHINDLER'S LIST ON CABLE LATE ONE NIGHT LAST YEAR.
CED
FORT MEADE FACILITY MARYLAND
SAD FLICK, BUT TRULY INSPIRING.
TOP OF THE CURVE FOR SPIELBERG MOVIES.
RESTRICTED ENTRY
CHECKPOINT AHEAD
I DECIDED TO PULL AN "OSKAR SCHINDLER" AND STOP WILLINGLY CREATING INSTRUMENTS OF DEATH.
DIFFICULT THOUGH SINCE I'M A WEAPONS DESIGNER IN A THINK TANK CONTRACTED THROUGH DARPA.
FJO/SB00070462
EX: TB
SE: 1/1
IM: 1/1
CED / FT MD
14:25:38:00
THAT'S DEFENSE ADVANCED RESEARCH PROJECTS AGENCY.
3-12
OR, "BETTER BOMBS AND PARDONS," AS I LIKE TO CALL IT.
8R
PORNO SCENE
L23
ASS

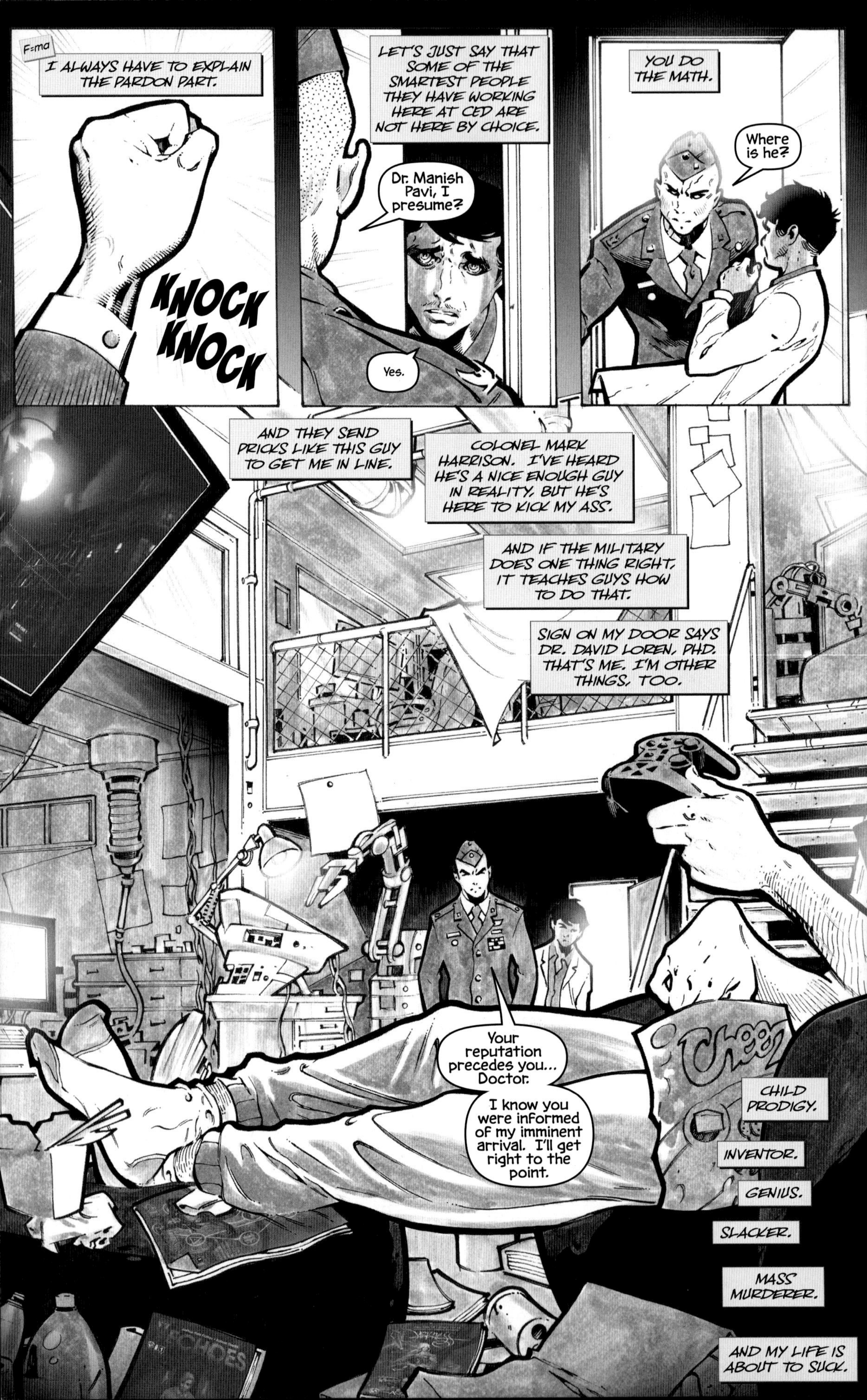
F=ma
I ALWAYS HAVE TO EXPLAIN THE PARDON PART.
KNOCK KNOCK
LET'S JUST SAY THAT SOME OF THE SMARTEST PEOPLE THEY HAVE WORKING HERE AT CED ARE NOT HERE BY CHOICE.
Dr. Manish Pavi, I presume?
Yes.
YOU DO THE MATH.
Where is he?
AND THEY SEND PRICKS LIKE THIS GUY TO GET ME IN LINE.
COLONEL MARK HARRISON. I'VE HEARD HE'S A NICE ENOUGH GUY IN REALITY, BUT HE'S HERE TO KICK MY ASS.
AND IF THE MILITARY DOES ONE THING RIGHT, IT TEACHES GUYS HOW TO DO THAT.
SIGN ON MY DOOR SAYS DR. DAVID LOREN, PHD. THAT'S ME. I'M OTHER THINGS, TOO.
Your reputation precedes you... Doctor.
I know you were informed of my imminent arrival. I'll get right to the point.
CHILD PRODIGY.
INVENTOR.
GENIUS.
SLACKER.
MASS MURDERER.
AND MY LIFE IS ABOUT TO SUCK.
ECHOES

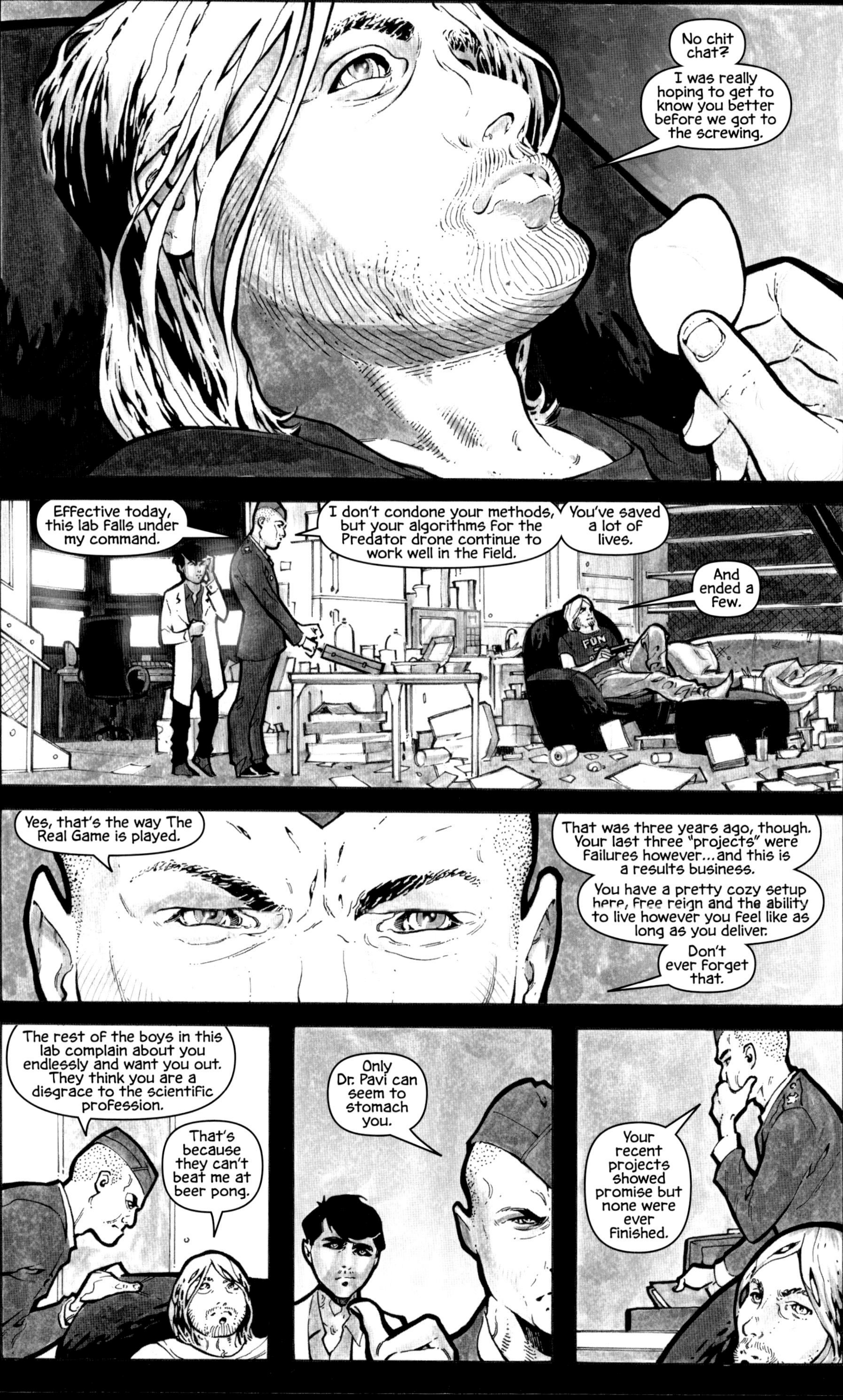
No chit chat?
I was really hoping to get to know you better before we got to the screwing.
Effective today, this lab falls under my command.
I don't condone your methods, but your algorithms for the Predator drone continue to work well in the field.
You've saved a lot of lives.
And ended a few.
FUN
Yes, that's the way The Real Game is played.
That was three years ago, though. Your last three "projects" were failures however...and this is a results business.
You have a pretty cozy setup here, free reign and the ability to live however you feel like as long as you deliver.
Don't ever forget that.
The rest of the boys in this lab complain about you endlessly and want you out. They think you are a disgrace to the scientific profession.
That's because they can't beat me at beer pong.
Only Dr. Pavi can seem to stomach you.
Your recent projects showed promise but none were ever finished.

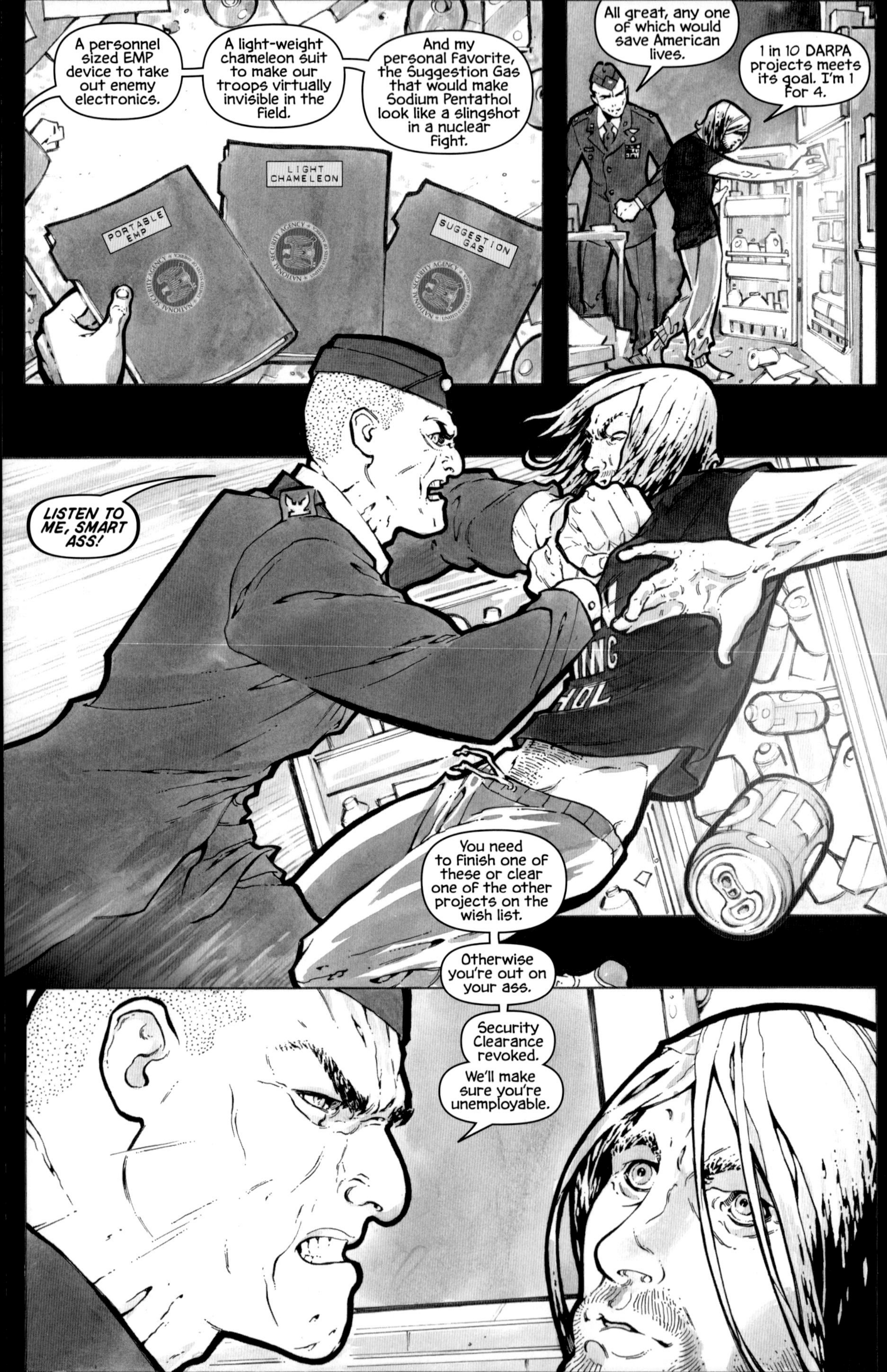
A personnel sized EMP device to take out enemy electronics.
A light-weight chameleon suit to make our troops virtually invisible in the field.
And my personal favorite, the Suggestion Gas that would make Sodium Pentathol look like a slingshot in a nuclear fight.
LIGHT CHAMELEON
PORTABLE EMP
SUGGESTION GAS
NATIONAL SECURITY AGENCY
All great, any one of which would save American lives.
1 in 10 DARPA projects meets its goal. I'm 1 for 4.
LISTEN TO ME, SMART ASS!
You need to finish one of these or clear one of the other projects on the wish list.
Otherwise you're out on your ass.
Security Clearance revoked.
We'll make sure you're unemployable.

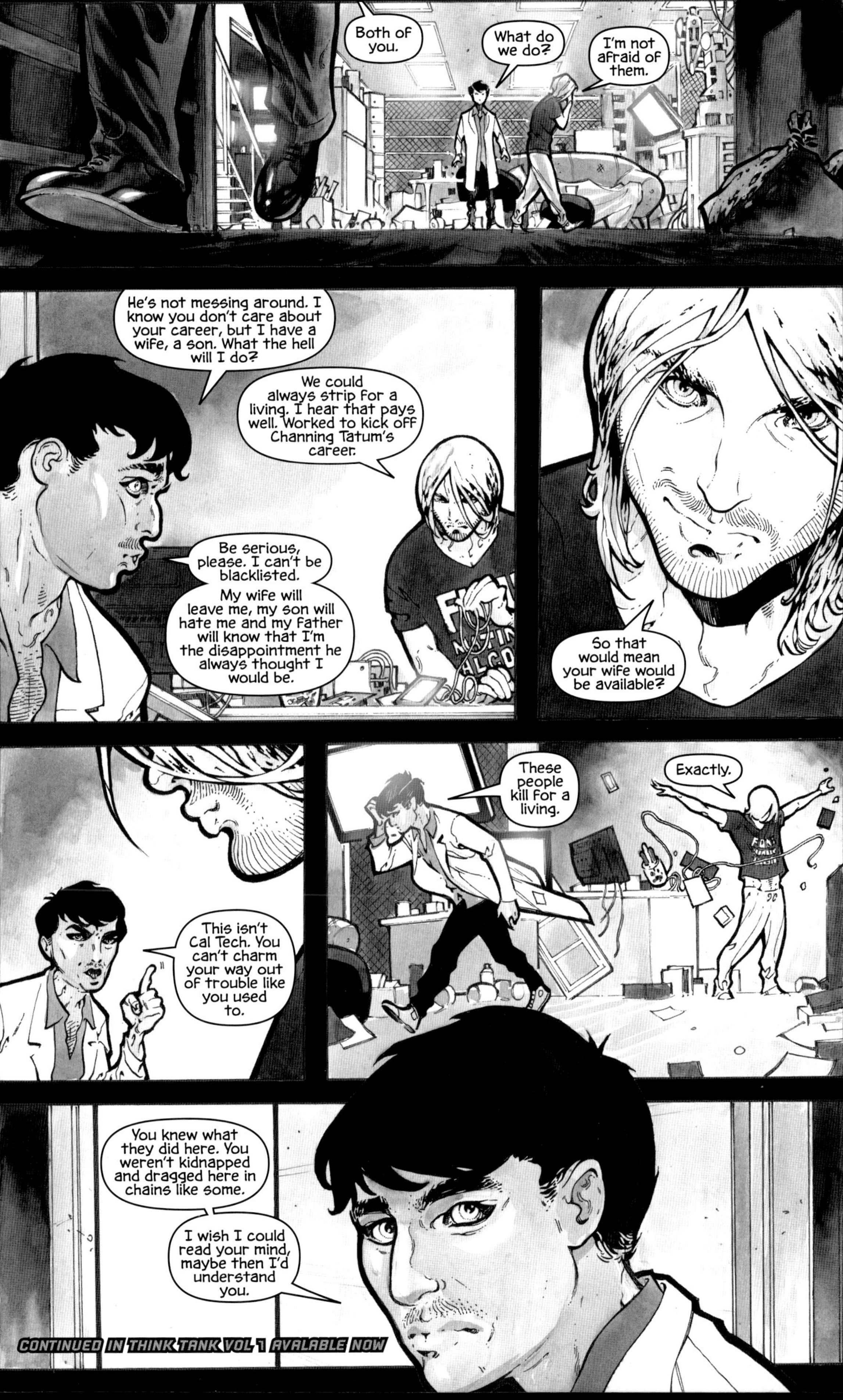
Both of you.
What do we do?
I'm not afraid of them.
He's not messing around. I know you don't care about your career, but I have a wife, a son. What the hell will I do?
We could always strip for a living. I hear that pays well. Worked to kick off Channing Tatum's career.
Be serious, please. I can't be blacklisted.
My wife will leave me, my son will hate me and my father will know that I'm the disappointment he always thought I would be.
So that would mean your wife would be available?
This isn't Cal Tech. You can't charm your way out of trouble like you used to.
These people kill for a living.
Exactly.
You knew what they did here. You weren't kidnapped and dragged here in chains like some.
I wish I could read your mind, maybe then I'd understand you.
CONTINUED IN THINK TANK VOL 1 AVAILABLE NOW

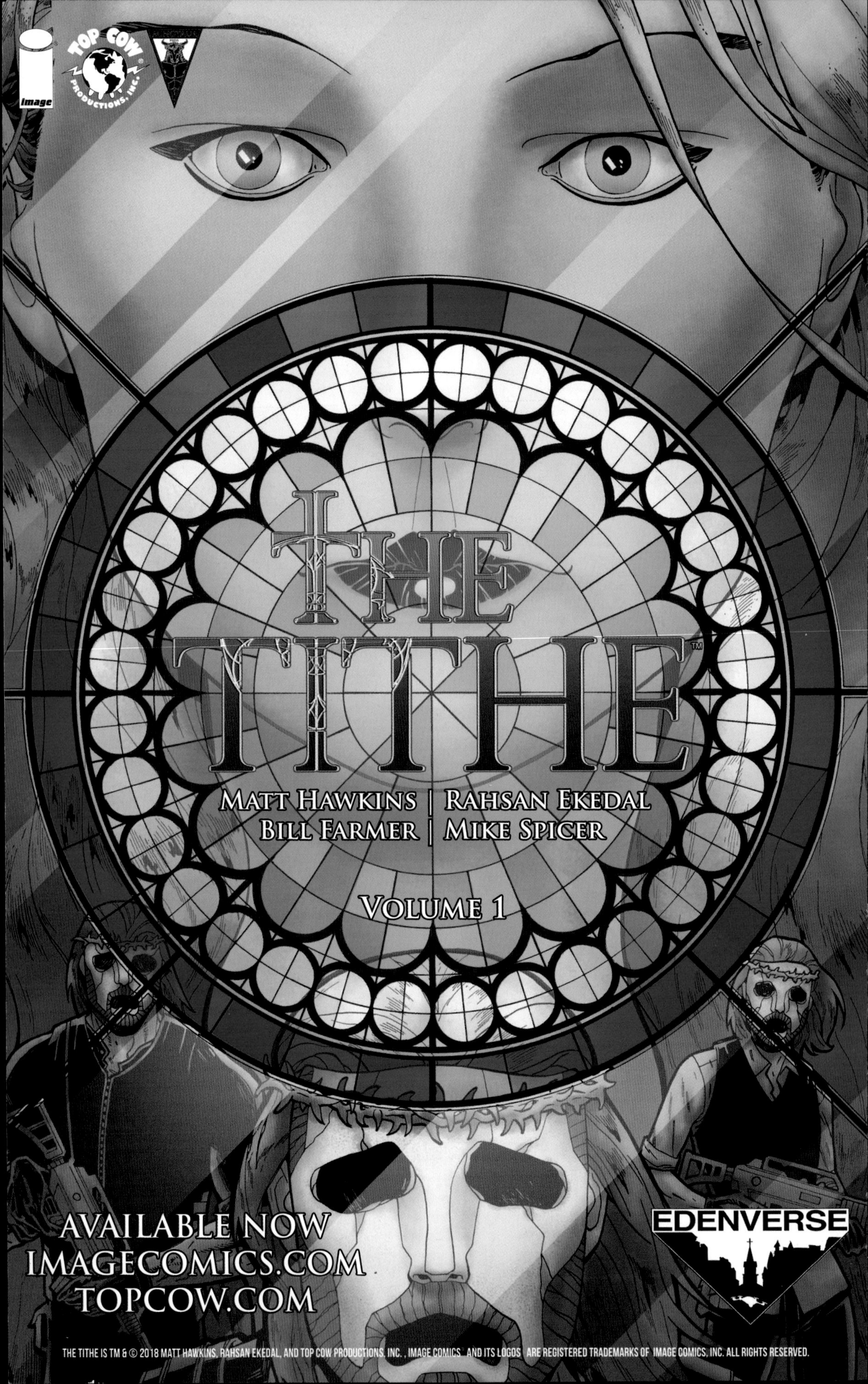
THE TITHE™
MATT HAWKINS | RAHSAN EKEDAL
BILL FARMER | MIKE SPICER
VOLUME 1
AVAILABLE NOW
IMAGECOMICS.COM
TOPCOW.COM
EDENVERSE
THE TITHE IS TM & © 2018 MATT HAWKINS, RAHSAN EKEDAL, AND TOP COW PRODUCTIONS, INC., IMAGE COMICS AND ITS LOGOS ARE REGISTERED TRADEMARKS OF IMAGE COMICS, INC. ALL RIGHTS RESERVED.

"GIVING TO OUR MINISTRY DOES THE LORD'S WORK."

-JIM BAKKER. TELEVANGELIST OF THE 700 CLUB AND THE PTL CLUB (PRAISE THE LORD)
CONVICTED OF FINANCIAL FRAUD IN 1989 WHO SERVED FIVE YEARS OF A
FORTY-FIVE YEAR SENTENCE. HE WAS BACK ON TV IN 2003 WITH
THE JIM BAKKER SHOW. WHICH STILL AIRS TODAY.

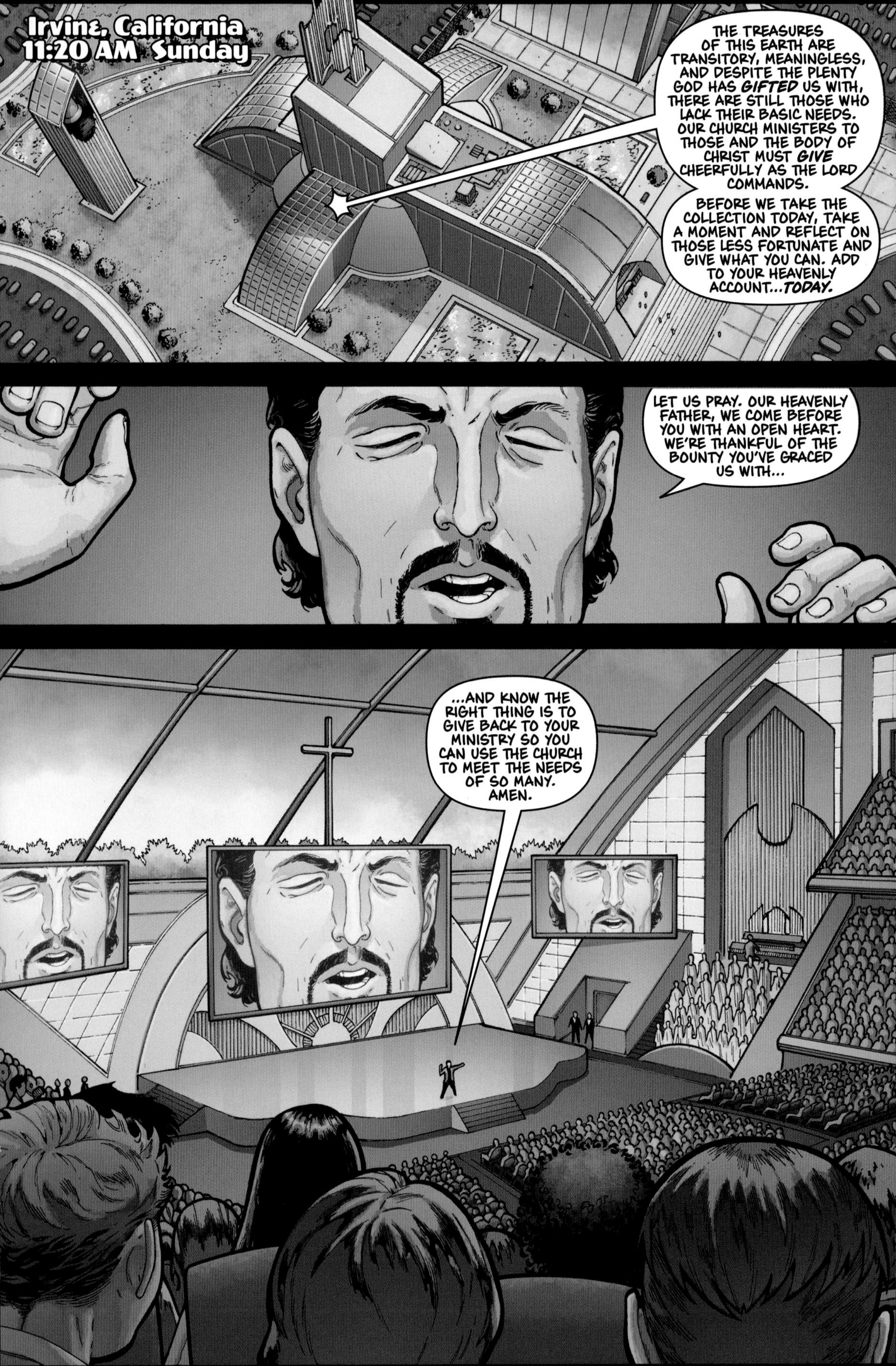
Irvine, California
11:20 AM Sunday
THE TREASURES OF THIS EARTH ARE TRANSITORY, MEANINGLESS, AND DESPITE THE PLENTY GOD HAS GIFTED US WITH, THERE ARE STILL THOSE WHO LACK THEIR BASIC NEEDS. OUR CHURCH MINISTERS TO THOSE AND THE BODY OF CHRIST MUST GIVE CHEERFULLY AS THE LORD COMMANDS.
BEFORE WE TAKE THE COLLECTION TODAY, TAKE A MOMENT AND REFLECT ON THOSE LESS FORTUNATE AND GIVE WHAT YOU CAN. ADD TO YOUR HEAVENLY ACCOUNT...TODAY.
LET US PRAY. OUR HEAVENLY FATHER, WE COME BEFORE YOU WITH AN OPEN HEART. WE'RE THANKFUL OF THE BOUNTY YOU'VE GRACED US WITH...
...AND KNOW THE RIGHT THING IS TO GIVE BACK TO YOUR MINISTRY SO YOU CAN USE THE CHURCH TO MEET THE NEEDS OF SO MANY. AMEN.

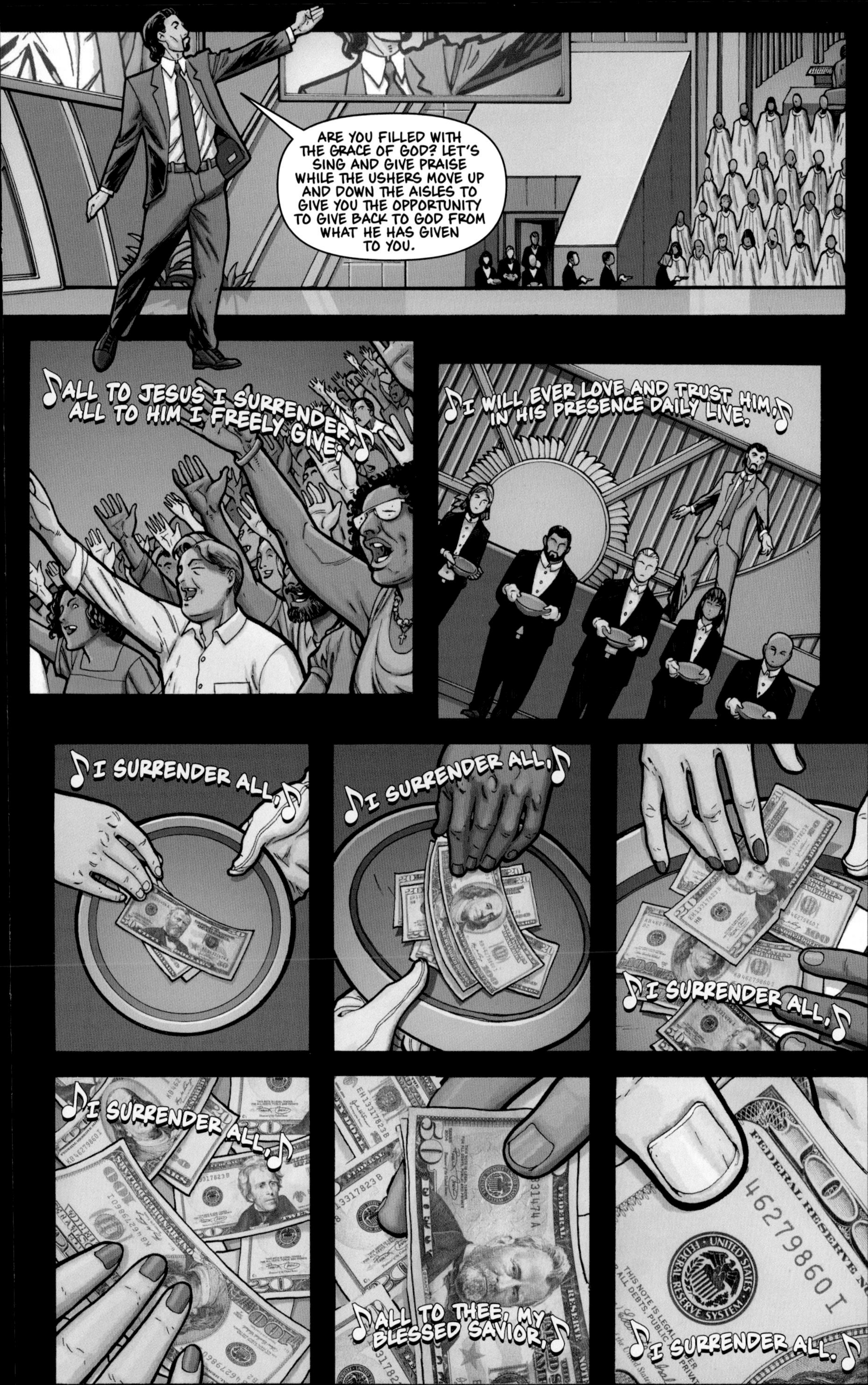

ARE YOU FILLED WITH THE GRACE OF GOD? LET'S SING AND GIVE PRAISE WHILE THE USHERS MOVE UP AND DOWN THE AISLES TO GIVE YOU THE OPPORTUNITY TO GIVE BACK TO GOD FROM WHAT HE HAS GIVEN TO YOU.
♪ALL TO JESUS I SURRENDER, ALL TO HIM I FREELY GIVE;♪
♪I WILL EVER LOVE AND TRUST HIM, IN HIS PRESENCE DAILY LIVE.♪
♪I SURRENDER ALL,♪
♪I SURRENDER ALL,♪
♪I SURRENDER ALL,♪
♪I SURRENDER ALL,♪
♪ALL TO THEE, MY BLESSED SAVIOR,♪
♪I SURRENDER ALL.♪

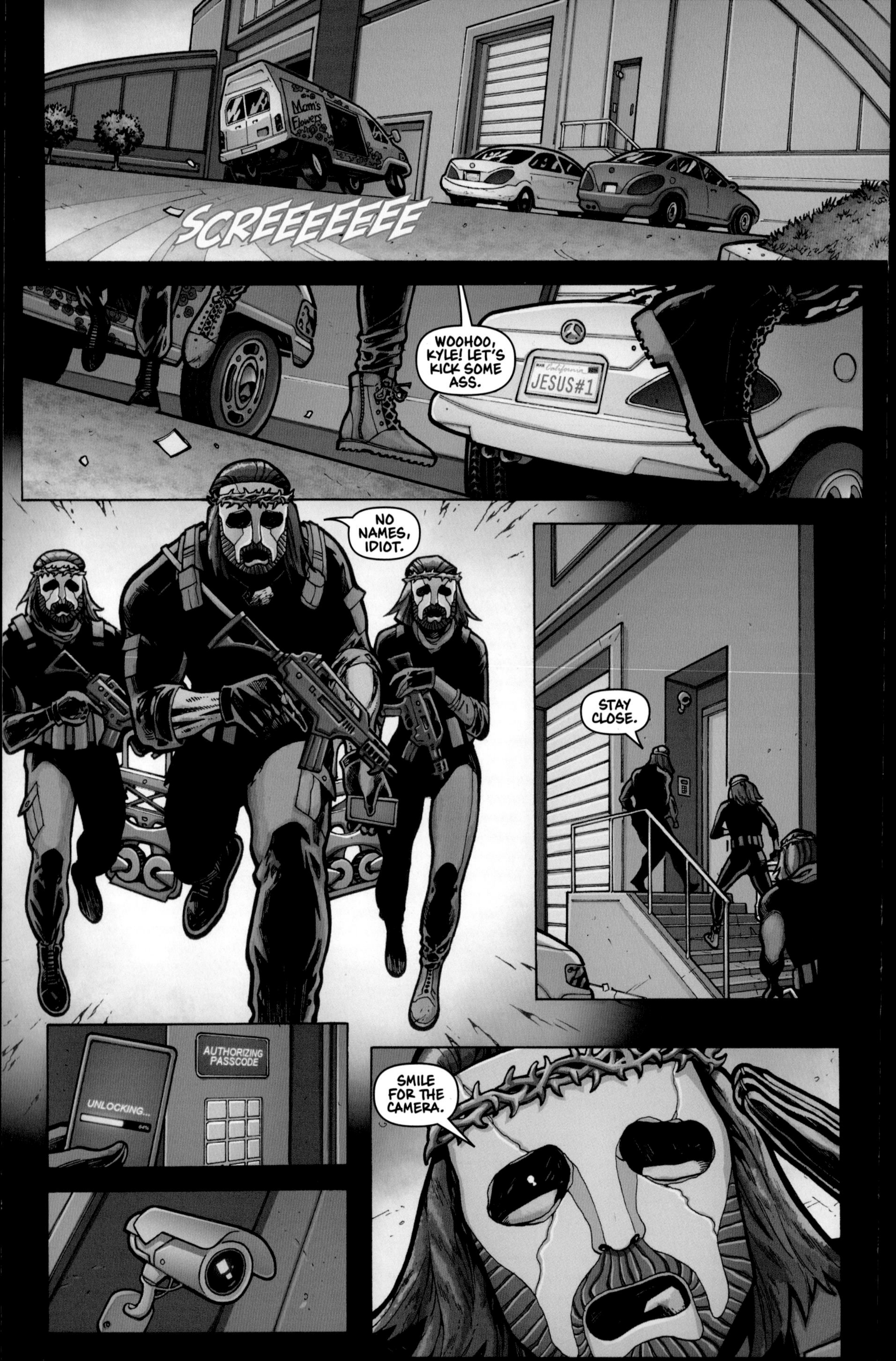
Mom's Flowers
SCREEEEEEEE
California
JESUS#1
WOOHOO, KYLE! LET'S KICK SOME ASS.
NO NAMES, IDIOT.
STAY CLOSE.
AUTHORIZING PASSCODE
UNLOCKING...
SMILE FOR THE CAMERA.

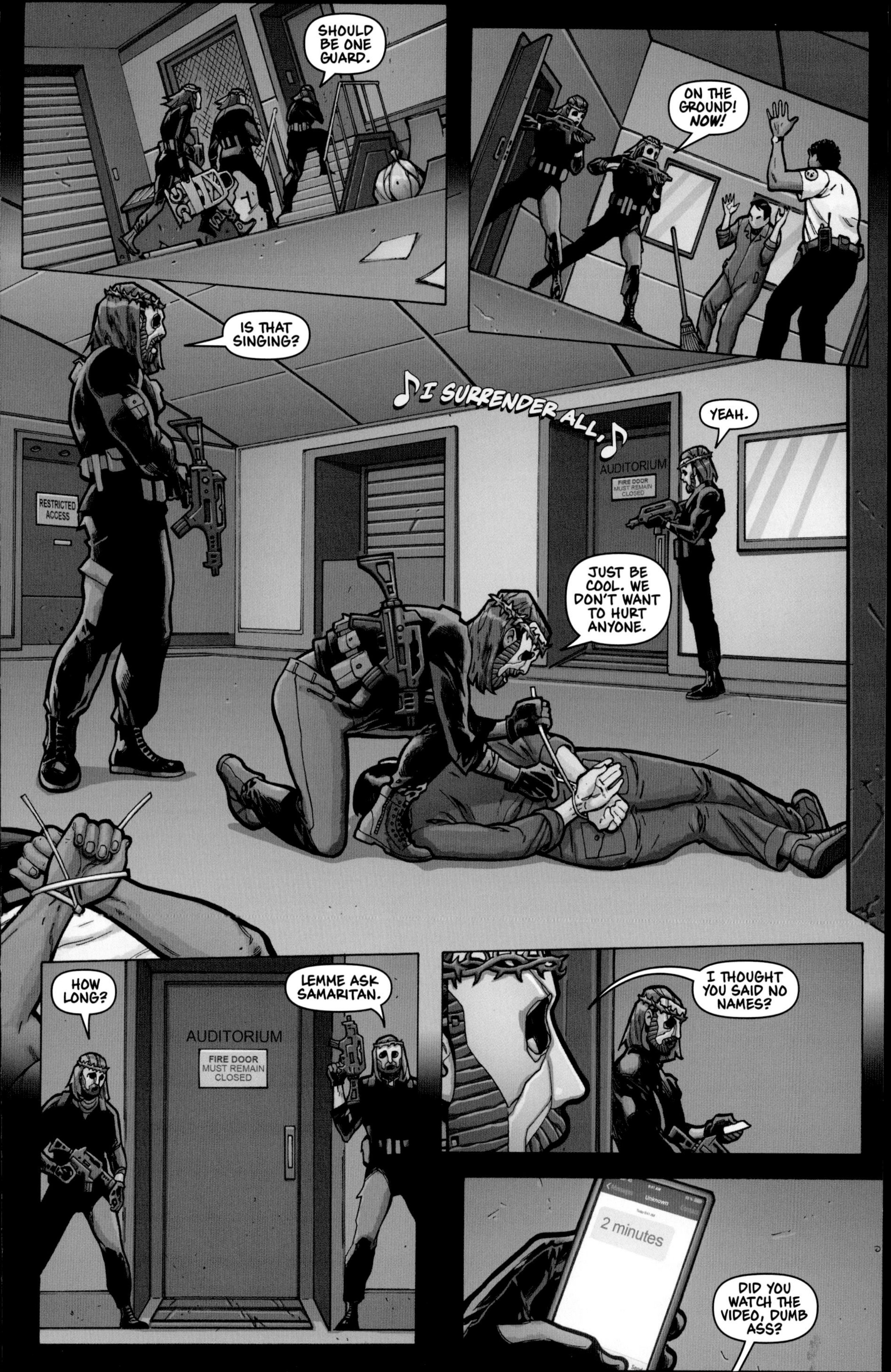

SHOULD BE ONE GUARD.
ON THE GROUND! NOW!
IS THAT SINGING?
♪I SURRENDER ALL,♪
YEAH.
RESTRICTED ACCESS
AUDITORIUM
FIRE DOOR MUST REMAIN CLOSED
JUST BE COOL. WE DON'T WANT TO HURT ANYONE.
HOW LONG?
AUDITORIUM
FIRE DOOR MUST REMAIN CLOSED
LEMME ASK SAMARITAN.
I THOUGHT YOU SAID NO NAMES?
Unknown
2 minutes
DID YOU WATCH THE VIDEO, DUMB ASS?

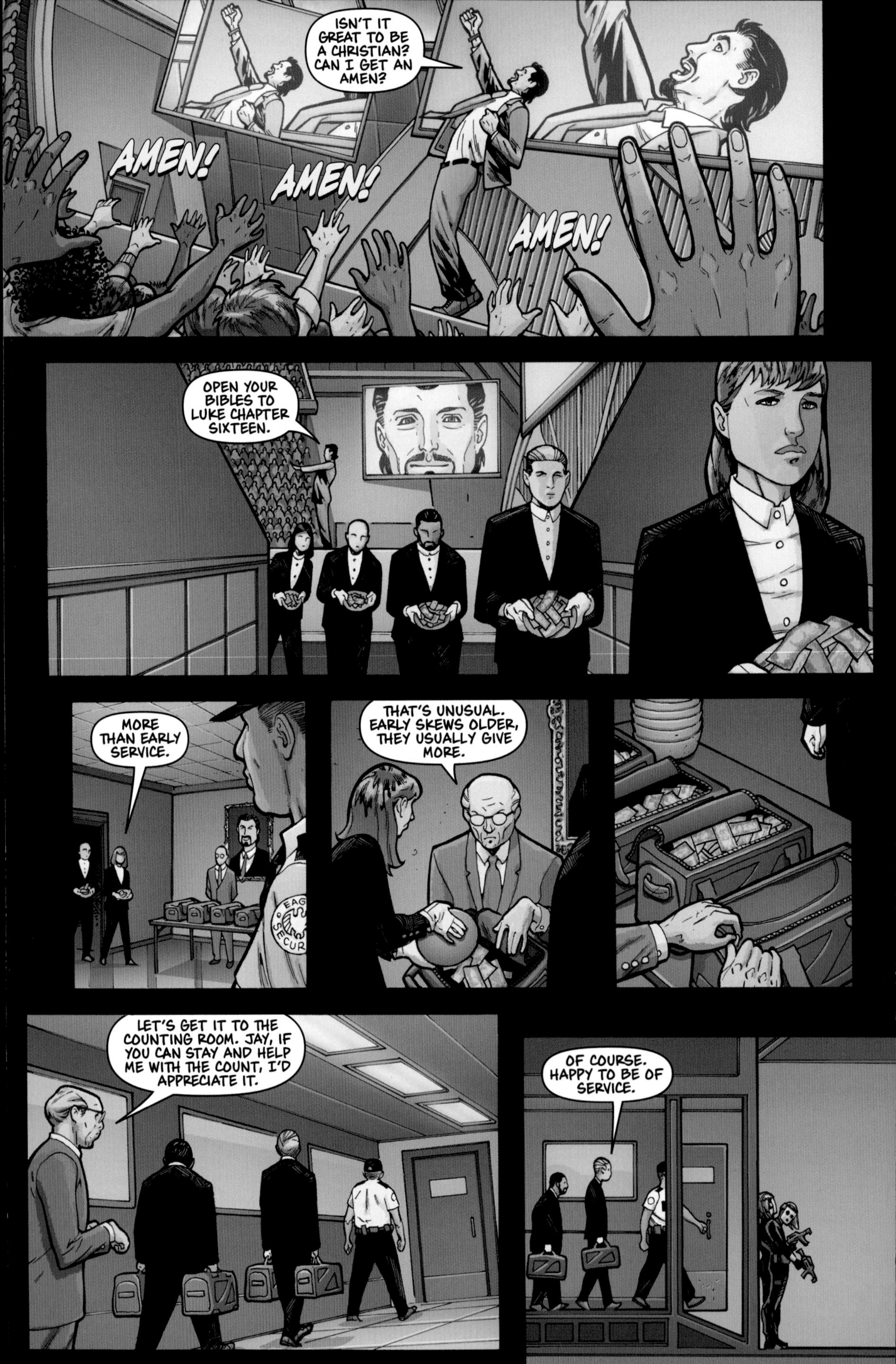
ISN'T IT GREAT TO BE A CHRISTIAN? CAN I GET AN AMEN?
AMEN!
AMEN!
AMEN!
OPEN YOUR BIBLES TO LUKE CHAPTER SIXTEEN.
MORE THAN EARLY SERVICE.
THAT'S UNUSUAL. EARLY SKEWS OLDER, THEY USUALLY GIVE MORE.
LET'S GET IT TO THE COUNTING ROOM. JAY, IF YOU CAN STAY AND HELP ME WITH THE COUNT, I'D APPRECIATE IT.
OF COURSE. HAPPY TO BE OF SERVICE.

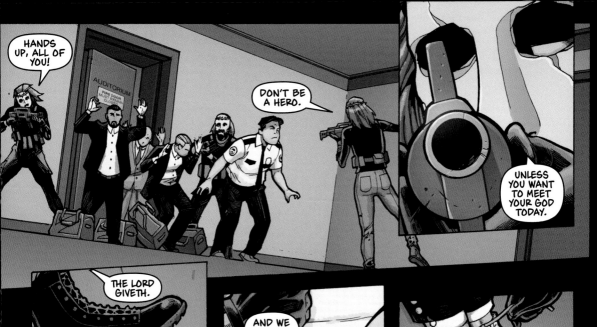

HANDS UP, ALL OF YOU!
AUDITORIUM
FIRE DOOR MUST REMAIN CLOSED
DON'T BE A HERO.
UNLESS YOU WANT TO MEET YOUR GOD TODAY.
THE LORD GIVETH.
AND WE TAKETH AWAY.
JUST TAKE THE MONEY AND GO. PLEASE DON'T HURT ANYONE.
THIS IS WHAT, SIXTY-K? WE WANT THE MONEY IN THE VAULT.
WHAT ARE YOU TALKING ABOUT? ALL THE MONEY IS TRANSFERRED AFTER EACH SERVICE.
WELL, JOHN TAGGERT OF 22 LOCUST LANE, FATHER OF THREE, GRANDFATHER OF SEVEN...WE BOTH KNOW THAT'S NOT TRUE, NOW DON'T WE?
WHAT DO YOU WANT?

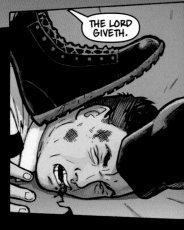

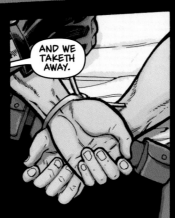

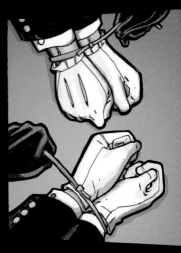

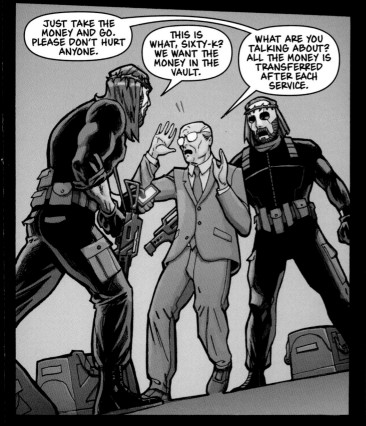

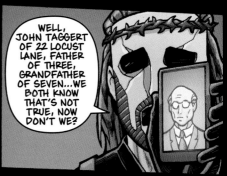

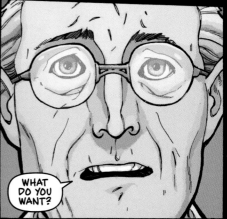

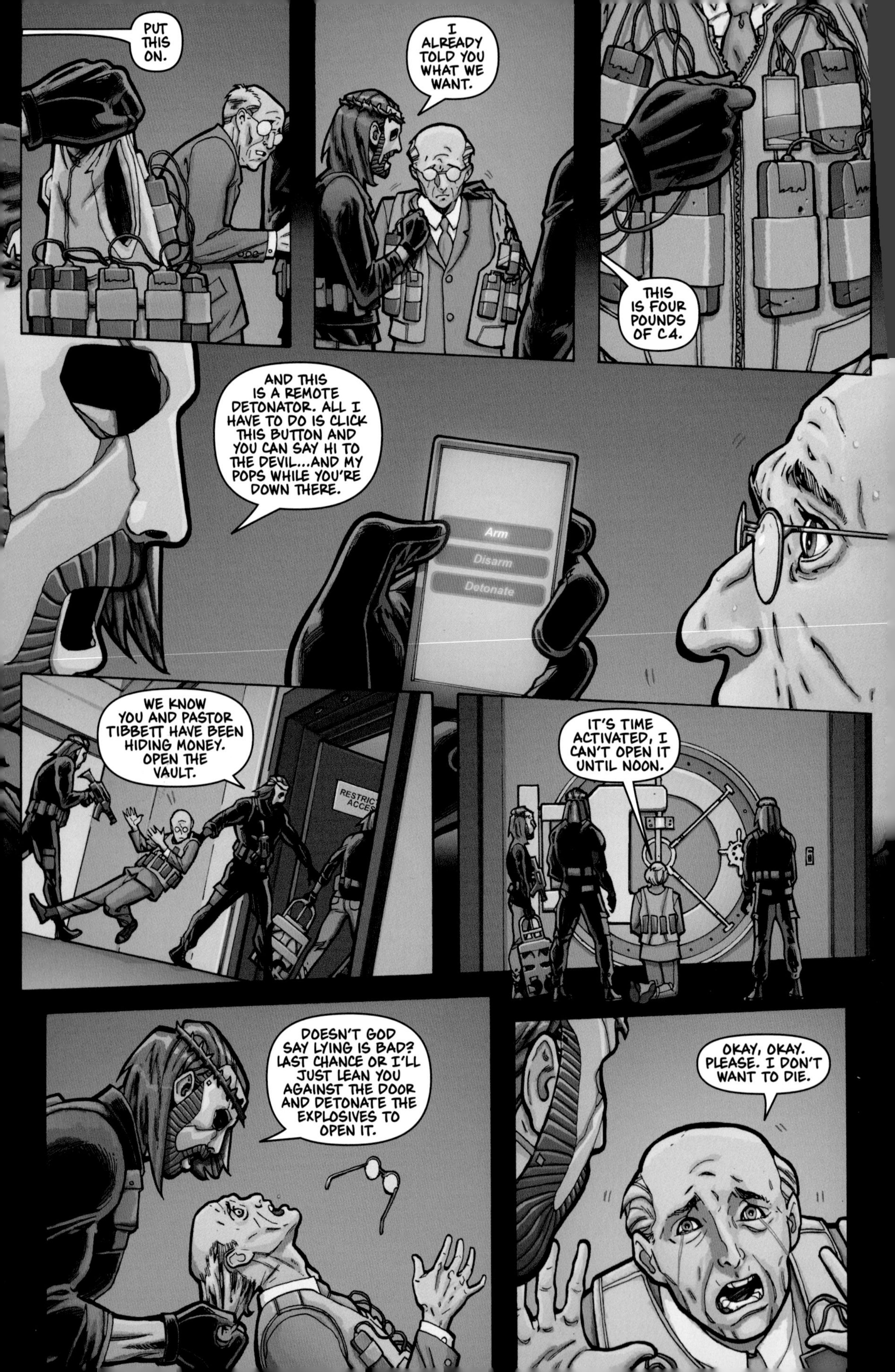
PUT THIS ON.
I ALREADY TOLD YOU WHAT WE WANT.
THIS IS FOUR POUNDS OF C4.
AND THIS IS A REMOTE DETONATOR. ALL I HAVE TO DO IS CLICK THIS BUTTON AND YOU CAN SAY HI TO THE DEVIL...AND MY POPS WHILE YOU'RE DOWN THERE.
Arm
Disarm
Detonate
WE KNOW YOU AND PASTOR TIBBETT HAVE BEEN HIDING MONEY. OPEN THE VAULT.
IT'S TIME ACTIVATED, I CAN'T OPEN IT UNTIL NOON.
DOESN'T GOD SAY LYING IS BAD? LAST CHANCE OR I'LL JUST LEAN YOU AGAINST THE DOOR AND DETONATE THE EXPLOSIVES TO OPEN IT.
OKAY, OKAY. PLEASE. I DON'T WANT TO DIE.

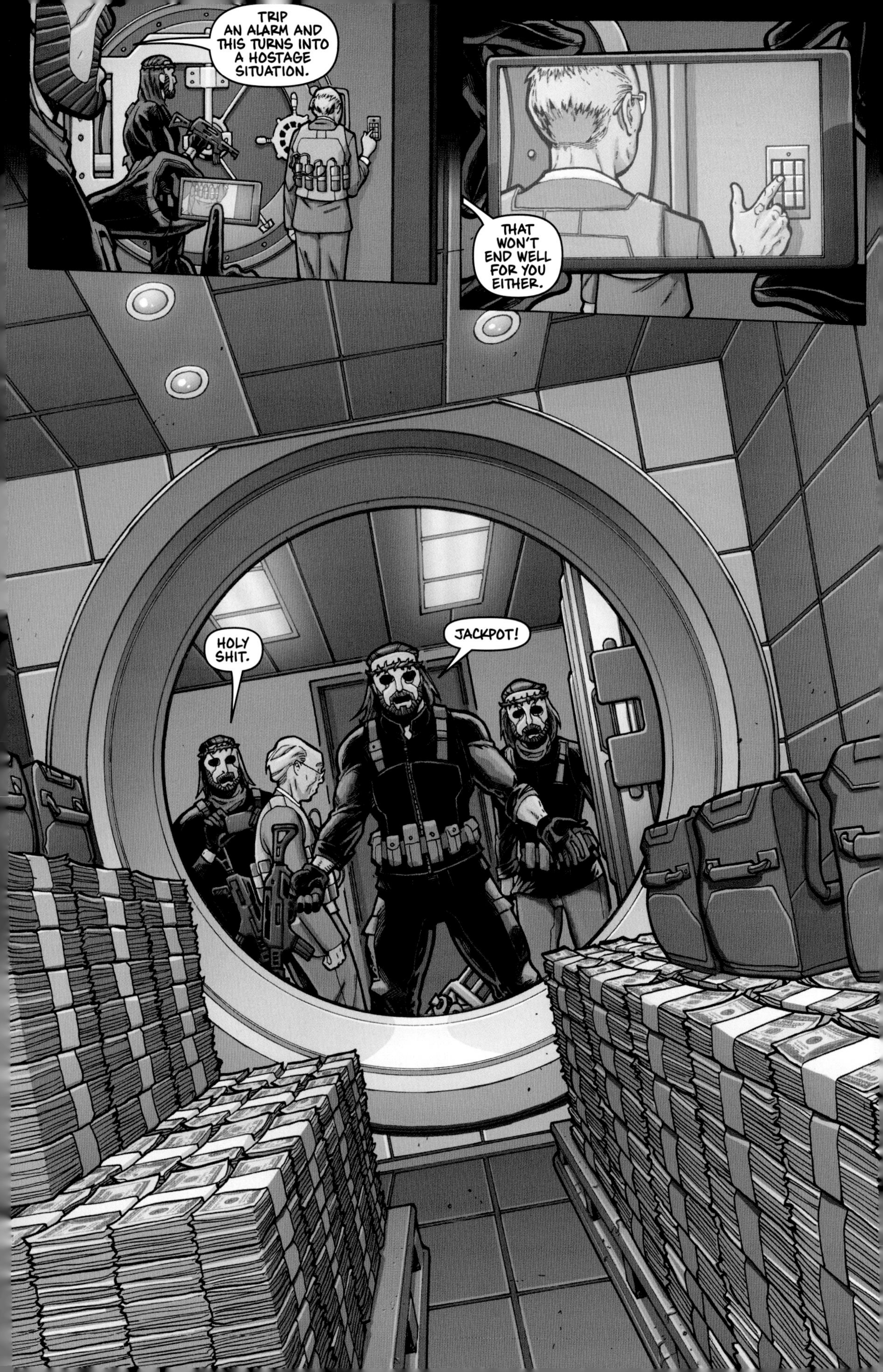
TRIP AN ALARM AND THIS TURNS INTO A HOSTAGE SITUATION.
THAT WON'T END WELL FOR YOU EITHER.
HOLY SHIT.
JACKPOT!

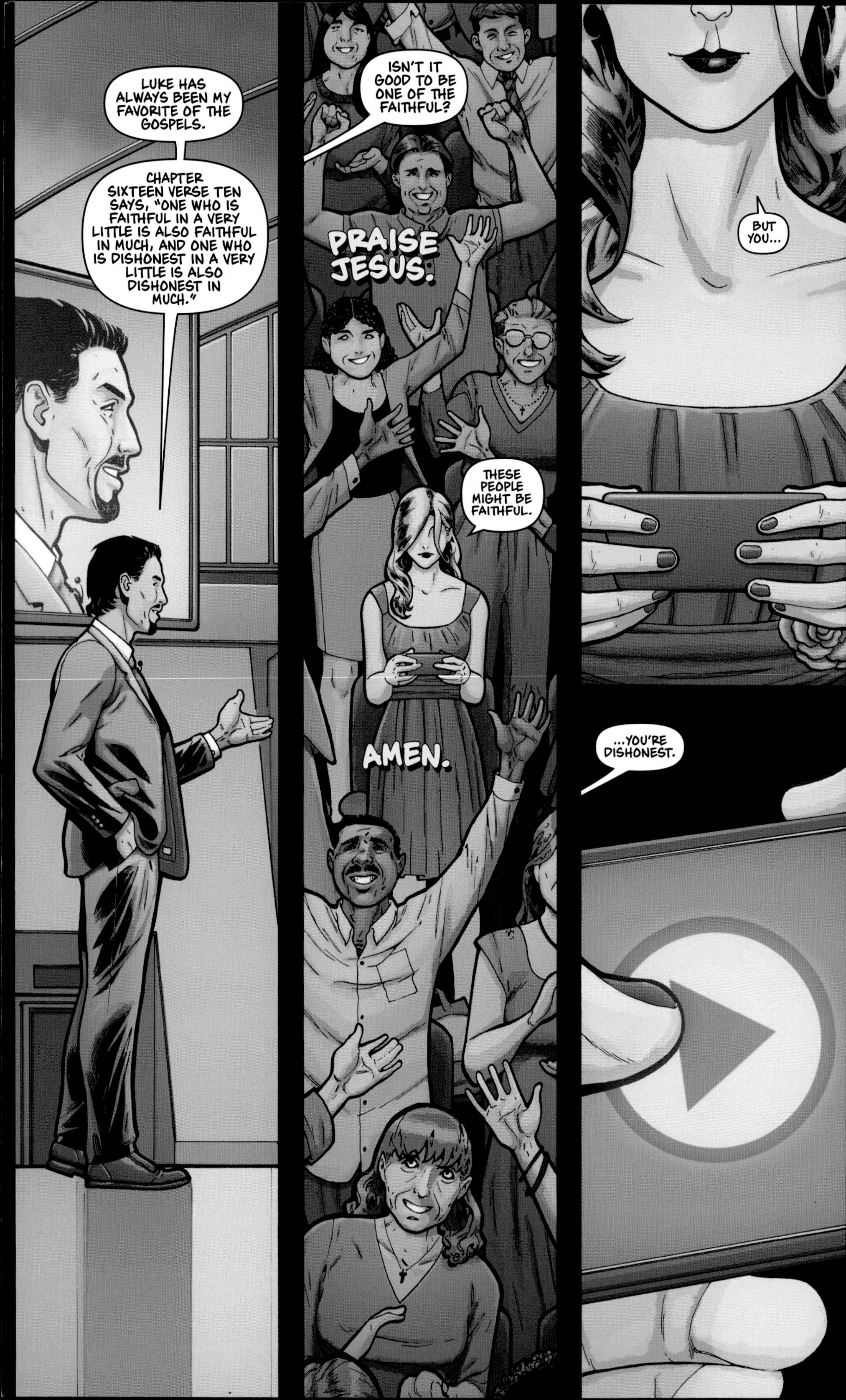
LUKE HAS ALWAYS BEEN MY FAVORITE OF THE GOSPELS.
CHAPTER SIXTEEN VERSE TEN SAYS, "ONE WHO IS FAITHFUL IN A VERY LITTLE IS ALSO FAITHFUL IN MUCH, AND ONE WHO IS DISHONEST IN A VERY LITTLE IS ALSO DISHONEST IN MUCH."
ISN'T IT GOOD TO BE ONE OF THE FAITHFUL?
PRAISE JESUS.
THESE PEOPLE MIGHT BE FAITHFUL.
AMEN.
BUT YOU...
...YOU'RE DISHONEST.

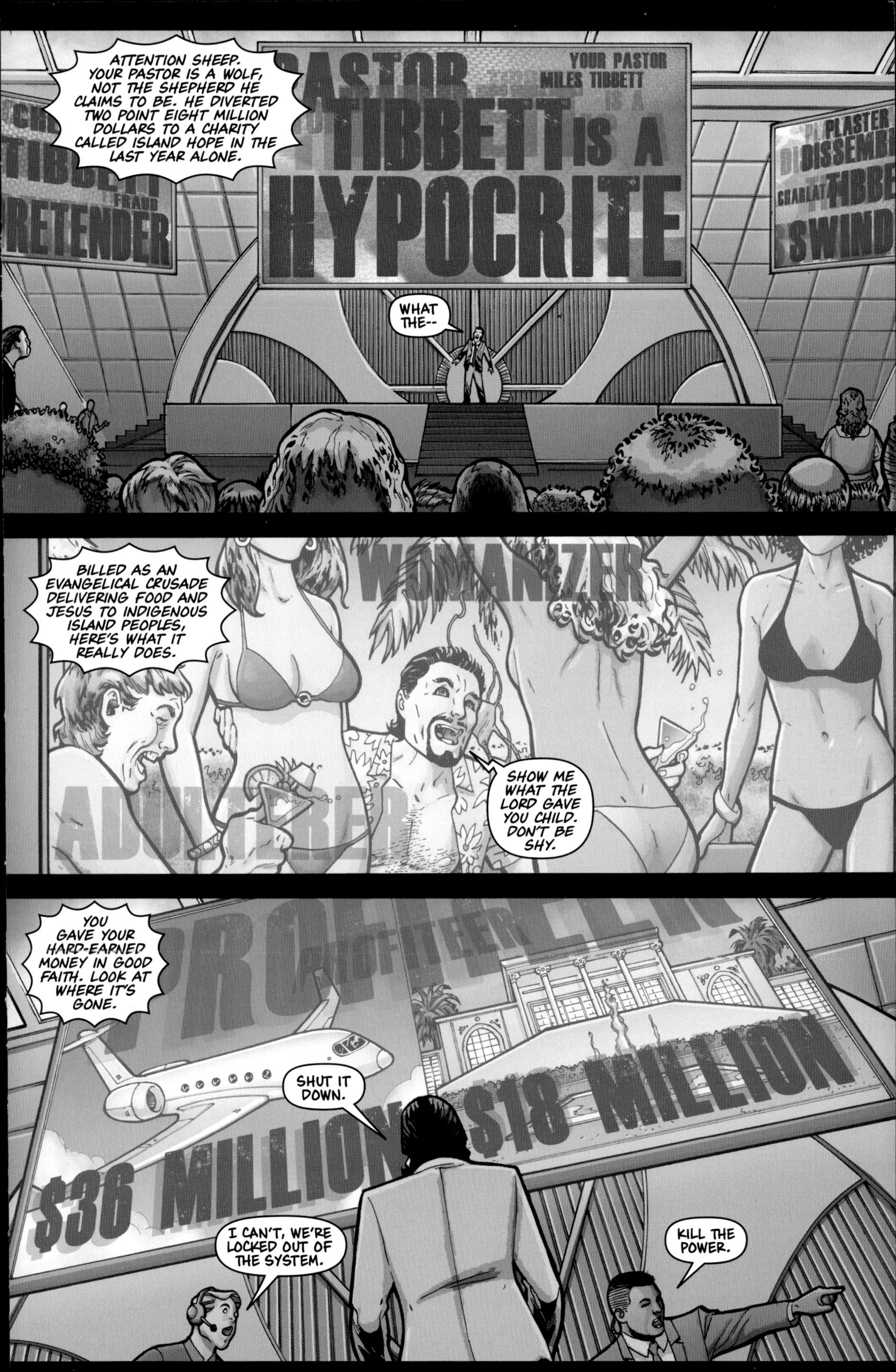
ATTENTION SHEEP. YOUR PASTOR IS A WOLF, NOT THE SHEPHERD HE CLAIMS TO BE. HE DIVERTED TWO POINT EIGHT MILLION DOLLARS TO A CHARITY CALLED ISLAND HOPE IN THE LAST YEAR ALONE.
YOUR PASTOR MILES TIBBETT
TIBBETT IS A HYPOCRITE
FRAUD
PRETENDER
PLASTER
SWIND
WHAT THE--
BILLED AS AN EVANGELICAL CRUSADE DELIVERING FOOD AND JESUS TO INDIGENOUS ISLAND PEOPLES, HERE'S WHAT IT REALLY DOES.
WOMANIZER
ADULTERER
SHOW ME WHAT THE LORD GAVE YOU CHILD. DON'T BE SHY.
YOU GAVE YOUR HARD-EARNED MONEY IN GOOD FAITH. LOOK AT WHERE IT'S GONE.
PROFITEER
$36 MILLION
$18 MILLION
SHUT IT DOWN.
I CAN'T, WE'RE LOCKED OUT OF THE SYSTEM.
KILL THE POWER.

CONTINUED IN THE TITHE VOL 1 AVAILABLE NOW

# MEET THE CREATORS OF POSTAL

### MATT HAWKINS

A veteran of the initial Image Comics launch, Matt started his career in comic book publishing in 1993 and has been working with Image as a creator, writer, and executive for over twenty years. President/ COO of Top Cow since 1998, Matt has created and written over thirty new franchises for Top Cow and Image including *Think Tank, Necromancer, VICE, Lady Pendragon,* and *Aphrodite IX* as well as handling the company's business affairs.

### BRYAN HILL

Writes comics, writes movies, and makes films. He lives and works in Los Angeles. @bryanedwardhill | Instagram/bryanehill

### ISAAC GOODHART

A life-long comics fan, Isaac graduated from the School of Visual Arts in New York in 2010. In 2014, he was one of the winners for Top Cow's annual talent hunt. He currently lives in Los Angeles where he storyboards and draws comics.

## K. MICHAEL RUSSELL

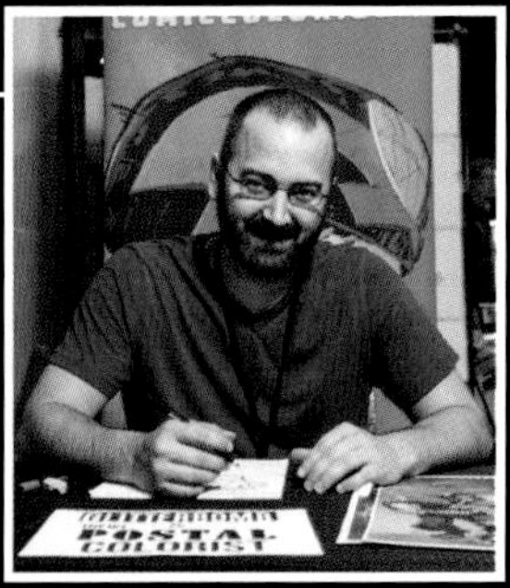

Michael has been working as a comic book color artist since 2011. His credits include the Image series *Glitterbomb* with *Wayward* and *Thunderbolts* writer Jim Zub, *Hack/Slash*, *Judge Dredd*, and the Eisner and Harvey-nominated *In the Dark: A Horror Anthology*. He launched an online comic book coloring course in 2014 at ColoringComics.com and maintains a YouTube channel dedicated to coloring tutorials. He lives on the coast in Long Beach, Mississippi, with his wife of sixteen years, Tina. They have two cats. One is a jerk. @kmichaelrussell

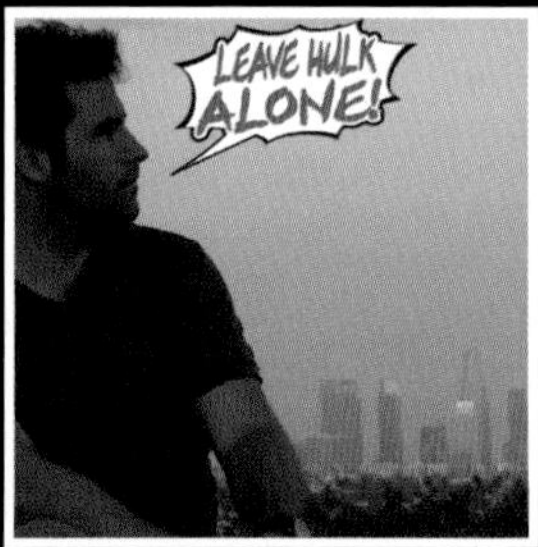
LEAVE HULK ALONE!

## TROY PETERI

Starting his career at Comicraft, Troy Peteri lettered titles such as *Iron Man*, *Wolverine*, and *Amazing Spider-Man*, among many others. He's been lettering roughly 97% of all Top Cow titles since 2005. In addition to Top Cow, he currently letters comics from multiple publishers and websites, such as Image Comics, Dynamite, and Archaia. He (along with co-writer Tom Martin and artist Dave Lanphear) is currently writing (and lettering) *Tales of Equinox*, a webcomic of his own creation for www.Thrillbent.com. (Once again, www.Thrillbent.com.) He's still bitter about no longer lettering *The Darkness* and wants it back on stands immediately.

## RAFFAELE "RAFF" IENCO

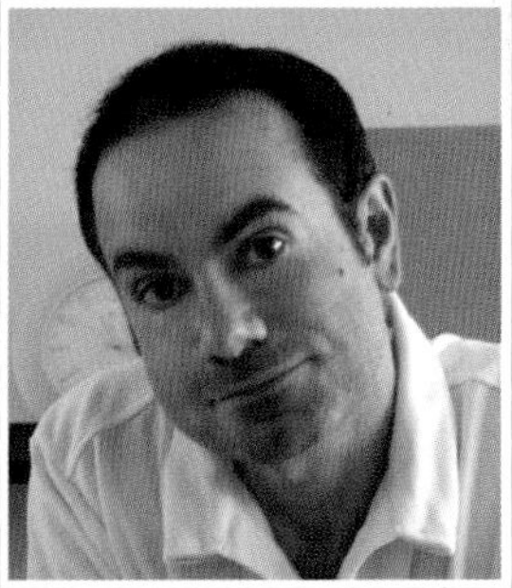

A comic book creator who has been in the industry for more than twenty years, and whose works have been published most recently by both Marvel and Image Comics. Raff's creator-owned works include the *Epic Kill* series and the graphic novels *Devoid of Life* and *Manifestations*. His work for Top Cow includes *Symmetry*, *Mechanism*, and *Postal*. He has also worked for DC Comics on *Batman: Sins of the Father*. Born in Italy, he came to Canada when he was 4 and currently lives in Toronto.

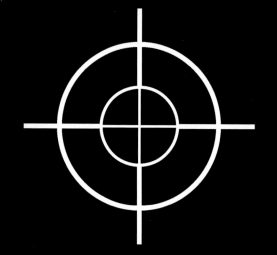

# The Top Cow essentials checklist:

**IXth Generation, Volume 1**
(ISBN: 978-1-63215-323-4)

**Aphrodite IX: Rebirth Volume 1**
(ISBN: 978-1-60706-828-0)

**Artifacts Origins: First Born**
(ISBN: 978-1-60706-506-7)

**Blood Stain, Volume 1**
(ISBN: 978-1-63215-544-3)

**Cyber Force: Rebirth, Volume 1**
(ISBN: 978-1-60706-671-2)

**The Darkness: Origins, Volume 1**
(ISBN: 978-1-60706-097-0)

**Death Vigil, Volume 1**
(ISBN: 978-1-63215-278-7)

**Eclipse, Volume 1**
(ISBN: 978-1-5343-0038-5)

**Eden's Fall, Volume 1**
(ISBN: 978-1-5343-0065-1)

**Genius, Volume 1**
(ISBN: 978-1-63215-223-7)

**God Complex, Volume 1**
(ISBN: 978-1-5343-0657-8)

**Magdalena: Reformation**
(ISBN: 978-1-5343-0238-9)

**Port of Earth, Volume 1**
(ISBN: 978-1-5343-0646-2)

**Postal, Volume 1**
(ISBN: 978-1-63215-342-5)

**Rising Stars Compendium**
(ISBN: 978-1-63215-246-6)

**Romulus, Volume 1**
(ISBN: 978-1-5343-0101-6)

**Sunstone, Volume 1**
(ISBN: 978-1-63215-212-1)

**Symmetry, Volume 1**
(ISBN: 978-1-63215-699-0)

**The Tithe, Volume 1**
(ISBN: 978-1-63215-324-1)

**Think Tank, Volume 1**
(ISBN: 978-1-60706-660-6)

**Witchblade 2017, Volume 1**
(ISBN: 978-1-5343-0685-1)

**Witchblade: Borne Again, Volume 1**
(ISBN: 978-1-63215-025-7)

For more ISBN and ordering information on our latest collections go to:
# www.topcow.com
Ask your retailer about our catalogue of collected editions,
digests, and hard covers or check the listings at:
## Barnes and Noble, Amazon.com,
and other fine retailers.

To find your nearest comic shop go to:
# www.comicshoplocator.com